"Beautiful sight, isn't it?"

Mattie turned back to Daniel; her cheeks hot at being caught staring. "I thought you said Caron was her partner."

"Main partner, yes. But not her only one. As the House Verity motto states, 'Baise tes Amis.'"

"I'm sorry, I don't speak French," she said with an apologetic smile.

He leaned in close, a mischievous glint in his eye. "It translates to 'kiss your friends' but we use it to mean…fuck your friends, bunny."

The words curled around Mattie, seeming to stroke their way up her cheek. "Oh. That's…quite the motto."

Maybe it was the whole surreal, wonderful day or the champagne, but the dark part of her unfurled, wanting her to be bold, wanting her to respond to the hungry way Daniel was regarding her. What would be the harm in giving in to that dark part of herself? Considering the motto of the House and the little she'd seen of the members, no one would judge her for it. Besides, she didn't know how long she would be working there. Shouldn't she learn and experience all she could while she was here?

Her tongue darted out to lick her lower lip. "Am I your friend?"

Champagne on Vice

by

Victoria Weyland

Champagne on Vice

COPYRIGHT © 2022 by Victoria Weyland

Cover Art by *Diana Carlile*

The Wild Rose Press, Inc.
PO Box 708
Adams Basin, NY 14410-0708
Visit us at www.thewildrosepress.com

Publishing History
First Edition, 2023
Trade Paperback ISBN 978-1-5092-4624-3
Digital ISBN 978-1-5092-4625-0

Published in the United States of America

Dedication

For Everyone Seeking More

Chapter One

New Orleans
1924
Mattie

Mattie wasn't a complete country bumpkin. After all, Lenny had taken her on shopping trips to Baton Rouge several times over the years. She reminded herself of these facts as she stepped off the stifling bus onto Canal Street. Despite her best efforts to appear nonchalant, her head swiveled this way and that, trying to take everything in.

There was an almost electric feel to the air, as if the city was buzzing with magic. With possibility. Like anything could happen.

Brick buildings towered over everyone, trapping the heat of the day, but not dampening anyone's spirit. The women in their smart day dresses and high heels walked arm-in-arm with men wearing hats low over their eyes, feathers of all colors decorating the brims. The sunlight glinted off the windows of the streetcar as it trundled along the wide grass strip that ran down the middle of the street.

The vibrant hum of the city filled her with anticipation, snapping the steel bands that had been clamped around her chest for so long. The crowd flowed around her, paying her no mind, as she stood in the middle of the sidewalk taking deep breaths. It was as if she'd been underwater to the point of drowning, and now her head had finally broken the surface and her lungs couldn't get enough air. Her body felt light as a hot air balloon, and *Sweet Baby Jesus*, she would not let anyone tie her down again.

"Come on, Ditzy Dora," she chided herself. "Stop standing around like a ninny and get a wiggle on!"

Clutching her carpetbag in front of her, she set off, her stride purposeful even if the rest of her was unsure where she was headed. Her sensible brown heels clacked on the pavement as she started down Royal Street.

Smart shops lined the road, selling everything from sweet pralines to lady's hats adorned with silk flowers and ribbons. Cafes nestled in-between the shops with their windows open to the street, spilling laughter and the clatter of silver on china. The smells of garlic, butter, and spices floated on the air, making Mattie's mouth water. The ham and cheese sandwiches she'd wrapped in parchment and tucked into her bag that morning seemed plain and unappealing by comparison.

The wail of a music rose up ahead. It wound its way through her and drew her further down the street until she found its source—a young Black man in a sharp zoot suit, playing a brass saxophone. The instrument had been polished to a high shine, and the man behind it leaned back as he played, his eyes closed as though he were blowing his very soul into the notes.

The music was almost a physical thing, slipping around Mattie's hips and setting her foot to tapping. It was the type of music Lenny had never approved of, wild and fast and full of life. Several folks stopped to listen, and two flappers were even dancing right there on the sidewalk! The glass beads lining the hem of their bright dresses sparkled against their shins as they shimmied.

Mattie fingered her gingham dress, her hand pale against the fabric. Its wide collar and pale blue flowers seemed terribly plain and old-fashioned in comparison. Another item for her mental list: an emerald green silk dress, short enough to cause the church ladies back home to faint. Her attention drifted back to the musician.

There was something about watching a person fully absorbed in what they loved, in what they were darn good at, that set Mattie's stomach aflutter. A bead of sweat rolled down the musician's puffed cheeks and trailed along the strong column of his neck. That dark, secret part of her stretched. The same part of her that had driven her to pack her bags and sneak out this morning wanted to use her tongue to lap at the sun-warmed saltiness of his skin. Back home she would have pushed that thought down in shame, but here, drunk on the feeling of freedom, Mattie savored it even if she would never act on it.

A rumble emanated from her stomach, so loud she could hear it above the music. She rubbed at her midsection, and the three thin bracelets on her wrist clinked. A frown tugged on her lips. Those three bracelets and the assorted coins in her pocketbook were all the currency she possessed.

For the first time since she packed her bags and got on that bus, a bit of doubt threaded through Mattie's mind. What if she couldn't find work? Would anyone even hire a single woman her age? Would they somehow know that she'd run away from her marriage and turn her away? What if she failed utterly and had to crawl back to Lenny? She gave a little shudder.

Worrying would get her nowhere. At least she had a lead on a boarding house. Not that she knew exactly where it was, but she could find someone to point her in the right direction—after she ate. As Granny Marie always said, never tackle a problem on an empty stomach.

She dropped one of her remaining pennies into the upturned hat in front of the saxophone player. A skilled musician deserved to be paid for his craft. He tipped his head to her without missing a beat. Halfway down the block, she found a set of steps that were mostly clean but close enough to let her still enjoy the music. Her foot tapped as she opened her bag and pulled out one of the waxed paper wrapped bundles.

Movement caught the corner of her eye. Something fluttered down a dim alley across the street. Halfway down the alley, two white children in short trousers, their faces streaked with dirt, were throwing pebbles at a black crow. Her eyebrows knit together as she stuffed the sandwich back into her bag, stood up, and took a hesitant step. The poor thing kept trying to fly away, but every time it would only get a few feet high before crashing back to the ground.

The taller of the children bent down, picked up a broken bottle, and raised it over their head.

Without thinking, Mattie grabbed her bag and took off toward them, shouting, "You there! Stop!" Her carpetbag bounced painfully against her leg as she ran.

The street urchin froze, the bottle slipping from their grubby hand to crash against the brick of the alley floor.

"Run!"

The two little hooligans took off in the opposite direction.

Skidding to a stop next to the injured animal, Mattie let out her breath in a huff. "Oh, you poor thing." She set her bag on the top of a broken crate and knelt down. "Someone should throw rocks at those ragamuffins and see how well they like it."

Up close, the crow was big—the largest Mattie had ever seen. The bird cocked its head to the side, chest heaving. It had stopped trying to fly away, which Mattie took as a good sign. She opened the bag and pulled out one of the wrapped sandwiches.

"It's a little stale, but I don't think you'll mind." She tore a bit of crust off the side and held it out.

The bird cocked its head toward her, and Mattie sucked in a breath. As the bird leaned forward to peck at the bread, it seemed to take pains to avoid Mattie's fingers.

Mattie forced her held breath out with a laugh. "For a second, I thought you could understand me. How silly is that? But what's that on your leg?" She offered more bits of sandwich to distract the bird as she leaned in. Around the bird's leg was a gold ring set with a small ruby.

"Help you, miss?"

The words made Mattie jump and nearly topple over backward. At the end of the alleyway stood a stunning young woman. Her light pink dress set off her dark mahogany skin, and loose curls tumbled out of her matching cloche hat.

Heat suffused Mattie's cheeks. Of course the bird

hadn't spoken. What nonsense.

The woman stayed several feet away and kept her head tilted toward the ground. She offered up a small apologetic smile. "Sorry to have startled you, miss. I just wanted to make sure you were all right. Alleyways aren't the safest place for young ladies."

Steadying herself against the crate, Mattie let out an embarrassed laugh. "I'm all right, promise. A couple of ragamuffins were tormenting this poor bird."

The woman's smile slid off her face as she hurried over, her timid demeanor dropping from her like a shawl. "Oh, Jo. Got yourself into trouble again?"

This woman knew the crow's name? Mattie looked between her and the bird, Jo, who seemed to hang its head in shame. That was just baloney. Wasn't it? Maybe the heat was getting to her after all.

"Thank you so much for looking after her." The woman drew a beautiful silk scarf from her handbag and knelt. With gentle fingers and taking care not to jostle its injured wing, she wrapped the bird up and gathered it to her chest. Standing up, she glanced at Mattie's carpetbag. "Just arrived?"

"Um, yes. I just came in on the bus, actually. That easy to tell?"

The woman's eyes tracked from Mattie's plain dress and worn carpetbag. "Alleyways aren't always the safest things even during the daytime round these parts. Got a place to stay?"

"Not exactly, but a gentleman at our church spent some time down here for work and mentioned the White Dove Boardinghouse. Do you know it?"

"Oh, Frannie's place." There was a deliberate polite neutrality to the woman's tone.

"Is that not a good place to stay? Do you know of a better one?"

"Frannie runs a tight ship. The White Dove's nothing fancy, but it's clean." The woman cocked her head in a move that wasn't dissimilar to what the bird had done moments ago. "Would you like me to show you the way?"

"I wouldn't want to impose…"

"No imposition at all. I need to get Jo back to the Lady, and it's on the way."

The Lady must be the bird's owner and someone of great import to afford jewelry like that for her pet.

A relieved grin broke across Mattie's face. "That would be wonderful."

"Attagirl! I'm Clementine, by the way." The woman pronounced it Clem-en-teen.

"Mattie."

Clementine nodded toward the end of the alleyway. "Let's get a wiggle on."

As she followed the fashionable young woman with a crow tucked against her, Mattie couldn't help but think maybe some of the New Orleans magic was rubbing off on her.

****

The two walked side-by-side through the French Quarter. Clementine was the perfect guide, pointing out the best places to get gumbo, chicory coffee, and oysters, and which shops overpriced their goods for unsuspecting tourists. Mattie's brown eyes were in constant motion, trying to take everything in. She especially loved the balconies that jutted from the buildings, overhanging the sidewalks. They were as colorful and varied as the building themselves. Some of them had so many plants they looked like miniature hanging gardens.

As they turned onto a street called Bourbon, the mood shifted. More men walked the sidewalks, and the shops and cafes mostly disappeared. Instead, the establishments had velvet curtained front entrances and posters featuring drawings of raised ruffled skirts, women's bare legs peeking out.

Heat flooded Mattie's cheeks. These were concert saloons or "dens of devilish sin" as Pastor Michals had called them. The rumor was the good Pastor was a frequent visitor to the Red Door club in Baton Rouge, so he must have been an authority on them.

Out of the corner of her eye, Mattie noticed a cheeky smirk on Clementine's face, and Mattie couldn't help but wonder if she'd picked this route on purpose to see how the country bumpkin would react. Keeping her head high, she refused to give Clementine the satisfaction. Still, she couldn't stop herself from sneaking peeks through the doors and wondering what was inside. What would it be like to go in?

"Hellooooo, Clementine!" called a voice from above them.

On a second-floor balcony sat two ladies at a small cafe table, arranged with tall glasses of iced tea and sandwiches on china plates. Ivy wound its way between the curlicues of the wrought-iron railing, giving the balcony the illusion of being suspended in the air, held aloft by the vines. Both the ladies were in patterned silk robes, and one had curlers in her blonde hair. The other's robe had slipped off her shoulder, showing off a truly impressive bosom, encased in an ivory corset. The color perfectly complemented the woman's glowing bronze skin.

"Afternoon, Darlene." Clementine said to the blonde woman. "BeeBee. How's the day?"

"Only June and it's hotter than the Devil's armpit. Who's your friend?" BeeBee asked, snapping open a lace fan and fluttering it near her open robe. Mattie dragged her eyes from the inviting curves up to the woman's heart-shaped face.

"This is Mattie."

Remembering her manners, Mattie bobbed her head. "Hello. Pleasure to meet you both."

"Why don't you two come up and join us?" Darlene said, leaning over the wrought-iron railing. One hand dangled over the edge, a ring set with an opal on one finger. "We've got sweet tea."

Clementine smiled. "Wish we could, but we have to get Jo here home."

"Jo, I wondered if that was you bundled in that scarf. What did you get yourself into this time, sugar lump?" BeeBee asked.

The bird pressed its head against Clementine's stomach as if ashamed.

"Tormented by some would-be hoodlums. Mattie here came to her rescue," Clementine explained.

"In that case, y'all better get her back to the Lady," BeeBee said, renewing her fanning. "See you on Tuesday?"

"Ab-so-lute-ly!" Clementine replied, drawing it out until each syllable was practically its own word. Mattie liked the way she said it and repeated it silently in her head. "I'll even save you a trip to the shop and bring you a bar of lavender soap."

"Appreciate it. Not that I don't love seeing all the

new wonderful things you cook up, but —" A loud wolf whistle sounded from down the street. BeeBee flashed the appreciative gentlemen a sultry smile, giving a little shimmy in her seat before turning back to Clementine. "But a gal's work is never done."

Clementine tilted her head back and laughed. "Not in this town, BeeBee. See ya Tuesday!"

The two ladies waved and went back to their afternoon libations. As Clementine and Mattie headed back down the street, Mattie forgot her pretense of worldliness and asked quietly, "Were those women…" She couldn't quite bring herself to say the word.

Her companion had no such reservations. "Women of the night? Hip peddlers? Flashtails? Short-time gals? Prostitutes? Why, yes. Yes, they are. And damn fine ones at that."

There was gentle teasing in Clementine's delivery, but the openness of her confession—the complete lack of shame—was…refreshing. There had been so much shame in Mattie's life, from herself, her family, the church, and especially Lenny. It had been used to bind and restrict her, to make her small. Except it had never felt like hers. They had always thrust shame upon her like an unwanted birthday gift she was too polite to return. But why couldn't she? Why couldn't she take that shame off and leave it? What if she said, "no thank you, that's not for me?"

Something else about BeeBee tickled the back of Mattie's brain. A memory, shoved deep into that dark place of hers, of a hayloft and a stolen afternoon. The feel of her best friend Samantha's lips as they kissed. They were both seventeen and soon to be married, Mattie to Lenny and Samantha to Jeremy who would take her west, far from Prairieville. They'd said it was to prepare for their wedding nights, but the affection had always been there.

Mattie could still remember the softness of Samantha's lips, the little gasps she made as Mattie had pressed kisses to the tender spot right below her ear. The feel of Samantha's breasts pressed against her own as they lay in the hay. They hadn't been brave enough for more than those gentle kisses, but the memory still set Mattie alight. In contrast, the thought of her wedding night and Lenny's practical application of his marriage duty left Mattie cold. She pushed thoughts of Lenny aside. She didn't want to think of him, not when there were more pleasant possibilities, like wondering what it would be like to rest her head on BeeBee's bosom.

"You're thinking about BeeBee's assets, aren't you?"

Mattie whipped her head around. Clementine gave her a knowing look as Mattie's cheeks heated. Again, there was no shame in the question, not even the gentle tease from before.

"Maybe." She swallowed hard and lifted one shoulder. "They were impressive."

"They are indeed impressive." Clementine leaned her head conspiratorially. "They feel just as lovely as they look."

Mattie returned Clementine's grin, and the two continued onward.

****

"Well, here we are," Clementine said brightly.

They had turned off of Bourbon and stopped in front of a set of steps that led to a sagging front door.

The dull brown paint was flaking away from the wood, but the steps were swept clean, and the brass knocker and doorknob winked in the sunshine. A wooden sign bore the likeness of dove worn by sun and soot until the dove looked like it had flown through a chimney then smashed into a plate-glass window.

It wasn't the most welcoming place she'd ever seen, but she could always find more cheery lodgings later. Once she had employment and knew the city better. She turned back to her walking companions.

"Thank you, Clementine. It was a pleasure to meet you." The crow chittered at Mattie. "You as well, Jo." She felt a little silly talking to a crow, but it seemed the polite thing to do.

"My pleasure and don't let Frannie fool you. Her bark is just as bad as her bite." Clementine grinned and turned away. Before she'd gone two steps, she stopped. She seemed to come to a decision and said, "Why don't you come with us and meet the Lady? I know she'll want to thank you for helping Jo. She might even have a job opening, if you're looking for work. She's a fair employer and provides room and board, as well."

From the protective circle of the woman's arms, Jo let out a cajoling *caw*. If Mattie was honest, having started the bird's rescue, she wanted to see it through, and she was curious to meet this Lady person. Still, it all seemed a bit strange.

"There's really no need. I'm sure this will be more than adequate. Thank you for the escort."

For a moment it looked like Clementine was going to say something else, possibly press the issue. Instead, she gave Mattie a smile and turned down the block.

With an oddly heavy heart, Mattie knocked on the

door of The White Dove. The flaking door swung open so fast, Mattie squeaked in surprise, nearly tumbling down the front steps. The woman in the doorway had a pinched mouth and speared Mattie with narrowed eyes. Her dress was clean and several years out of fashion. The collar and long sleeves sported stiff white lace despite the sweltering summer heat. Her salt and pepper hair was pulled so tightly back, it made the skin at Mattie's temples ache in sympathy.

"Yes," the woman snapped. "What is it?"

"Um. Hello ma'am." She had a feeling that if she tried to call this imposing older woman Frannie, the door would swiftly shut in her face. "My name is Mattie, and I was wondering if you had a room for rent."

The eyes narrowed further. "There's a room available. You'd have to pay the first week's rent up front and abide by the house rules. Any violation will result in you being escorted from the premises and forfeiting of rent."

The sinking feeling settled firmly into Mattie's stomach. "The house rules?"

"No visitors of the opposite sex. Curfew is eight p.m. sharp. Cigarettes and other tobacco products are to be smoked only in the courtyard. All rooms must be kept clean and tidy. Church services are strongly encouraged every Sunday and alcohol is strictly prohibited." The list had been fired off with a rapidness that spoke of frequent recitation.

The last conversation Mattie had with Granny Marie came back to her. Illness had turned the woman who'd been such a force of nature all Mattie's childhood into a frail shadow of herself. One gnarled hand had snaked out of the heap of quilts to grip Mattie's wrist, the conviction behind Granny Marie's words strong despite the ragged wheeze of her breath.

"Mattie bird, don't let these fools clip your wings. There's so much out there beyond this narrow-minded little town. Don't you settle for the small life that's been shoved on you. You live it as *you* want to."

This boardinghouse would be the safe option with the rules clearly laid out. Rules that she'd been following pretty much her whole life. Coming to New Orleans, though, that hadn't been the safe option.

Involuntarily, she looked down the block. Clementine's pink dress was a splash of sunshine against the grey sidewalk. Mattie turned back to the stodgy woman standing before her, in front of her stodgy building, with her stodgy rules.

"Thank you, ma'am, but I'll be seeking lodging elsewhere." Mattie didn't wait for the woman's stunned reply, she just hiked her carpetbag higher up her arm and took off down the street. Her heart soared in her chest, as light as dandelion fluff, as one hand gripped her carpetbag, the other held her straw hat to her head.

Chapter Two

Officer Boudreaux

New Orleans had always been a lawless place, poised on the banks of the Mississippi, populated by criminals, thieves, and those who enjoyed the seedier aspects of life. The only thing standing between these shady criminal elements and the good Southern folk who respected the law and went to church every Sunday were the men of the New Orleans Police Department.

At least that was Officer Boudreaux's opinion.

His nightstick swung against his thigh with every step. It was a comforting feeling. Less comforting was the sweat that slipped down his collar and between his shoulder blades. At least his uniform's coat was dark blue, making the damp fabric harder to see in the bright afternoon sun.

As he walked the streets of the French Quarter, Officer Boudreaux kept his head high and on a swivel, always on the lookout for lowlifes and thugs. Not on his watch! He was the only thing keeping the Quarter from devolving into a lawless pit of vice, booze, and sin. Him and the other boys who patrolled these cobbled streets were the glue that held civilization together. They were bright shiny beacons against the night. They were—!

Officer Boudreaux's inner monologue was cut short as he turned a corner and nearly ran into two young ladies.

Backing up a step, he straightened his jacket, buttoned up proper despite the heat, and tipped his hat. "Miss Clementine, good afternoon."

The young Black woman who owned the store over on Barracks, or was it Hospital Street? Sold smelly lady products, creams and whatnots. Miss Clementine tipped her head in deference and gave him a friendly smile. "Good afternoon to you, Officer Boudreaux."

He turned to Clementine's companion. "And who is this, young lady? I don't think I've seen you around these parts before." The white woman wore a plain dress with a wide collar. Her hands tightly clutched the handle of a faded carpet bag. Large brown eyes were set in a round face and her long hair was pulled up in a sensible bun. There was a nervous air around her that tickled Officer Boudreaux's highly trained police senses.

"This is Mattie, Officer. A dear family friend who's just came in on the bus. We're just going to drop this injured bird off with a lady I know who rehabilitates them." Clementine raised the scarf wrapped bundle in her arms. A black beaked head swiveled to regard Office Boudreaux, who nearly took a step back in surprise, but caught himself. Officers should never show that they were caught off guard. Wasn't professional. "Afterwards, I was going to take Mattie to her rooms at The White Dove Inn."

Mattie looked at Clementine with a blank expression before nodding hard. "Yes, that's right."

Ah, that must be why the young lady was nervous.

First time in the big city.

"Well, Miss Mattie, have no fear. Me and my fellow officers keep the Quarter ship-shape and ruffian free. Besides, the White Dove is a fine establishment. Clean and well run. You tell Frannie I said hello for me when you see her. Fine Christian woman, Frannie." He reached a hand up to smooth the edges of his mustache. A man's mustache said a lot about a person. That's why Officer Boudreaux always kept his thick and well-groomed.

Mattie stared at him for a moment before nodding slowly.

"We'll happily say hello," Clementine cut in. She hooked an arm through Mattie's and pulled her down the sidewalk. "Well, we don't want to keep you from doing your good work, protecting the Quarter and all. Good afternoon, Officer!"

Officer Boudreaux puffed with pride. "Ladies."

As he continued on his patrol, nothing escaped his keen eye. Still, Officer Boudreaux couldn't help but think back on the newest member of his little community. Mattie seemed like a proper young lady, not as flashy and daring as some of the flappers that went around these days. Still, he couldn't help but think that she'd be a whole heap prettier if she smiled a bit more.

Chapter Three

Mattie

Clementine steered Mattie down an alley, not dissimilar to the one she'd found her in barely half an hour previously. Except this one had a distinct lack of dirty puddles or general refuse. Her guide took a sudden left through an opening in the brick.

As Mattie followed, her breath caught in her throat. They were in a hidden courtyard, the ivy-covered walls of the adjoining buildings rising up like protective mother hens on all sides. A small stone fountain splashed in the center with decorative benches dotted here and there. Set in the far wall were three stone steps leading up to a massive set of wooden doors.

Her eyes gazed upward. Carved into the stone archway above the door were the words "Tonique & Lace." Her eyes kept going up to where a statue loomed on a ledge. It was a great hulking thing with the torso of a muscular man. It sat on a hound's haunches, the ends of its hands and feet stretched into sharp talons. Whoever had carved it was a master. Even from this distance, the details were incredible. Every muscle and plane of its chest were rendered so perfectly, her palm itched to smooth along the stone surface.

She squinted, trying to get a better look. Was that a ring around one of its taloned fingers? Why would the creator of the statue give it ring?

Giving a little shrug, her gaze roamed over the rest of the sculpture. The head was carved with a hound's long snout, sharp teeth jutting down over the lower lip. Two large, pointed ears seemed poised, alert to any sound of danger. There was intelligence in the eyes that captivated Mattie. At least, until one of them winked.

Startled, she took a step back. That couldn't have been right. It was probably just the way the light had shifted or the heat of the day getting to her. Stone statues definitely didn't wink.

"Do you want to gawk some more, or do you want to come inside?" Clementine said with a laugh.

"Can't I do both?" Mattie wondered as she headed after Clementine, who had shifted Jo into the crook of one arm, her free hand resting on her hip.

Without bothering to knock, Clementine opened the door and walked in. As Mattie stepped over the threshold, a shiver went up her spine, but still she set one foot in front of the other and carried on. Dark, heavy drapes slid across her sun-kissed skin as she pushed through into an enormous room. She couldn't shake the feeling that the drapes marked a boundary, a liminal place between worlds.

Tables with dark marble tops and low-backed chairs were spread around the enormous room. The ceiling arched overhead, and two crystal chandeliers threw rainbows of sunlight across the walls and floor. A raised stage complete with golden footlights and deep red curtains took up an entire end of the room. A polished wooden dance floor waited at the base of the stage. On the wall to the right was a massive bar made of gleaming redwood with brass details. Behind it rose shelf after shelf of bottles. Some had elaborate labels in every color of the rainbow, while the rest were unadorned.

The tall white man standing behind the bar, cleaning a glass with a pristine white cloth, could only be the barkeep. The man's blonde hair was slicked back in the latest fashion, his mustache dark with wax and twisted up on the ends. His crisp white shirt nearly glowed in the sunlight that streamed in from the high windows, and black armbands encircled both of his biceps.

"Hello, Clementine," the man said, his hands never stopping their work. A gold ring adorned with a ruby winked as it shifted in and out of a sunbeam. "What brings you in before opening?"

"Afternoon, Francis. Special delivery," Clementine replied, holding up Jo in her scarf.

Caw.

This time Mattie was sure that the bird had called an embarrassed hello. She shook her head. It may have been the strangeness of the day, but she was starting to worry she was losing her marbles.

"Oh, Jo. What are we going to do with you?" he said with a sigh. "Let me fetch the Lady." Francis set the sparkling glass down on the polished wood of the bar and disappeared behind another set of velvet curtains. As they fluttered closed behind him, Mattie had a quick glimpse of a long hallway.

Clementine strolled up and gently set Jo on the bar before going around the back. "Have a seat," she called as she hunted through the bottles on the shelves.

Hesitantly, Mattie set her carpetbag down and perched herself on one of the velvet-cushioned stools near Jo. "Should you be doing that?"

"Francis only gets mad when you upset his strict organization, but Lady Lorna doesn't mind a bit. Ah-ha!" Clementine stood up on her tiptoes and pulled a bottle from the rest, holding it up triumphantly before turning back to Mattie. "Why? You aren't a teetotaler, are you?"

"No, not at all!" What she didn't say was how inexperienced she was with alcohol. She'd enjoyed the few glasses of wines she'd had before Lenny had declared solidarity with the "drys" and banned it from the house. The spiteful part of her wondered if he'd done it solely because it was something that had brought her pleasure.

"Good, because while prohibition is the law of land; it's not the law of New Orleans." Clementine pulled out two delicate crystal glasses from behind the bar and filled them with the amber liquid. She handed one over to Mattie and raised her own. "Cheers."

"Cheers," Mattie replied, raising the glass to her lips. She could have sworn the bottle contained wine, but the ruby liquid was sweeter than any wine she'd had previously.

"I see you've found the good sherry. Again." Francis swept back through the velvet curtain. The warmth and affection behind the words gave away the lie of the annoyed frown that pulled the corners of his mouth.

Clementine saluted him with her glass. "You know, I always do. Do you really think I'd drink coffin varnish?"

"Do you really think I'd allow inferior booze in my gin mill? Still, I don't know how you keep finding it."

"As I keep having to remind you, Frances, you may be king behind the bar, but Tonique & Lace is still *my* gin mill. Finding the good sherry is just one of our Clementine's many talents. Along with finding lost souls, it seems."

Mattie nearly spilled her sherry. She hadn't heard the woman's approach or even the rustle of the curtains. As her eyes widened at the sight of her, Mattie's words of greeting lay forgotten on her tongue.

This must be the Lady Lorna, and she was the most beautiful woman Mattie had ever seen. Tall with skin like spilled ink, the Lady held her head proudly like a queen or a goddess. A dress of deep purple silk cascaded over shapely, perky breasts, down a narrow waist and hips. Her hair was done in perfect finger waves to her chin, and her lips were painted a brilliant red. Mattie was so struck that it took her a moment to notice the Lady was missing her left eye. In its place was a polished gold sphere.

An amused smile tugged at the corners of the Lady's mouth as Mattie fought the urge to stumble from her stool and bob a curtsey. Not that she'd ever curtsied before in her life, but it seemed like the appropriate response.

Lady Lorna held out a long-fingered hand tipped in gold-painted nails. "Lady Lorna, and who may you be?"

A pleasant shiver went up Mattie's spine as she shook the offered hand. "Mattie St—…um. Mattie Logan, ma'am."

"Welcome to my speakeasy, Miss Mattie Logan," Lady Lorna said with a smile before her eyes flicked to the bar top. The smile disappeared and worry creased her forehead as she ran a hand down the back of Jo. The crow arched into the touch. "Josephine, ma cherie, what happened?"

The bird gave an affectionate *caw*. For the second time, Clementine explained how she'd come across Jo and Mattie in the alley.

Lady Lorna arched an eyebrow and speared Mattie with a look. "It seems I owe you a debt."

"Oh no," Mattie said, holding up her hands. "You don't owe me anything. I just happened to be in the right place. Anyone would've helped if they could."

"No, not just anyone would have." Lady Lorna stroked Jo's head before gently checking her injured wing. The bird didn't even flinch or try to peck at her hand. "I don't think its broken, but I know Evangeline would prefer to treat you in human form. She's never fully forgiven you for pecking her that time you flew into the bramble bush chasing that calico who lives on the convent grounds." The bird fluffed its feathers indigently.

Human form? Mattie's forehead wrinkled, but try as she might, she couldn't make sense of what the Lady had said.

"Now that you are safe and back home, do you think you could change back?"

The bird nodded, before rubbing its head against the Lady's palm one last time. The Lady smiled as she unwound the scarf and took a step back.

Mattie blinked rapidly, trying to clear her vision, but it wasn't a trick of the eye, the bird was growing…changing, right there on the bar top. Its edges blurred and expanded. Mattie glanced down at her glass. It was still about two-thirds full, and while it had been a long time since she'd imbibed, she was fairly sure it wasn't enough to make her hallucinate. The blur on the bar seemed to be changing colors and things that looked like limbs came into focus.

A part of Mattie wanted to stumble back off her barstool and run screaming from the building, but the larger part of her, the curious part, that dark part that had made her pack her bag and get on the bus that morning, wanted to know what was happening. Besides, none of the others seemed the least bit concerned about what was going on.

The blur resolved itself into a slight woman with warm peach skin and black straight hair cut into a choppy bob. Her face sported a pointed chin, a long, sloped nose, and large green eyes rimmed with thick black lashes.

And naked.

The woman was stark naked. Not that it seemed to bother her at all. Still, heat rose in Mattie's cheeks, and she averted her eyes from the woman's soft curves. Again, none of the others seemed to think anything of it. Clementine and the Lady were looking at Jo with concern, but no shame, no blushing cheeks, no downcast eyes. As if a naked woman on the bar was an everyday occurrence.

Curiosity burned through Mattie, and she peeked at Jo through lowered lids. Jo didn't raise her arms to cover her small, perky breasts or shift her knees so that no one could see the black curls between her thighs. She just sat there completely at ease in her own glorious skin.

"Here, Jo," Francis said, pulling a folded silk robe from under the bar. Apparently, this kind of thing happened enough to require spare robes conveniently at hand.

"Thanks!" Jo chirped. She pulled the robe over her injured arm with a wince. Mattie noticed that the ring had transferred from the bird's leg to one of the woman's fingers.

That made little sense.

Shouldn't it have been on her wing then when she was in bird form? It was an odd thing to fixate on, but it seemed easier to worry about this detail than to drive herself mad with the bigger questions. Like how a crow turned itself into a girl.

"Clementine, may I inconvenience you to bring Jo round to Evangeline's?" Lady Lorna asked.

"Of course." Clementine pushed off from where she leaned against the back shelf and finished her sherry. "Cheers, Francis. Better luck next time." She patted his cheek as she flounced past him. Francis's face maintained his stern look of disapproval, but Mattie could see the corners of his mouth twitch with the effort.

As Clementine passed by, Lady Lorna leaned to press a lingering kiss to her cheek. "Thank you, cherie. Always a pleasure to see you."

Clementine leaned into the kiss. "Always."

A startling pang of jealousy coursed through Mattie at the casual act of affection. When was the last time she'd been kissed with even half that tenderness? Probably that afternoon in the hayloft with Samantha. The idea sat bitter as lemon peel on Mattie's tongue.

Jo hopped down on Mattie's side of the bar, holding her left arm carefully against her side. "Thank you for coming to my rescue. You're a peach."

Mattie froze in utter surprise as the woman, who until very recently had been a crow, leaned in and kissed her full on the lips. Her mouth was so soft and tasted of cherries, and Mattie melted against that softness.

"Josephine." Lady Lorna's voice was sharp, making both Mattie and Jo jump apart. "What is the rule?"

Jo's face fell. "Always ask before kissing."

"And?"

"If they say no, you do not kiss them, because respecting their 'no' is another way to show you care about them." Jo finished her recital and turned back to Mattie. "My apologies, Mattie."

"Um, it's all right, Jo."

"May I kiss you?"

Mattie sat blinking at Jo for a long moment. The girl looked back at her with such sweet anticipation. That dark part of her wanted to say "yes, yes please!" but she was feeling so far out of her depth, she wasn't sure she should. "Maybe later?"

Jo's face lit up with a smile. "Deal! See you soon!" she called as she started for the door.

"Jo! This way. We've got to get you into proper clothes. And probably some shoes," Clementine said from the back doorway, her voice full of affectionate exasperation.

"Oh, right!" Jo changed direction and went through the curtain Clementine held open.

"Pleasure, Mattie. I'm sure we'll be seeing you soon." With that, Clementine disappeared through the doorway before Mattie could respond.

"Francis, I know you have to get ready for tonight,

but I'd like a private word," Lady Lorna said with a wave of her hand toward Mattie.

"Of course, Lady." He gave her a respectful nod of his head before doing the same to Mattie and heading back into the bowels of the building.

"You may want to finish that sherry. You're looking a bit peaked."

Mattie glanced down to find the glass still in her hand. "Oh. Yes." She took another sip, as if maybe more alcohol would encourage the world to make sense again.

"Please forgive our Jo. When she gets excited, she forgets her manners. It's a work in progress."

"She's… ah…" Her voice trailed off as she desperately searched for the right word. "Delightful." It seemed the safest choice while also being true.

The Lady gave her an amused smile before leaning on the bar. Mattie swallowed and suppressed the urge to squirm on her barstool as the woman regarded her. Up close, the outline of a pupil surrounded by elaborate curlicues was etched into the surface of her gold eye.

"Now. What brought you to New Orleans, Mattie Logan?"

She thought about lying, but the lie sat her on tongue like paste. There was something about this woman or this place or what had just happened that made the lie untenable. But mostly, it was how the Lady Lorna had been genuinely concerned about Jo and her safety. That sense of care and family that had been missing from Mattie's life for so long.

"I was born Mattie Logan, but I became Mattie Stumps. Lenny's not a bad man, not really. But there was no love in our marriage unless you count Lenny's love of the Lord. Or how that love gave him control over me." She tried to keep the bitterness out of her voice. To only convey the facts.

Lady Lorna gave her a look of sympathy, and Mattie thought maybe she didn't need to elaborate more than that. Maybe the graceful woman just knew, and it was a comforting thought.

"When I got married, Granny Marie, my grandmother, gave me five gold bracelets." Mattie held out her wrist. The three remaining bangles clicked against each other. "She told me they were insurance. That pretty jewelry hid in plain sight and was easy to sell. That if I ever needed them, they would be there. I didn't know what she meant at the time."

"But you do now."

There was no judgement in those words, and for that, Mattie could have leaned over and wrapped her arms around Lady Lorna's regal shoulders, but she restrained herself.

Her heart ached in her chest at the thought of Granny Marie wasting away in her bed. Her somber funeral and Lenny's stiff words of comfort. The Granny Marie of Mattie's childhood would have loved every minute of this. A speakeasy tucked behind an alley. A bird who turned into a crow. A whole other world shimmering beneath the surface.

Mattie let out a long breath. "Yes, now I do. Early this morning, Lenny went on a fishing trip, and I packed my bag, sold two of my bracelets, and hopped the bus here."

"Where you stumbled upon a member of my House in distress," Lady Lorna filled in with amusement in her voice.

"Clementine also mentioned a House earlier."

"As long as there has been a New Orleans, there's been Houses. Each run by a Lady or Lord and dedicated to one aspect of the city's virtues or its vices. Tonique & Lace is the home of House Verity, my House. Members wear a ring signifying their loyalty," she said, reaching out a hand to Mattie. On her finger was a ring similar to the one Jo and Francis wore, but larger. The oval ruby on it nearly taking up the full space between her knuckles. "House rings can only be given or removed by the Lord or Lady of the House."

"It's beautiful." It was, but something about a ring that couldn't be removed sent a shiver down Mattie's spine. She thought back to the plain band she'd left on Lenny's bedside dresser that morning. Taking it off had been the hardest and easiest thing she'd ever done. The idea that the ring could have resisted, could have stayed stuck on her finger forever, or until Lenny removed it, made her pulse spike with fear. Jo's ring made more sense in that context, but still didn't explain why it had been on her foot and not her wing in bird form. That was probably a better question for Jo.

"Thank you, but please call me Lorna. Or Lady."

"Is Clementine a member of your House, Lady?" Mattie thought of calling her Lorna, but it felt too intimate, too casual for the regal woman before her.

"No. As much as we would love her to be, Clementine is currently unaligned. Though she does grace us with her presence often."

"You said each House has a specialty. Is alcohol the specialty of House Verity?" Mattie asked, taking another sip of sherry.

Lady let out a laugh that reminded Mattie of bells.

"It's more of a perk. Our specialty is vice. Specifically, those of the flesh."

Mattie nearly choked on her drink as her cheeks heated. "Like the ladies of the night over on Bourbon Street?"

"No, prostitution is House LeBlanc's bread and butter. Not that there is anything wrong with the oldest profession, mind you. I have great respect for those ladies and gentlemen and their entrepreneurial spirit. But I've found that when money gets involved in the bedroom, typically only one party truly enjoys the experience.

"Here, we provide a space for the lowering of inhibitions—drinking, dancing, and enjoying each other's company. And then, of course, there is the burlesque show."

"Oh." Mattie's glass of sherry hovered in her hand, forgotten. Questions churned in Mattie's mind, begging to be asked. The world had shifted so drastically in the last few hours, the very laws of the universe, changing, shifting into something new. It overwhelmed her. But, instead of wanting to run home to the safe, predictability of life on Lenny's farm, she wanted to stay. She wanted to know more. About the Houses, about Jo, about the statue out front that she was sure had winked at her, now that she thought about it.

It was all simply too exciting, like something out of her father's pulps. She'd found the rough papered magazines with their bright, evocative covers in a bin covered by an old horse blanket in the barn. Even though she knew he'd tan her hide for just finding them, let alone reading them, she couldn't help sneaking away to leaf through their pages. For hours, she'd get lost in the wonderful, sometimes frightening, stories of Weird Tales, or go on adventures in the Arctic or deepest jungle with Adventure magazine. Her favorites, though, were the ones always hidden at the very bottom of the bin: Spicy Detective.

The covers featured beautiful women in distress, her dress strategically ripped with her arms bound or being menaced by a dark figure at the edge of the page. She couldn't really be bothered about the plot of those stories. Rather, she'd flip through until the intrepid detective would inevitably have his way with the gorgeous dame he'd just rescued from the mob or an evil uncle who wanted her inheritance or, in one memorable story, an overly amorous gorilla.

Lady Lorna gave her a slow smile that made Mattie's heart flutter. "What do you want, Miss Mattie Logan?"

A sigh escaped Mattie at the sound of her full name, the name she'd chosen to be once more. Was it really as easy as that? Could she just step into the pages of one of her father's pulps? Wouldn't it be much safer to return to the White Dove and beg a room from Frannie?

The thought of returning to the dingy border house and Frannie's tyrannical rules were enough to force the words out of Mattie's mouth, "A job. If it's not too much trouble."

A smile quirked Lady Lorna's lips. "As a dancer?"

"Oh no! Well, rather, I don't know how to dance. Not really. But I could serve drinks and Clementine mentioned you might be in need of another waitress." Mattie had never before served drinks, but she was a quick study and something deep in her wanted to stay.

Not to be a part of the Lady's House with its rings, but to be near it. At least until she got her feet under her. Until she got the lay of the strange land that was the French Quarter.

"Hmm. Francis has been complaining that we're a gal short." Lady Lorna speared Mattie with a look she couldn't read. "However, before I hire you, we must go see Grace."

Chapter Four

The Lady Lorna

There was something infinitely appealing about watching a man smoke a cigarette with care. The way his lips wrapped around its length and let the smoke drift from his mouth in lazy whorls.

Francis sat smoking at the kitchen table. The small courtyard with its tiny raised vegetable beds were visible through the open back door.

Lady Lorna paused in the doorway, enjoying the view. As with everything he did, Francis was precise with his movements, deliberate. Whether it was mixing a perfectly balanced Manhattan or tapping the ash of his cigarette gently into a crystal dish. She stepped into the room, her heels making a low clack against the tile.

"You're going to keep that one, aren't you?" Francis asked, looking up at her.

"You and Nelly have both been complaining about needing more help. Still, I'm going to take her to see Grace first. She looks harmless, but so few things are what they seem."

Francis tilted his head in agreement. "Clementine's instincts are hardly ever wrong, but double checking with the Oracle is always aces. I'll keep an eye on things here."

"I know you will. Thank you," Lady Lorna said,

resting an affectionate hand on Francis's shoulder.

After retrieving her handbag, she gathered Mattie from the bar and headed out. After closing the front door, she looked up and gave Daniel a wave. The gargoyle gave a small head nod in return, and Lorna steered Mattie toward Grace's shop in the Bywater.

As they passed by the small boutiques and restaurants that lined Decatur Street, several of the Vieux Carré's residences tipped their hats and called out greetings. If it hadn't been so close to opening time, Lorna would have happily paused to chat, asking about family members and if she'd see them at Tonique & Lace later that evening. Instead, she returned the greetings with a dip of her head and a warm smile as the two carried on their way.

"Mattie, cherie, could I ask you walk on my right side so I can see you?"

"Oh goodness! Because of your—Yes, yes, of course."

The girl hurried to Lorna's other side with a swiftness that made her lip twitch.

"Lady, would it be all right if I ask a question?"

"Of course."

"Back at the Tonique & Lace, who were you waving to? Was it the statue over the door?"

"Yes, his name is Daniel. He's on day duty. Several gargoyles are members of the House and take turns both guarding the premises during the day and providing muscle in the evenings in case things get out of hand with the customers."

"So the statue is alive?" A note of wonder threaded through Mattie's voice.

"They prefer the term gargoyle. Statues are decor;

gargoyles are living persons who can change their shape."

Mattie's steps faltered. Apparently seeing a crow turn into a girl was not enough to startle this one, but the idea of a living gargoyle was. Or maybe it had more to do with the flicker of desire that had rolled off the girl when she'd looked at Daniel. Between that and the way she had watched Jo on the bar, filled with both wonder and want, Lorna knew taking her to see the Oracle was the right choice.

They came to a compact shotgun house painted a sunny yellow and brilliant white. A wooden sign hung next to the door proclaiming the word "Tattoo" was the only indication of what lay within.

"After you, cherie." Lorna swept an arm in front of her.

The girl walked up the white steps to the front porch, her sensible shoes clicking on the boards. Her head swiveled back and forth, seeming to take everything in with quiet curiosity. The House didn't necessarily need such a green young woman, but Lorna had to admit, there was something appealing about the nearly greedy, open-eyed way the girl approached the world.

Not bothering to knock, Lorna waltzed through the door. The front room served as Grace's studio, where she created her masterpieces. It was currently unoccupied. A large leather barber's chair took up one corner along with a wooden stool. A cupboard held the needles and dyes she used to ink fantastic pictures into people's skin.

"Grace," Lorna called into the next room of the house.

"Lady! Give me a moment, I'll be right there." The voice coming from deeper in the house was full of light. A ray of sunshine as bright as her home.

While they waited, Lorna watched as Mattie eyed the art that covered the walls. Some pieces were Grace's, explosions of color and light, examples of her work that could be translated into tattoos. Others, though, were from local artists. Lorna knew that every wall in the house was as stuffed as the front room. Grace collected art like others collected stamps or porcelain dog figurines. Mattie's mouth hung slightly open as she drifted from wall to wall, pausing here and there to admire specific pieces.

"Do you like them?" Grace leaned against the door that led to her kitchen.

She was a sight to behold. Black and grey tattoos covered every visible inch of her porcelain skin from the chin down. They peaked out of the cuffs and hem of her black satin robe. The gold and red of her House ring was the only color in sight. Other than that, she was a walking monochromatic masterpiece.

Mattie finally remembered to snap her mouth closed. "Yes. They're wonderful."

"Thank you so much." The tattoo artist sauntered next to Lorna. "I had a feeling you were coming by today."

Lorna's lips stretched into a smile. "I can never surprise you, cherie."

"Difficult to surprise an Oracle." Grace's grey eyes sparkled with amusement. "I'm assuming you aren't here for a tattoo." Grace's gaze roamed over Mattie's creamy, uninked skin.

A blush rose to the girl's cheeks as she shook her

head. The curiosity was there, though. Lorna wondered what image Grace would pick to prick into the girl's skin. That was part of Grace's talent—she would take requests from her clients, but at the end of the day, she would only tattoo what she wanted to. Even if that meant the client left disappointed to find another artist who would.

"May I introduce Mattie Logan? She's newly arrived in our fair city and interested in working at Tonique & Lace. Mattie, this is Grace Benoit, the city's finest tattoo artist."

"And the first female one at that," Grace added with a grin. "Pleasure to meet you, Mattie."

"Pleased to meet you." Mattie bobbed her head in reply, the picture of southern politeness, and Lorna had to smother the urge to grin. This bunny was too sweet.

Grace inclined her head. "You'll be wanting to know if she's on the level."

Mattie's eyebrows knit together in confusion as she looked between the two women.

"Before the House takes anyone under its wing, I consult Grace. It's a safety precaution for the good of all House members."

"All right," Mattie said with a swallow, squaring her shoulders. "What do I have to do?" Mattie's eyes darted to the leather barber chair.

Lorna's lip stretched into a smile. "Oh, you don't have to do anything. Grace's prophecies are unique and require an act of a sexual nature. If that makes you uncomfortable, you are more than welcome to wait on the front porch. However, Grace does love an audience."

"Especially one as cute as you," Grace interjected

with a wink.

"So, you are more than welcome to stay and watch," Lorna finished with a wave of her hand toward the tattoo chair.

Mattie froze in her spot like a bunny in the headlights of a Model Ford. Her eyes flitted between Lorna and Grace as spots of color rose into her cheeks. A pink tongue darted out to wet her lips as she swallowed hard. With slow, careful movements, she crossed the room and perched on the very edge of the chair. The leather gave a soft squeak under her weight.

Grace crossed to the front door and bolted it before drawing the curtains across the windows and turning on several lamps. The room comfortably dim, she returned to stand next to Lorna. Grace held her hands in front of her, palms up. Her inky hair framed her face, the impish smile gone, replaced with a serene professionalism. Lorna stepped to face her and placed her own palms against Grace's. The two women took a deep breath in and out together.

"Oracle, House Verity requests your help. Will you exchange a little death for the answer to our query?"

"Yes, the Oracle accepts. What is your question?" Grace asked, her tone weighty with ritual. "What do you wish to learn?"

Lorna didn't answer out loud but held the question of Mattie's future with the House on her tongue, in her mind, and near her heart. She increased the pressure on her hands against Grace's who nodded once in response. Normally, Lorna would start right into the next steps, but they had an audience this time. She stepped next to Grace's shoulder so her real eye could still see Mattie. Her gold-tipped fingers caressed

Grace's chin before she pulled her in for a kiss. The other woman's lips parted hungrily, and Lorna's tongue stroked hers in a long stroke, eliciting a moan that Lorna ate greedily. Her hands undid the tie at Grace's waist, slowly slipping the satin fabric off her shoulders and down her tattooed arms to her elbows.

From the corner of her eye, Lorna watched Mattie, who was sitting rapt in her chair, her cheeks twin spots of red.

A thread of desire rolled off the girl, surprising in its depth. Inhaling, Lorna tasted it across her tongue, bright as champagne with a hint of sweet honeysuckle. She couldn't help grinning into Grace's mouth before trailing kisses down the long column of the woman's neck, nibbling at the place where it met her shoulder. A tattoo of an egret in flight. Lorna loved the way the bird's wings draped over Grace's chest and back as if it were embracing her.

The black robe slid to the floor, offering the full, exquisite view. A sharp inhale came from the corner.

Lorna knew what a breathtaking sight Mattie was taking in. Beyond Grace's lovely curves and valleys, there was her art. Animals, plants, symbols of all kinds, each one rendered and shaded to perfection. All those disparate pieces, separate but somehow cohesive as a gorgeous whole, an incredible canvas of ink.

Grace's head tilted back as Lorna's hands cupped her heavy breast. When she pinched the tattoo artist's pink nipple, a delighted gasp escaped. The Oracle's desire was always a complex thing. Burnt sugar, layered with hints of cinnamon and clove. Brushing her hand down Grace's stomach, which heaved with each of her panting breaths, Lorna drank deeply of that desire, enjoying the way Mattie's mixed with it.

Her fingers cupped Grace's sex, and the woman sagged against her, whimpering for more. Being nothing if not merciful, she slipped one finger into the Oracle's dripping wetness, relishing the gasp it elicited.

She worked her finger in and out, finding the spot she knew sent electric shivers up Grace's spine. Soon the tattoo artist wasn't the only one panting in the room. As Lorna drove Grace higher and higher, she kept her eye on Mattie. The girl's knees pressed together, her hands clasped so tightly, her knuckles were turning white. The girl trembled, her desire a heady perfume, but restrained, subdued. Lorna wondered at that restraint, at the way the girl held herself back or at least tried to. Had her husband been the one to bind her desire, bind her bright spark of life? Was that leash the reason she had run off to New Orleans?

What would the girl do if she was set free?

"Mattie, cherie, do you really want to help?"

The bunny licked her lips, her voice only a whisper. "Yes."

"Touch yourself. Show Grace how much you're enjoying the view."

Mattie inhaled sharply, her eyes flicking between Lorna and the panting Grace, who nodded encouragement. To prove how much Grace wanted her to take part, she bit her lower lip, one hand coming up to cup her own breast.

Mattie's pink tongue darted out again, wetting her lips before she unclenched her hands, releasing them from her knees. She didn't spread them wide as other members of the House would have, rather she only opened them only far enough to slip one hand under the hem of her plain dress. The shadows kept things vague, but there was no mistaking the reason for the gasp that fell from Mattie's lips. The girl leaned back, her hand working herself as her eyes locked on the other two.

Lorna moved her hand in time with Mattie's, drinking in the desire that flooded forward. Savored how it swirled and mixed with Grace's around the room like a heady perfume. The two women feeding off each other. Before long Mattie's breathing became ragged, her movements intense and jerky. Similarly, Grace's breathing was equally quick, her body warm and ready.

"Please, Lady," Grace begged. "Please."

Lorna pressed the heel of her hand to the bundle of nerves above Grace's trembling sex, her finger increasing its pace in her depths.

"Yes! Oh, God." The Oracle's body trembled, poised on the precipice. "Shoulder....right...side."

Keeping her hand exactly where it was, Lorna stepped back to see where Grace had indicated. The trembling woman gave a stuttering cry, her body clutching around Lorna's hand. Her preference would have been to fully enjoy Grace's heady release, but that wasn't possible when a prophecy was involved. She'd just have to make it up to her later.

As the aftershocks faded, the tattoo on Grace's shoulder started to move. Water lapped against Cyprus trees; their roots sunk into the muddy bank. A woman's hand floated next to a half-sunken log. The log opened one split-pupil eye. Lorna blinked and the scene reset. This time it was a man's hand wearing a large gold ring. It wasn't a House ring as there was no gem, just a design carved into its flat surface, but she couldn't make out the details. Again, the log became an alligator who opened one eye, but this time, its mouth also opened in a wide, toothy grin.

The tattoo was still once more, a static scene of the swamp. Lorna used her free hand to rub comforting circles along Grace's back as the Oracle leaned heavily against her. Lorna looked at where Mattie sat slumped in the tattoo chair, one hand still pressed beneath her dress, looking wide eyed and satisfied. Damn. She'd been so caught up in the prophecy, she'd missed the girl's orgasm. The traces of it lingered in the air. She could tell a lot about a person in those precious, vulnerable moments. Lorna's own hunger itched and writhed beneath her skin. She thought of her powers as a panther that lived in her stomach. Now, it paced and snarled, wanting more. She ran a mental hand down its back. Soon. There was business that needed to be tended to first.

"Absolutely beautiful, cherie. Thank you." Lorna pressed a kiss to Grace's damp temple. "I'm going to remove my hand now, all right?"

Grace nodded, taking a deep breath. As Lorna's hand slid free, the Oracle let out a little mew of overstimulation. Prophecies took a lot out of her. After picking up the discarded robe, Lorna helped the woman slip it over her shoulder. She was pleased to see Grace's hands were mostly steady as she tied the belt.

"Would you like me to make you a tea?"

"Oh no, I have some sweet tea in the ice box already." Grace pulled her dark tresses out of the neck of her robe, letting them fall down her back.

"You had a feeling you'd need it, didn't you? Clever girl."

Her laugh was bright and infectious. "I'll be fine,

promise." Grace glanced between the clock on the wall, a wooden octopus held the clock face in its carved tentacles, and where Mattie still sat watching them, though the hem of her dress was back in its proper place. "Francis will be opening the bar soon, and I suspect you two have much to talk about."

"Indeed, cherie."

Lorna pressed a last kiss to Grace's mouth, wishing she had more time to properly tend to the Oracle. "I know you aren't scheduled to dance, but why don't you come by the bar for a drink?" An apology and a promise laced her words.

"Ab-so-lute-ly."

Extending her elbow to Mattie, Lorna said, "Walk with me?"

The stunned girl pushed herself to her feet, relying heavily on the arms of the chair for support. As Mattie placed one hand lightly on Lorna's offered arm, the Lady couldn't help taking a deep inhale of the desire still lingering on the girl's skin.

At the door, Mattie paused. "Thank you for letting me... You are... It was a pleasure to meet you."

"The pleasure was all mine."

The sound of Grace's warm laughter followed them out the door and into the street.

While they'd been inside, the sun had slid near the horizon, making the shadows stretch but doing nothing to cut the thick summer heat that made itself known in April and refused to leave until September.

Lorna turned them down Esplanade. She loved this street with its massive oak trees planted in the middle, arching over both sides of the road like protective sentinels. They waited for an automobile to pass, a sleek black thing of chrome and metal. The fabric top had been rolled back so the occupants, a couple dressed to the nines, could enjoy the evening air.

Once it was past, they crossed the street. Lorna kept the pace slow, savoring the sounds and sights of the city on the cusp of evening. When the whole town seemed to hold its breath in anticipation for the night ahead.

After several blocks of silence, Lorna said, "What's going on in that pretty head of yours?"

Mattie stopped on the sidewalk. Her mouth pressed together, but her hand never left the crook of Lorna's elbow.

"When Grace...you know. Her tattoos told you something, didn't they?"

"Yes. When she orgasms, her tattoos tell the future or answer a question. That's how her particular brand of prophecy works."

"What did they tell you about me?" Mattie regarded her with big, serious eyes.

"Sometimes they provide a clear path forward. Other times, they show possibilities. Things that could come to be given different choices."

Frustration pinched the corners of her mouth. "That isn't an answer."

"No, cherie, but it is the only one you will receive for now," Lorna said with a small smile. "The question is, once again, what do you want, Mattie Logan?"

Instead of blurting out an answer, Mattie stood stock still, contemplating the question. Lorna appreciated a woman who was careful with her choices. Especially one so curious and eager to jump into New Orleans' dark and deep depths.

Mattie's mouth set in a determined line. "I would very much like to work at Tonique & Lace."

The desire in those words, the hope, warmed Lorna through like a long drink of brandy. "I'll hire you on a trial basis. If you can convince Francis to keep you, you'll be paid a salary and board at the House." Lorna leaned forward, fixing her with her stare. Lesser men had quailed beneath the gaze of her one brown, one gold eye, but to the girl's credit, Mattie held her ground. "However, if you do anything to jeopardize the safety of House Verity or any of its members or friends, I will end you so slowly and painfully that you will pray to your God you had never stepped foot in New Orleans."

Mattie swallowed hard. "Understood."

"Good." Lorna straightened. "As for becoming a full member of the House, that will be another trial all of its own."

The girl's eyes flicked to Lorna's House ring, fear pinching the sides of her mouth. Now, that was interesting. Lorna would bet her gold eye it had to do with a certain Lenny Stumps still at home in Baton Rouge, but that was a subject for another day. She gently tugged the girl forward.

"Come on, we need to get you back if you want to start your shift on time. Being late is a surefire way to start things off on the wrong foot with Francis. I'm sure Jo will lend you some glad rags since you came to her rescue after all, and you're about the same size."

At the words, Mattie's face lit up, her whole body humming with excitement for the night ahead. But after a few more blocks, the girl quieted, growing thoughtful once more.

"Lady, may I ask another question?"

"Of course, cherie. In the future, would you do me the favor of just asking the question? Not asking to ask the question?"

"I'll try. It's all been a test, hasn't it? Clementine taking me to Bourbon Street, Jo's transformation on the bar, and Grace's prophecy."

Lorna flashed her a fierce grin. "Clever bunny. Yes, it has."

"What would have happened had I failed?"

"I would have slipped a Forget-Me potion into your drink and sent you on your way. All memories of things strange and unusual softened and blurred to mere dreams."

A shudder went through the girl. "I'm glad I didn't fail. I don't think I ever want to forget this afternoon."

"I'm glad you didn't either, cherie."

Chapter Five

Daniel

From the outside, you would never know Tonique & Lace existed. Even before Prohibition had become the law of the land, that was the way House Verity preferred things. No lights or noise gave it away, thanks to some very expensive wards the Lady maintained around the House. Passing it on the street, you'd think it just an old building; a little shabby, a little worn, but nothing special. But obscurity could only take you so far, especially in New Orleans. The rest of the security fell to the gargoyles.

"What are you doing working tonight? Thought you were on day shift."

Daniel clasped Leo's dark brown hand in his own lighter one. "I swapped with Mac." When he'd asked the head of security for House Verity to take their shift, they'd lifted an eyebrow but agreed.

The two stood just inside the velvet entry curtains of Tonique & Lace. Daniel had changed into his human form and donned his usual white shirt, dark pants, and deep red suspenders. Compared to most of the patrons, he was underdressed, but those that frequented speakeasies expected the muscle to be rough around the edges. Besides, Daniel had ruined enough jackets in bar brawls over the years.

"You don't say." Leo's eyebrow rose. It had a small scar running through it that Leo insisted made him even more debonair. "Does this switch have anything to do with the new tomato I've been hearing rumors about all afternoon?"

That was exactly why Daniel had offered to take Mac's shift, but he wasn't going to admit it out loud. Especially not to a wing. They may both have been gargoyles and members of the same House, but still. Some things were best kept close to the chest. Like an adorable little bunny that bothered to look up. Especially ones who turned such a delightful shade of pink when winked at.

Despite his best efforts, his eyes wandered to the bar where the new gal was currently leaning, waiting for a drink order from Francis. Jo must have let her raid her closet, because the drab, shapeless dress of the afternoon was gone, replaced with a deep blue flapper number. It was cut low with thin straps that left an expanse of skin exposed across her shoulders. The white feathers that lined the hem brushed her knees, leaving her long calves exposed. She even had her hair done up in curls at the back of her head. Mismatched jeweled pins stuck up at odd angles that could only be Jo's handy work.

"I'm going to take that as a yes."

Daniel turned back to Leo, whose smug face was particularly punchable at that moment. "Yeah, yeah. And you're only here on your night off because T&L is the only place in this entire booze-soaked city to get a drink, and not because Hazel is dancing tonight curtesy of Jo's busted wing?"

A slow, wicked grin crept across Leo's face as he

clapped Daniel on the back. "Why can't it be both? Besides, you know I love to watch my baby work."

Shaking his head, Daniel returned the grin. Leo may be a wing and a bastard, but he was a good-natured bastard. Leo headed off to the bar, stopping to greet friends along the way.

The place was already in full swing. The House band, affectionally called The Crawfish Brothers, though none of the members were related, was playing tonight. The sound of horns and piano wove in-between the laughter and chatter of the patrons. The dance floor in front of the stage swirled with couples in all colors of the rainbow, two-stepping, swinging, and jitterbugging. The tables in the rest of the room were populated with folks taking a break from dancing or enjoying a drink or both.

Daniel kept one eye on the room and one eye on the new gal as she wove her way between tables, delivering drinks and chatting with customers as comfortable as if she'd been working at the joint for years and not a few hours. She set a drink, a Grasshopper by its distinctly pale green color, on a table. The three men were well on their way to ossified if the volume of their voices and gestures were any indication. As she bent to deliver the drink, Daniel was offered quite the view, the blue material stretching over a perfect heart-shaped bottom. His hand twitched at his side as he wondered how those pert globes would fit into his palm.

The grasping hand of a man in a dark brown suit with a bright blue feather in the brim of his hat marred the view. The sight sent a ripple of anger down Daniel's spine, and he was halfway across the room before he'd made the conscious choice.

He was still several feet away when the bunny straightened up, one hand reaching back to grip the offending wrist. And twisted. Not enough to seriously hurt, just enough to get the man's attention. A bunny with teeth. Daniel's lip twitched in approval, but he wiped his face neutral as he came up to the table.

"Fellas. Is there a problem?"

The bunny turned to smile up at him, nearly rocking him back on his heels. "No problem at all. I was just reminding this gentleman here of the House Rule: Always ask permission." She turned back to the customer, who was looking distinctly uncomfortable. The bright smile vanished. "Because if he doesn't keep his hands to himself, he will be asked to leave this fine establishment and never be welcomed here again. And that would be a shame. Wouldn't it?"

The man's eyes darted between her and the way Daniel's muscles strained his shirt as he slipped his thumbs into his suspenders.

His companion leaned over. "Please pardon our friend. He forgot himself. It won't happen again."

"Make sure it doesn't. Because if it does, your *friend* won't be the only one on banned from the premises." Daniel held the eyes of each man driving his point home, saving the fella with the blue feather for last. "Either way, I think you owe the lady an apology."

The bunny kept ahold of the man's wrist as he stammered on about how sorry he was and that it would never happen again.

That brilliant smile flashed. "All gravy, darlin. You gentlemen enjoy your evening."

She let go of his hand. The fella set it on the table,

waiting until her back was turned to rub it. With one last glare, Daniel turned to catch up with the bunny as she headed back to the bar. Her back was straight, and that smile was there, but now it was brittle around the edges and the tray in her hands wobbled.

"Hey, bunny, you all right?"

She stopped, clutched the empty tray to her chest, and let out a long breath. "Swell. Just a bit of nerves. I've never done anything like that before."

Daniel smirked. "Seemed to know your onions from where I was standing. You handled them like a champ."

A pink blush crept up her throat. Coals lit in Daniel's belly as she left out a low laugh and pushed a curl back from her face. Gods and monsters, she was gorgeous when she blushed.

"Jo gave me some pointers. She said not to take any lip, or anything else, from the customers. That we have the power to throw anyone who hassles us out on their rears."

"You only have to say the word."

"I'll try not to let that kind of power go to my head." That smile flashed at him again. "I'm Mattie."

"Daniel."

Mattie's eyes went wide. "Oh, you're Daniel." Her gaze flicked down his body and back up, lingering on his narrow waist and muscled forearms, exposed by his rolled-up shirtsleeves. When he smirked at her, the blush went from pale pink to distinctly rosy.

"I mean, of course you're Daniel. All I meant was the Lady told me your name earlier today. When you were…" Maggie's nervous ramblings faded out.

"A gargoyle? Yes, I was on watch when you

brought Jo in. To be honest, I've been wanting to meet you properly ever since. You'd be amazed at how many people don't bother to look up."

"Oh, really?" came the breathless answer.

The lights from the chandelier dimmed as the music faded. Mattie gazed toward the ceiling with a puzzled expression.

"Showtime," he explained.

"Oh!" The sound held a mixture of curiosity and a hint of apprehension.

The lights on the stage flashed against the heavy velvet curtain.

"Watch it with me?"

"I'd love to, but I should get back to the bar. Francis probably has drinks ready."

"Not during the show, you don't. House Rule. Besides, the customers get rowdy if the waitresses walk back and forth, disrupting the show. Though, for you, they might make an exception."

Mattie ducked her head at the compliment, but grinned and nodded. Daniel maneuvered them to the wall near the entrance. He stepped close behind her, but as much as he wanted to, he didn't touch her.

He leaned down to whisper into her ear, "Did Jo tell you about the show?"

The shake of her head brought her hair close, smelling of vanilla. He held himself back from burying his nose into it and taking a long inhale. He might be a gargoyle, but he had manners.

"No, she said, she wanted me to be surprised."

"Even better."

The din of the room quieted; every eye pointed at the lit stage. A single saxophone rent the silence, sending a shiver down Mattie's spine and making the feathers at the hem of her dress flutter against Daniel's pant leg. As the other instruments joined in, the curtains slid open, revealing a stunning black woman. The flood lights turning her long, sequined dress into a river of light. Her body began moving to the music, all lean limbs and swaying hips. She turned her back to the audience, reaching a hand up to slide one strap off her shoulder and then the other. She looked at the audience over her shoulder, a wicked gleam in her eye as she let the dress fall to pool around her feet to a chorus of cheers and whoops from the audience. A wolf whistle cut through the other cheers, making the side of Daniel's mouth pull into a grin. Even without looking, he knew the enthusiastic appreciation came from Leo.

"Her name is Hazel."

"She's…um…beautiful," Mattie said, her voice low and breathless.

And she was. Her skin was bare except for the satin and matching lace of her underpants hugging the curve of her hips. Which drifted up and down to the time of the music.

"Her specialty is fans."

Without turning around, Hazel snapped her wrists and unfurled two large white feathered fans. Holding them just so, she turned back to the audience, completely covering the front of her with the feathers. In a blink, she switched the positions of the fans, leaving the audience only the barest flash of skin as they moved. With half-lidded eyes, Hazel began moving to the music, timing the fluttering movements of her fans to allow only a tease of skin as she danced. A flash of hip here, a bit of stomach there.

Tension filled the air, heavy and waiting, like the calm before a thunderstorm. The entire audience focused on Hazel, mesmerized by her every move. Hell, Daniel had seen her dance hundreds of times, and he couldn't tear his eyes from her. It wasn't the same as Leo's particular appreciation, but anyone still breathing and maybe not a Southern Baptist Preacher would admire her craft.

From the little panting breaths coming from Mattie, it was clear the bunny was enjoying the show as well.

"This is the Lady's favorite part of the night," Daniel whispered.

Keeping her eyes on the stage, she tilted her head to him. "What?"

His arm snaked around her shoulder and paused. "May I?"

"Oh, um, yes."

The words were low, but the sound of them made Daniel want to hear them again. Giving her plenty of time to pull away, he gently took her chin in his hands and turned her head to where the Lady stood with Caron, whose hands were wrapped around her arms. The Lady's head tipped back onto his shoulder, and her eyes closed as she took deep, long breaths.

"She looks like she did at Grace's. When she was helping her...prophesize. What is the Lady doing?"

He let out a low chuckle at her choice of phrasing. "Didn't she tell you?"

Mattie shook her head, the edges of her pinned-up curls tickling the end of his nose, allowing him to inhale the vanilla scent of it again.

"Our Lady is a succubus."

From her confused silence, he guessed she hadn't

heard of one before. "She's feeding off the energy of the crowd—the sexual desires created by Hazel and her dance. Sips it like wine."

"Oh." Mattie spent a moment watching as Caron ran his hands up and down her arms. "Who is that with her?"

"Caron."

"Is he a gargoyle or a succubus?"

Daniel laughed softly. "No, if he stepped out to enjoy the day, he'd burn hot enough to light a cigarette."

She whipped her head back to look at him, eyes questioning.

"He's a vampire and the Lady's main partner."

"Oh!" Mattie turned back to watching the two. After a moment, she leaned back into Daniel's chest as if she'd been rocked back by surprise. Her bare shoulders were now tantalizingly close to his mouth.

"So, he...drinks blood? Like in the penny dreadful stories? I've heard stories that New Orleans was full of dark beings, but I didn't think it was literal."

"While not all vampires are honorable, our Caron only dines on the willing." He couldn't resist the temptation to nuzzle the curve where her neck met her shoulder. She let out the most delightful squeak, followed by a giggle. It took all his willpower not to try to get her to make that adorable noise again.

"He's a member of House Verity?"

"No, just a friend of the House, same as Clementine." He nudged her chin back toward the stage. "Don't miss the grand finale."

As the song crescendoed, Hazel shook her fans in time to the music. As the final notes crashed down, she lifted the fans up behind the back of her head, like a feathered halo. The smirk on her face was far from saintly, though. Particularly with the long, gorgeous display of flesh beneath the fans. The crowd whooped and clapped as the curtains slid close.

The lights brightened once more. Mattie stepped away, and Daniel fought the urge to pull her back against him.

"I knew there would be dancing, but she was incredible!" Mattie grinned, bright and eager. Then she looked down at the tray still pressed to her chest. "Oh! I should get back. Job to do."

"Buy you a drink after closing?"

The corner of her mouth turned up as she pinned Daniel with a stare. "Jo also said that we all get free drinks after our shift."

He gave her a shrug and a grin. "Can't fault a fella for trying."

Turning on her heel, she paused. "Maybe I'll take you up on it," she said over her shoulder before heading back to the bar.

Daniel took a moment to appreciate the sway of her hips. With a grin, he went back to his post next to the door. The end of the night couldn't come soon enough.

Chapter Six

Mattie

It was closer to sunrise than it was to midnight, and every muscle in Mattie's body was stiff and aching. She didn't want to even think about the pain radiating from her feet. One-by-one the customers had paid their tabs and headed out the door, mostly in groups of two's and three's. Most of them leaned heavily on their companions, either from too much alcohol or in hungry anticipation. Sometimes both at once.

Now, the only ones left were members of House Verity. Mattie had been introduced to everyone, but now the names and faces were blurring together. A happy fatigue had settled into her bones, making everything soft and unreal. It had been less than twenty-four hours since she'd woken up in Prairieville, but she felt like she'd been awake for days.

Her eyes roamed the room. The lights were brighter now. The dancer, Hazel, was sitting in the lap of a man who Mattie was fairly sure was a gargoyle named Leo. The man had broad, powerful shoulders. Relaxed against that large expanse, Hazel looked even more beautiful than she had on stage, laughter making her eyes sparkle.

"A French 75 is the only way to celebrate a first night." Francis handed over the champagne flute, a lemon twist swirling up the middle of the glass.

The bubbly drink was sweet and tart. And dangerous. Something she thought she could drink until her head swam if she wasn't careful. "Thank you, Francis. It's delicious."

The man slid a bundle over to her, the printed face of George Washington wrapping around the fold. "Your cut for the evening."

Mattie's hand shook a bit as she pulled the money close. When Francis turned to take another order, she counted them as inconspicuously as possible. The stack contained nine one-dollar bills. A giddy giggle rose in her throat. It was the most money of her own she'd ever had—had ever been allowed to have. Lenny had controlled the finances, only giving her a dime or two every Sunday for the collection plate. A dollar if it was Christmas or Easter. He'd even had credit with the grocer and other stores in town, so he hadn't needed to give her shopping money. That way he'd been able to review and critique her purchases every month.

Shoving the past into the past, her mind turned to practical matters like where to put her newly earned dough. The dress Jo had lent her was beautiful but didn't have pockets, and she'd left her handbag in her new room. She looked around and spotted Francis handing another bundle of cash to the other waitress, a human named Nelly. Nelly had helped with Mattie with her whirlwind introduction to waitressing. With an air kiss for Francis, Nelly took the money and promptly stuck the whole thing down the front of her dress without a hint of reservation. Francis gave her a good-natured eyeroll and headed back to the bar as Nelly continued pushing the broom across the dance floor.

Even though the band was long gone, she shimmied and twisted with each step. How did she have so much energy?

Mattie shrugged, stuffed the money into her own brassiere, and took another sip of her cocktail. When Francis had asked what she wanted, she'd been too embarrassed to admit that she knew nothing about cocktails and had simply said, "Surprise me."

"I thought you were going to let me buy you a drink."

Mattie smiled into her glass, refusing to turn and look at the man leaning next to her on the bar. "You were taking too long."

"Ouch!" Daniel cried, full of exaggerated hurt. "Fair enough. Shame on me for keeping a beautiful dame like yourself waiting. Can I get a bourbon, Francis?"

Francis gave him a small salute before turning to the shelves of bottles behind him.

"How was your first night?"

"I can't wait until tomorrow night."

Daniel tilted his head back and let out of a laugh. Mattie admired the sight from the corner of her eye. He had been impressive in gargoyle form but was an absolute dish of a man as a human, with dark brown hair just long enough to be shaggy and a jaw that could cut glass. His eyes were the same in both forms. Keen, taking in everything happening around him, and a startling shade of light grey. White dress shirt and black pants hid lean muscles, hinted at by the way the fabric stretched and the powerful grace with which he moved.

She couldn't help but wonder about the process of how he shifted from the gorgeous man in front of her into that of hound-faced, muscled gargoyle she saw earlier in the day.

"Glad to hear it, but the next shift is sooner than you think. It's actually tonight. Not tomorrow."

"Oh, yes. It's after midnight. Tomorrow is, in fact, today."

Francis handed a glass filled with a large chunk of ice and amber liquid to Daniel. Over the course of the night, she had learned that the fat, low-walled glassware was called a lowball.

"A saint, my friend," Daniel said as he took the glass. He held it out to Mattie with a slight smile. His House ring was the only decoration on his long-fingered hands. "To the first night of many at T&L."

She turned and clinked her glass against his before taking a drink. Movement caught her eye. The lady and her partner, Caron, were walking toward the internal hallway with Grace between them. The three of them slowed their steps as the Lady lifted Grace's hand to kiss the inside of her wrist. The Oracle closed her eyes, leaning her head against Caron's shoulder as he wrapped a hand around her waist.

Mattie's cheeks heated as she watched. A part of her thought she should look away from the intimate moment, but her gaze remained fixed. Caron's other hand came up to caress the Lady's cheek, before sinking into her finger waves and pulling her head back sharply. The look on her face wasn't one of pain, only pleasure. He pulled her close, kissing her deeply as Grace kissed her way along the Lady's shoulder. The three broke apart and headed deeper into the House.

"Beautiful sight, isn't it?"

Mattie turned back to Daniel; her cheeks hot at

being caught staring. "I thought you said Caron was her partner."

"Main partner, yes. But not her only one. As the House Verity motto states, 'Baise tes Amis.'"

"I'm sorry, I don't speak French," she said with an apologetic smile.

He leaned in close, a mischievous glint in his eye. "It translates to 'kiss your friends' but we use it to mean…fuck your friends, bunny."

The words curled around Mattie, seeming to stroke their way up her cheek. "Oh. That's…quite the motto."

Maybe it was the whole surreal, wonderful day or the champagne, but the dark part of her unfurled, wanting her to be bold, wanting her to respond to the hungry way Daniel was regarding her. What would be the harm in giving in to that dark part of herself? Considering the motto of the House and the little she'd seen of the members, no one would judge her for it. Besides, she didn't know how long she would be working there. Shouldn't she learn and experience all she could while she was here?

Her tongue darted out to lick her lower lip. "Am I your friend?"

A low chuckle rumbled out of Daniel's throat as he took a long drink. The sound warming Mattie's lower belly.

His eyes never left hers. "Nothing I'd like more than to be your friend. If you'd let me."

Mattie's mind flashed back to the afternoon and Jo's recital of the Rule. He hadn't said the exact words, but she knew the meaning behind them. The question they contained. She finished her glass in one drink, hopped off her stool, and held her hand out to the beautiful man who was also a gargoyle. Her heart beat wildly in her throat as he looked at her.

He didn't even finish his drink. Just left it on the bar and took her hand. It was warm and slightly rough in hers as she led him through the back curtain and up the stairs to the second floor. They turned right down the hallway, making their way to the room she'd stopped in briefly that afternoon to dump her carpet bag and change into Jo's dress.

Her room.

One with a lock on the door and that she didn't have to share with anyone else. Not unless she wanted to. Not unless she invited them explicitly in. Like she was doing now.

It was small, but cozy, with a good-sized bed with a simple metal frame. A table and two chairs sat in the corner, and cheery pale pink curtains hung over the tall windows. A mirror set over a chest of wooden drawers rounded out the extent of the furniture. Hooks for her dresses hung on the wall next to a door that led to her own private bathroom.

Mattie's eye fell on the bed where her open carpet bag spilled all her worldly possessions into a disordered heap. Maybe she should have waited to bring Daniel up here until she'd settled in. Tidied up.

The thoughts were pushed out of her head as the man in question closed the distance between them, pulling her gently against his chest. She could feel the strength in his arms as he wrapped one around the small of her back, holding, but not trapping her. His thumb brushed along the edge of her chin, tipping it upwards. Heat flared in her stomach, sending sparks like fireflies into her chest. How could such chaste touches make her nearly dizzy with need?

"Still want to be friends, bunny?"

The question wasn't want stunned her—it was the look on his face. The one that said if she changed her mind, he would respect that decision.

Her eyes roamed over his face, taking in the day's scruff on his square jaw and the banked intensity of his grey eyes.

The rest of the room disappeared as her tongue darted out to wet her lips. "Yes."

A slow smile curled up the sides of his mouth, causing Mattie's heart to beat faster in response. With deliberate care, his fingers cupped the back of her head as his lips pressed against hers. It sent an electric pulse through her, curling every bit of her up into it, from her fingers all the way to her toes. She pressed herself against him, reveling in the warm, hard planes of his body. His tongue flicked against her lips—the barest of questions. Mattie's lips parted like church doors on Easter Sunday, welcoming him in. She could feel his smile before his tongue claimed her, tasting her in long, purposeful strokes. The electrical pulses had built into lightning storms, racing along her nerves as he tilted her head back, claiming more of her mouth.

It wasn't anything like the sweet, brief kiss she'd gotten from Jo. It was the type of kiss that she would've had with Samantha in the hayloft if they'd been braver. The type of kiss she had dreamed of Lenny giving her on their wedding night, but never had. Not then, and not any other night they'd been together either.

Lenny.

Mattie drew back, fighting the pull of Daniel's lips, the heat of his skin through his shirt. Fighting her own desperate need to be touched and to touch. "Um, Daniel?"

His eyes were sharp as they searched her face. The hand cupping her head moved to stroke his thumb against her cheek. "Yes?"

Her hands kneaded the muscles of his bicep while she tried to pull her scattered thoughts together. She got distracted by the way his muscles bunched under her hand. It was a very shapely bicep. Had she ever found biceps appealing before?

Giving herself a mental shake, she stilled her hand and forced the words out. "I need tell you—I think it's only right that you know…" She licked her buzzing lips. "I'm married."

Daniel stiffened. His hand didn't leave her cheek, but he increased the distance between them. That hungry look shuttered away behind his grey eyes.

Mattie's heart fell into her pinching shoes. "I've mucked it all up, haven't I?"

"No, you haven't mucked anything up, but I think we should talk." He let her go and headed for one of the chairs next to the table.

The sudden loss of his embrace nearly made her cry hot, frustrated tears. Her entire body ached for the brief glimpse she'd had of what being intimate could be like. With someone who actually wanted her.

Silently, she chided herself for being a ninny. She'd only just met the man, and if he couldn't handle her situation, she would just find someone who could. But she would not lie about who she was or where she came from. She walked to the other chair with her head held high.

As she passed where Daniel sprawled, he reached

out and snagged her by the waist, dragging him onto his lap. She let out a surprised squeak.

"I meant it when I said you hadn't mucked anything up, bunny," Daniel said, his voice rumbling against her shoulder. "Now, tell me about your old man."

Warmth raced to pool in her belly. Maybe the evening wasn't over yet. "Lenny. The marriage is over. Not legally, mind you, but for me there's no going back. Every aspect of my life was dictated the way he wanted it. And I couldn't do it anymore." Mattie left out the part where sex to Lenny had been about duty to God to bear and raise children, and anything beyond that was a mortal sin. Or how he had reduced Mattie's life to the farm and the church, cutting her off even from her family and the few friends she'd had before they were married. "What he wanted out of our marriage and what I wanted were two different things. He wanted a perfect pious doll of a wife to show off at church…"

He leaned forward, nudging her with his chin. "What did you want?"

She took a deep breath and let it out. "To be me and all the messy, wicked things that entails. To read pulp magazines and drink wine until the room spins. To dance. To live jazz and eat foods from places I've never heard of. To live life now and not just wait around until the next one. I just…want to live and love as I choose."

She tilted her head down, loose curls swinging to hide her face. "I know it sounds silly."

"No. Everyone in House Verity is here for that same reason, because we want to live as ourselves—not as others would want us to. We're all looking for more." He used one finger to force her to look at him. "Do you love him?"

"I wanted to. I desperately wanted to, because a wife should love her husband, you know? That's what I've been told my whole life, by my parents, Pastor Michals, the story books. But, no, I don't love him, and I don't think he loves me either. Not really. He loved the idea of me. The control he had over me."

Mattie realized her hands were clenched in her lap, and she forced them to relax, smoothing Jo's dress over her legs, savoring the silky feel of it. "I know I've only been in New Orleans for a short time, but I don't think I could ever go back to the farm. Not to the farm, and certainly not to him. To shut myself up into that windowless box of a person he wanted me to be. To live only by his rules. It would suffocate the life out of me. I know it would."

"I believe you." He reached a hand up and gently tucked a strand of hair behind her ear. "And it would be a tragedy."

"Does it matter?" She bit her lip to stop the tremble in her voice. "That I'm still married?"

He gave a slow shake of his head, the corners of his mouth turning down. "If it's over for you, that is all that I care about."

She slumped against his chest, nearly giddy.

"But since we're doing some housekeeping, might as well ask if you've been to see Clementine's shop?"

She was loath to remove her head from the crook of Daniel's neck—he smelled like sun-warmed granite—so her words were muffled. "Haven't had time, but Jo promised to take me tomorrow. Why?"

"Ask her for some of the special tea. The one she

makes with Evangeline."

Curiosity forced Mattie to sit up. "What makes it special?"

"Prevents consequences of the family way."

"There's a tea for that?" Mattie thought about the harried women back home with their hordes of children. A tea like that would give them more control over their lives. Then she thought of what Pastor Michals would say. Probably would call it the devil's brew or some such nonsense. She thanked anyone who would listen that Lenny's occasional attentions had never resulted in more than a vague disappointment for her.

He nodded. "They make one for the ladies and one for the fellas. It works best if both parties drink it every day."

Mattie's shoulders slumped. "So, I guess that's curtains for tonight."

"Hold up now. Who said anything about curtains?"

"But I don't have any of the tea yet?"

"Just because the menu changed, doesn't mean we need to cancel the reservation." He leaned in and nibbled the place just below her jaw, sending little spikes of pleasure rippling down her neck. "Assuming," he continued between nibbles, "that you're still hungry."

Mattie tilted her head to the side, allowing him more access. "Starving."

His talented mouth worked its way down Mattie's neck and across her shoulder, alternating between kisses, licks, and nibbles as he pleased. Every fiber of Mattie's being focused on his progress, her banked desire roaring back to life in an instant. When he came across the barrier of the strap of his dress, he moved the fabric aside, letting it slip down her arm. His lips blazed a trail of fire down her heaving chest to the top of her brassiere.

"Well, seems I've found buried treasure," he murmured against her skin.

At the words, her eyes flew open, and her head snapped upright. "What?"

He grinned, pulling the bundle of ones from her undergarment, and set it on the edge of the table. "I'll just put them over here for safekeeping."

Before she could even thank him, his lips were back to work on the top of her breast. The fabric of her bra moved to the side, exposing one nipple to the warm night air. A growl of appreciation rumbled from his chest as he kissed the pink nub before sucking it between his lips. Her breath caught, and she arched back, drowning in the sensation. Heat was building in between her legs, persistent and needy. On instinct, she wiggled, trying to sate the sensation. The movement did little to lesson her need, but it did result in a groan from Daniel. Seems she wasn't the only one enjoying themselves. The long, hard length of him pressed into her hip, and she did another slow experimental wiggle, marveling at the size of him, wondering what it would look like outside the confines of his black pants.

"Woman." The word was low and rough, both with desire and a warning. It curled in the bottom of Mattie's belly. She wanted to make him say it again. To see what the unspoken consequence would be.

Before she could find out, his hands were on her waist, standing her up in between his splayed legs. As his hand worked their way up her ankles to her calves, he said, "Let's get you out of that dress before I rip it off you. I wouldn't want to get on Jo's bad side. She is mighty fond of her sparkles."

Mattie nodded. Shivers ran up her body as his hands explored the backs of her knees. Had her knees always been so sensitive? She couldn't remember. His hands worked further up, gathering up the feathered hem of the dress, but still cupping the outside of her thighs, pulling the fabric up her body. He rose with the dress until he was standing next to her, the garment in one hand. His eyes roamed over her, and she felt a stab of self-consciousness. Jo's beautiful dress had made her feel fearless, transformed, but underneath, she still wore the plain cotton underthings she'd packed from home. Her mind thought of the beautiful lace bras and silk panties that had spilled from Jo's chest of drawers or BeeBee's ivory corset and the way it had shaped her impressive bosom. As she crossed her arms over her chest, she added more items to her mental shopping list.

"Stop that." Daniel had laid Jo's dress over the back of the other chair and now pinned her with his gaze. "Don't cover yourself. I want to see all of you."

Mattie froze at the quiet authority in his voice. There was a possessiveness there that tore her open, made her want to obey. She uncrossed her arms.

"Much better."

She shivered at the praise, at the obvious approval in his gaze as he looked at her. In half a heartbeat, his hands were on her waist again, lifting her up as she if she weighed less than a bag of flour and set her down on the edge of the table. His leg pushed hers wide, leaving no room for modesty, and stood between her knees.

One hand tangled in her hair, heedless of the multitude of hairpins contained within, and tilted her head back. His mouth caught hers in a softly brutal kiss. His tongue invaded her mouth, exploring every inch as his free hand undid her brassiere. As she kissed him back and her tongue tangled with his, she removed the straps from her arms and flung the undergarment in the general direction of the bed. Her back arched as his hand cupped her breast, his thumb skimming her nipple as it tightened into a stiff peak. A gasp escaped as his fingers pinched just hard enough to send a jolt of pain racing through her pleasure and stoking the fire building low in her abdomen.

His hand explored lower, stroking the skin of her stomach until reaching her cotton panties. He ran one finger just along the edge, pulling away to give her a smirk.

"I'm not gonna find golden doubloons in here, am I?" A glint of mischief flashed in his grey eyes. "Uncut diamonds? A priceless statue?"

Mattie swatted at his shoulder as he let out a laugh. The breather reminded Mattie that while she was practically naked; he had on too much clothing. She pulled his dark red suspenders over his shoulders, letting the loops fall down his arms to hang at his sides, dangling from the buttons on his trousers. Her fingers found the top button of his shirt and undid it. She leaned forward and pressed a kiss to the newly exposed skin at the base of his throat, marveling at the taste of him.

Daniel rumbled approval as his hands stroked slowly up and down her back. Her fingers went to the next button, her mouth pressing kisses as she went until she couldn't bend forward anymore. As her hands finished unbuttoning his shirt, her lips trailed over his collarbone and shoulder, trying to imitate the little nips of teeth that had trailed fire along her skin earlier. She pushed the fabric down his shoulders, letting it slip to the floor and spread her hands over the hard planes of his chest. Oh, he had definitely been sculpted by a master. Even in this form, he was muscled and toned in all the right places. Her tongue darted out to lick her lips, wanting to press her mouth to every inch of him.

He'd been watching her undress him with his head tilted back, his eyes half closed. With a lazy hunger, he moved forward, gently pressing her down until her back was flat against the table. He kissed down her collarbone and up the mound of her breast until he sucked her nipple into the wet heat of his mouth. She arched with a cry, a wordless plea for more. He alternated between flicking his tongue and sucking on the stiff peak until Mattie thought she'd squirm off the table.

With one last kiss, his mouth moved further south, kissing and nipping his way down her stomach as his hands undid the clasps at the top of her stockings. He left her plain garter belt in place but slid her panties down her legs. He knelt down, pulling her hips until she was on the very edge of the table, spread open before him. Her heart hammered in her chest as she came up to her elbows. Her thighs quivered with the desire to close, to press back together. His earlier admonishment the only thing keeping her from trying to hide herself from him. His mouth found the tender skin of her thigh, inching its way to where her legs met. Her legs shook, torn between her desire to spread herself further open for him and the little voice in the back of her head, demanding that she close her legs at once. That his mouth was too close to her ladyhood and wanting him to press that mouth to her was wicked and sinful.

"You…um, you don't have to," she said, a bit breathless.

He paused and looked up at her. Goodness, he was gorgeous. His hands kept rubbing small circles at the tops of her thighs.

"If I do something you don't want or like, I want you to tell me. But know that I don't do anything I don't want to. And I expect the same from you."

The intensity of his gaze speared her, held her in place. She swallowed and nodded slowly. He leaned down, his mouth hovering just above her aching sex. His lips parted and hot breath brushed against her, making her tremble under his hands. His tongue licked up the entire length of her slit in one slow lick. Sensation exploded through her, and she fell back to the table with a cry she cut off with her hand. Sweet baby Jesus, how could one little lick completely undo her like that?

"Don't hide from me, bunny. Let me hear how much you enjoy it." The soft command was back in his voice, allowing no room for second guessing. She obediently removed the hand from her mouth and balled it at her side. If he wanted to hear her, she'd let him. If this gorgeous man…gargoyle wanted to do those wonderfully sinful things with his tongue, she was more than happy to let him. With a happy sigh, she pushed her worries aside and let herself just enjoy the experience.

His tongue was back, exploring her folds, darting

into her wetness. His hands were heavy on her hips, keeping them in place so she couldn't squirm away from his attention as small cries and pants fell from her mouth. When his lips closed on her tight bundle of nerves, it sent an electric bolt through her and drove a harsh cry from her lips. How could a body experience so much pleasure and not explode into a thousand pieces?

His tongue flicked that little bundle of nerves in a smooth steady rhythm, driving her pleasure higher and higher. She felt this pressure building in her, filling every bit of her. Her whole body hurtled toward a cliff edge, driving on by Daniel's unrelenting attention. For one glorious moment, she was suspended in time before every muscle clenched and she spilled over. Her nerves lighting up like fireworks at the July 4th picnic.

Awe filled her as she tried desperately to regain her breath. This is what an orgasm could be? Not that it was her first one. When she was sure Lenny was out of the house, she would lock the doors and use her hand to relieve the tense ache that was her body's constant companion these past years. But those fluttery little bits of relief were like an overturned cart horse compared to the train wreck she'd just experienced.

Even the one she'd had watching Lady Lorna and Grace earlier that day couldn't compare. Had that really only been that afternoon?

He pressed kisses onto her hip as her shivers subsided. Still a little out of breath, she tried to sit up, only to be stopped by one long-fingered hand on her stomach.

"You aren't done."

Three words and a wicked smile had her heart beat

like a jazz drum. She eased back down as his mouth pressed feathered kisses onto the trembling skin of her inner thigh. Her heart rate slowed, but soon the memory of what he could do with that clever mouth relit the fire in her belly. As if he sensed the shift, his mouth worked its way back up to settle between her thighs once more. The kisses increased in pressure and intensity, occasionally replaced by the flat of his tongue. The build was slower this time, but the anticipation so much greater.

One of his hands came up, his fingers caressing her dripping entrance. She groaned as one fingertip teased but did not enter her. The wanting grew until it was its own beast, prowling in her chest. Her fingers tangled in his dark hair, unsure if she wanted to pull him closer or push him away. His mouth grinned against her as her hands clenched. Still, his hand stayed maddeningly shallow. Slow little dips that never relieved the growing pressure inside of her.

When she thought she'd burst, she let out a whimpering plea. "Daniel. Please."

"Tell me what you want. Say the words."

"Please…please won't you fill my pussy?" She'd never said the word for another human. Only whispered it in her mind as she worked her own fingers into herself. The word felt round and soft on her tongue, and she liked the way it tasted.

"How could I say no when you beg so pretty?" He pushed his finger into her with one slow thrust, the feeling of it curling Mattie up off the table with a cry. His other hand pressed on her stomach, keeping her still as he pulled out and thrust into her again, slow and steady.

Her mind tried to flash back to those few, quick times Lenny had done his husbandly duty, where beyond a general discomfort, she really hadn't been aware of what was going on down below. Now, it felt as if every inch of her was focused on the feeling of his long, blunt finger causing delicious friction as it moved in and out of her. And this was just one finger! What would it feel like to have his manhood, his cock, deep inside her?

The thought sent little shivers down her spine. There was no way around it, she'd just have to stop by Clementine's tomorrow. The thoughts vanished from her head as his tongue wrapped around her pearl, sucking in time to the rhythm of his finger, sending her soaring higher with each flick, each thrust. When his fingertip pressed into a place deep within her, electric fire coursed through Mattie and she cried out, curling her whole being around Daniel's head as her body clenched and pulsed. When the initial wave ended, she flopped back to the table, her head spinning, her blood fizzing like the champagne in a French 75.

If this gargoyle kept giving her orgasms like that, she might not make it. But what a sweet death it would be.

Chapter Seven

Daniel

Daniel stood up and leaned over Mattie's sprawled form, one hand cradling her cheek. His thumb rubbed soothing circles. "Still with me, bunny?"

Her eyes remained closed as she let out a drowsy "mmhmm," the corners of her lips tugging up into a grin. His own mouth pulled into a smug grin. Splayed out on the table, she looked like a debauched wood nymph from a classic painting. That must mean he was the wicked satyr leading her into temptation. It wasn't his usual role, but there was something about her eager curiosity that had completely ensured his attention.

Unable to help himself, he reached out to slide his palm down the soft skin of her side. The sweet, tart taste of her was still on his tongue. He wanted to force those desperate, breathy noises from her again, but contented himself with rubbing up and down over her hip. He didn't want to overstimulate her, at least, not too much. The poor thing was so starved for touch, even that much had been a lot for her.

One of her hands found his shoulder and tugged down, and he obliged her with a long, slow kiss. Her hands roamed the planes of his chest, down the slope of his stomach to the little dips where his hips disappeared into his trousers. With how they were positioned, she couldn't get her hands further down to where his hard cock pressed into the softness of her belly.

He let her push him up, and he stood back, watching as she sat up on the edge of the table. The tip of her tongue wet her full lower lip as she eyed the tented front of his pants. The heady mixture of sweetness and desire on her face made his cock ache as she began unbuttoning his trousers. As the last button slipped free, his cock sprang up, straining the silk of his underpants. Her fingers brushed up his length, finding the shape of him through the thin fabric. Daniel made a rumbling sound of approval in the back of his throat as she pushed his pants and underwear down his thighs.

"Oh, my." The words were breathless. Her eyes large and hungry as she surveyed him.

Daniel knew he had no reason to be shy about his endowments, but there was something very appealing about the genuine wonder in Mattie's face.

"Enjoying the view?"

Her fingers dug into his hips. "Very much so."

With an adorable look of concentration, she brushed her fingertips along his shaft, sending a ripple of pleasure down his back. He wanted to thrust into her touch but forced himself to be still while she explored him with her hands.

"You're…um…quite large," she said as her hand curled around the base of him, her fingers not quite meeting.

"I'll take that as a compliment." Gods and monsters. She stared up at him in wide-eyed hunger. Like he was a plate of beignets, straight from the fryer.

She bent forward, but the angle was all wrong. Letting out a frustrated little mew, she pushed him back. He sat in the chair with a huffed laugh, his pants still tangled around his thighs. After removing his shoes, he pulled them all the way off before leaning back in the chair and spreading his legs. He brought one hand up and gripped his shaft, moving up and down in a lazy stroke as he watched her. She pushed off the table and sank to her knees, not caring about the stockings that bunched and slipped down her thighs. Small, eager hands rested on the tops of his legs. Liquid brown eyes watched his hand wrapped around his cock, slowly moving up and down.

"Is this what you want?"

Mattie looked up at him and nodded.

"Say the words, bunny."

"Yes. I want to suck your cock."

Holy hell, he enjoyed the way the filthy words tumbled out of that sweet mouth of hers. "Open your mouth."

Mattie shivered as she leaned forward and obeyed. His cock brushed her lower lip and the tip of her tongue darted out to swipe along the head, lapping at the bead of moisture poised there. There was a curious, almost tentativeness, to the movement. A part of him wondered if this was the first time she'd ever put her mouth on a man before.

With a little hum of excitement, she leaned forward and worked her way up from the edge of his hand back to the broad head. The eager curiosity with which she explored, using her tongue and lips, made his balls ache. Being the sole focus of that much intensity was intoxicating.

He let out a groan as those perfect lips parted and she took as much of him as she could into her mouth.

She sank down until her lips met his fingers still curled around his shaft. There she let out a little choked noise and backed up, but didn't fully release him. His other hand come up to tangle in her dark curls, gently drawing her head up and moving it slowly back down. Pleasure knotted at the base of his spine as he guided her head up and down as she worked him over with her eager lips and tongue.

A part of him wanted to draw it out as long as possible, to savor the sight of her mouth stretched so prettily around him. To savor the hot, wet warmth. The little muffled noises that slipped around his cock as her head bobbed up and down. The way her fingers dug into the tops of his thighs, reflexively, as if she didn't know she was doing it. The way her eyes never closed, but watched intently as his breathing changed, becoming ragged and harsh. She redoubled her efforts, sucking hard, trying to take even more of him into her mouth.

"Mattie…"

The word was pure need as his body stiffened, and his balls tightened. His entire world narrowed as pleasure ripped through him. A harsh, rough cry tore from him as he pumped into her mouth. The long muscles of her throat working to swallow him down.

Utterly spent, his grip relaxed on her hair, and he slumped back in the chair. She sat back on her heels, licking those luscious lips now red and swollen from her effort.

He reached out to push a sweaty curl behind her ear. "How are you doing?"

"I feel like I should ask you that question," she replied with a huffing laugh. Mattie rubbed her cheek against his palm. His hand felt rough and calloused compared to her exquisite softness.

"I asked first." He couldn't help the slow grin that split his face. Just touching her face wasn't enough, so he leaned forward and scooped her off the floor and into his lap. She melted into his chest, tucking her head under his chin. She let out a little contented sigh as his hand slowly drifted down the curve of her spine.

"I'm ab-so-lute-ly lovely."

"Good. You deserve nothing less."

He felt her stiffen slightly in his arms. His hand stopped his soothing strokes. "What's that thought, bunny?"

She turned her face further into his chest as she confessed, "I made you…um…come." There was a note of sweet pride in her voice.

"You did. Spectacularly, as well. It's not often I lose control like that."

Leaning her head back, she looked at him, a pleased smile on her lips. "You are a big, beautiful man with a big, beautiful cock." She paused and ran light fingers over his bare chest. Amazingly, his deflated member stirred under her attention. "And I made you groan and pant and come. The power of that is delicious."

Daniel gave her a slow, lazy smile. "Anytime you want to taste that power again. Just let me know. I'd be happy to oblige you."

"Deal." She grinned back at him before giving in to a jaw-cracking yawn. Ignoring his half-mast cock, he pressed a kiss to her forehead and stood. As her head rested against his chest, he moved her carpetbag and other things from the bed before pulling back the quilt and setting her down.

Only, she didn't let go. As her hands pulled him down next to her, he froze. Not staying the night was one of his cardinal rules. Sex was one thing but sleeping next to someone was a whole other ball of wax. That way led to feelings and complications. Not to mention, he wouldn't get a good night's sleep.

Her eyes were already closed as she gave another gentle tug. Brown curls spread out over the pillow in a dark halo, and there was a look of sweet satisfaction on her face. If he pulled away now, she'd wake up and that look would morph to one of disappointment. What kind of monster would he be if he caused that?

Besides, one night wouldn't hurt. Would it?

Resigned to a long night, he slipped into the bed. As she snuggled into his chest, he pulled the sheet up over the two of them. One soft leg tangled with his as her breathing evened out into the gentle rhythm of sleep. The weight of her was surprisingly comforting, not confining. The last thing he remembered before he fell into sleep was the feel of her hair under his hand, as soft as satin and moonlight.

Chapter Eight

Mattie

The next afternoon Mattie walked arm-in-arm with Jo up Hospital Street. She'd awoken that morning with Daniel's lips pressed against hers and a promise to see her after work that night. After a quick bath, she'd gotten dressed and wandered down to the kitchen in search of food. She'd found Jo making eggs and toast with a large pot of coffee already brewed. Mattie nearly kissed her again. After they'd both stuffed themselves silly, she asked if Jo minded taking her to Clementine's shop. When they'd left Tonique & Lace, Mattie had looked up to wave at Daniel on his perch. A sense of wonder had settled into her chest at the sight of those sharp talons, so at odds with his nimble fingers of the night before. The sides of his snout pulled up into a sharp-toothed grin. He gave Mattie a wink, and she realized his eyes were the same in both forms. Grinning, she'd blown him a kiss as Jo had grinned and waved.

Now, the two strolled through the French Quarter, talking about anything and everything. After they crossed Chartres, Jo's bright chatter trailed off. The further they got down the street, the stiffer Jo became, and her eyes kept shifting to the last house on the left-hand side. The house was a large three-story affair with the typical wrap around balcony on the second story, extending over the sidewalk. Windows with arched casements lined the cream-colored walls.

As they come up next to the house, Jo's mouth went into a hard line, her eyes focused on the building across the street.

"Um, Jo, what is it?"

"Have you heard of Madame LaLaurie?" Jo said the name with a fierce hate that surprised Mattie.

"No, I don't know who that is."

Jo stopped and turned to stare at the building. "That's the LaLaurie mansion, named for its mistress Delphine LaLaurie. Wealthy, a member of high society, and purest evil."

"Evil?"

Jo's dark hair swung as she nodded once. "In 1834, a fire broke out in the mansion. When neighbors rushed to make sure everyone had gotten out, they found that the sweet-faced mistress of the house had been performing experiments on her enslaved people. Horrid things… The fire had been started by a woman chained to the stove. She didn't make it, but because of her sacrifice, the authorities took LaLaurie's enslaved people away."

Disgust and horror gripped Mattie's stomach. Living in the South, she'd grown up hearing stories about slavery. Seen for herself the horrific effects it still had on both their society and Black folks themselves. Considering the evils of slavery, she shuddered to think how monstrous a person would have had to be for the authorities to step in.

"It made the papers. A mob attacked the mansion. That snake, LaLaurie, escaped in a carriage, but the mob destroyed the house—nearly burned it to the ground. She escaped to Paris and eventually the house was rebuilt. But that much suffering. That much pain. It leaves its imprint on a place. Makes it sick."

The house hadn't looked particularly welcoming before, but now it seemed like shadows clung to the corners, to the windows. A shiver went down Mattie's spine.

"That's horrible, but Jo, if you don't like passing the house, why don't you take a different route?"

"Avoiding terrible things doesn't make them go away."

Shame burned in Mattie's cheeks as Jo continued, "We can't sweep the ugly under the rug. If we do that, it could happen again."

Squeezing Mattie's arm, Jo gave her a small, sad smile. "Come on, time to wing it."

Clementine's shop was located down one of the less trafficked streets of the French Quarter, tucked between a bookshop on one side and a small grocer on the other. The painted wooden sign over the door said Arbor Gifts in fading letters. A chipped teapot and a couple jars of desiccated herbs sat on a small table in front of a faded curtain, blocking the view inside. This was Clementine's shop?

"If you want a shrimp po' boy, that's where you go," Jo said, pointing to the grocer. "Their muffulettas are also top rate, but I would pass on their fried catfish unless you like it on the thick side."

"I've never had a muffuletta before."

"They're the bee's knees of sandwiches. Ham! Cheese! Olives! We'll grab one to take back to the House on our way home." Jo opened the door to Arbor

Gifts and Mattie followed her through. After Tonique & Lace, Mattie thought she'd be used to places whose exteriors didn't match their interiors, but the inside of Clementine's shop nearly rocked her back on her heels.

Every wall of the small shop was covered in white shelves, housing jars of tea with neat hand-written labels, bars of soap, and pots of face cream. The exposed walls were pale green, and tendrils of a massive ivy plant crisscrossed overhead. It even wound around the silver lighting fixtures that hung from the ceiling, and potted ferns lined the walls. The smell was heavenly, a mixture of rose, lavender, mint, and the green of growing things in summer. It felt as if you'd stepped off the street and straight into a greenhouse.

Clementine sat at a small table, an open book in front of her. "Heya, dolls," she said brightly, rising to give first Jo and then Mattie a hug. "How's the wing?"

"Worlds better. Evangeline says I should be shipshape in no time. Though, she did say I can't dance for another night or two."

"It's only a couple of nights. It won't kill you." Clementine let out a laugh at Jo's exaggerated pout.

"It might kill me. You don't know."

The look on Clementine's face said she thought death to be a highly unlikely outcome. She turned to Mattie. "It's good to see you again. Welcome to my store."

"It's wonderful," Mattie gushed, her eyes roaming over the shelves.

"Thank you. Come on, I'll give you the nickel tour. The teas are all the highest quality I could find, and I make all the skincare products myself."

As Jo sat at the little table, swinging her feet,

Clementine walked Mattie through the shop, explaining the various wares, their uses, and having her smell each of them in turn.

Mattie looked up from a bar of soap that smelled of lavender and a hint of juniper. "This is the soap you were talking to BeeBee about yesterday."

"Uh-huh, that's her favorite."

"I can see why." Reluctantly, Mattie put the bar of soap back on the shelf. She'd only brought a few of the dollars she's made the previous night, and while she desperately wanted the chamomile and rose lotion and the orange spiced black tea, she needed to save her pennies. At least until she had a financial cushion, then she'd be back.

Trying to keep her words casual, she asked, "What about the tea you make with Evangeline?"

Clementine whipped around from where she was straightening bottles, a look of intense curiosity on her face. "Miss Mattie, how did you come to hear about our Mother's Friend Tea?"

"Mother's Friend? But I thought it was supposed to prevent you from being a mother?"

"It's the term they use in ladies' magazines to advertise contraceptive products. Truth be told, most of those do more harm than good and are about as useful as a raincoat in a hurricane at keeping a girl from getting in the family way. Ours is much safer and more effective. But you just dodged my question, didn't she, Jo?"

Jo had her elbows up on the table, her chin in her fists. "Probably because the news around the House is our Miss Mattie took Daniel home last night."

Heat flooded Mattie's cheeks. Did everyone really

know? After only one day, did she already have a reputation?

"Well, aren't you hitting on all eight," Clementine said, nodding her head up and down.

Mattie blinked at her a moment. "Pardon?"

"She's saying he's a catch," Jo explained.

"I hear that man has a fine set of credentials." The way Clementine wiggled her eyebrows as she said credentials made Mattie think she wasn't talking about his list of accomplishments. The lack of judgement from either of them was a relief. In fact, their response made her a little proud.

"His, um, credentials are top rate. I'd like to give them a more thorough going over, though. With the help of Mother's Friend."

Clementine's laugh was joyful and a little suggestive. "I bet you do. Be back in two shakes." She headed through a white door in the back of the shop and returned with a plain tin and a stack of muslin tea bags. "One heaping teaspoon steeped for at least three minutes every day."

"It tastes better if you add a spoonful of honey," Jo added with a knowing bob of her head.

"Jo, you add honey or sugar to your tea regardless of what kind it is. And without even tasting it first." Clementine said this as if it was one of the worst sins a body could commit. With a disdainful shake of her head, she put the items in a paper bag and handed them to Mattie. "At least try it on its own first before you go adding a bunch of sugar. We add rosehips and lemon zest to the mix to make it more palatable."

Over Clementine's shoulder, Jo mouthed the word "honey" and Mattie tried to keep a straight face as she promised Clementine to try it plain first.

"Just the tea, today?"

Mattie looked around the store, her gaze lingering on the glass jars and bars of soaps in their bright paper wrappers. "Yes. But I promise to be back."

She handed over her money, and Clementine went to get her change from a metal lockbox she kept hidden under the counter that ran along the back wall. The tea was expensive, but if it worked, it would be worth every penny since she had no desire to be a mother yet. Especially not from a man she'd only just met. When Clementine brought Mattie her coins, there was also a small paper-wrapped square in her palm.

At Mattie's quizzical look, Clementine explained, "I make sample soaps so customers can try new varieties without having to buy a whole bar. Why don't you try this one?"

Mattie pocketed the change, took the soap, and held it to her nose. The smells of vanilla, strawberry, and a sharp tang of mint came from beneath the paper. "Oh, that is heaven. Thank you, Clementine."

"We should get a wiggle on," Jo called from the table. "I still want to get that sandwich before our shift."

"Muffulettas from next door?" Clementine asked.

"Ab-so-lute-ly!" Jo said out loud with Mattie silently chorusing her in her head.

Clementine squeezed both their hands, pressing kisses to their cheeks with promises of seeing them at the speakeasy the following night.

The girls popped into the grocery which smelled of fried cornmeal, butter, and garlic. Jo ordered a sandwich, asking the older gentleman behind the counter to split it into two for them. While they waited, Mattie perused the aisles. Jars of pickled okra, canned vegetables, and loaves of crusty French bread lined several shelves.

Sandwiches in hand, they headed back to the House. As soon as they were on the street, Jo unwrapped hers and took a small, but vicious bite. A look of pure joy suffused her face. Mattie had never eaten while walking before. Her mother had always said she'd rather walk naked into church than eat on the move, but her mother wasn't around to see, was she?

Mattie looked between where Jo was taking another bite and her own wrapped sandwich. She tore the paper back and bit into it, the ham and cheese, a warm contrast to the cool olive and carrot, mixing into a delicious burst of flavor in her mouth. A little groan escaped her as she bit off another mouthful. Jo grinned and bumped her shoulder against Mattie's. Mattie bumped her back, and the two continued on. There was something decadent about eating while walking down the street with the late afternoon sunshine warming the air around them like an embrace. It was something Mattie could definitely get used to.

****

Mattie's second shift at Tonique & Lace started with disappointment. Daniel wasn't on door duty.

"Buck up, doll. It's not like Daniel can keep pulling doubles just to see you. No matter how cute your tush is," Nelly teased as she bumped Mattie with her hip.

Straightening her slumped shoulders, Mattie gave Nelly a half smile. "I'm sure I don't know what you mean. My tush is glorious!"

Nelly threw her head back in a bright laugh. Mattie envied the way Nelly's burnt orange dress brought out the golden undertones in her copper skin. She even had a matching headband of brown and amber beads.

"But seriously, Nelly. Who is that on door duty?"

"That's Mac. They're the head of security for the House and keep the rest of the gargoyles in line. Go introduce yourself."

Mattie stole another glance to where Mac stood next to the entrance curtains. Built like Daniel, Mac was tall and leanly muscled but with dark brown skin. Mac wore a sophisticated pin-striped suit that was expertly tailored. Only a fool would underestimate the lean line of muscles under the expensive fabric. Black hair hung in a long bob. Intense brown eyes surveyed the room from above cheekbones so sharp they nearly glinted in the light from the chandelier.

When Mattie hesitated, Nelly bumped her with her hip again. "Go on! Mac doesn't bite. At least, not unless you ask politely."

Mattie stuck her tongue out at the laughing Nelly and headed over to the door. With her friendliest smile in place, she stuck her hand out and said, "Hi, I'm Mattie."

One side of Mac's mouth pulled up in grin as they shook Mattie's hand. "So, you're Mattie. I'm Mac."

She was unsure what Mac meant by that comment but kept her smile in place. "Nelly said you're head of security for the House?"

"Yes. I also prefer they/them when being referred to."

"Oh, sure!" Mattie repeated they/them over and over in her mind to associate them with Mac. "Well, I just wanted to introduce myself, but I should probably get a wiggle on before Francis gets grumpy. Well, grumpier."

The comment earned her another half-smile from the gargoyle who tipped their head in agreement.

Replastering the smile onto her face, Mattie headed to one of her tables, reminding herself she had a job to do, and she certainly couldn't mope over a missing gargoyle all night. Especially since there was no reason to mope! It was one night of fun, and if it happened again, fabulous, and if not, that would be aces as well. So she told herself.

Once the night was in full swing and the dance floor crowded with hot, sweaty bodies dancing to the live band, Mattie had lost herself in the work. It helped that there was a singer tonight, a gorgeous Black woman with a voice that sounded like smoke and bourbon. Even more couples than the previous night packed the dance floor, bobbing and twirling, hypnotized by the woman's crooning voice. Mattie's foot tapped as she darted between couples and tables, taking orders and dispensing drinks.

She stopped by a table occupied by an older couple dressed to the nines. The woman was wearing a sleeveless velvet dress with matching gauzy wrap. Her date was in an older style, well-made suit and vest. The band of his fedora matched the light purple of his companion's dress.

"Evening folks. What can I get you?"

"The lady will have a glass of sherry," the gentleman said as the woman next him gave an appreciative nod.

"Isabella, ma fleur." Lady Lorna bent down and

planted a kiss on the beaming older woman's cheek. "It's been much too long."

"Lady. You look gorgeous as ever. We've been visiting Harold's relatives in New York. The only thing that could keep us away."

Mattie felt like she was intruding on the reunion but running away seemed rude since the gentleman hadn't given her his drink order yet.

"Good evening, Harold," Caron said, joining the Lady at the table and shaking the older man's hand. "Isabella." He took Isabella's offered hand and pressed a kiss to her fingers that was more sensual than polite. With her hand still in his, Caron glanced back to Harold, who was remarkably calm given the circumstances. "Harold, old friend, may we borrow your ravishing wife?"

Isabella blushed, the wrinkles around her eyes deepening. Now, Mattie couldn't have left the table even if she wanted to. Curiosity had sunk its claws deep into her, and she wanted to see how this all would play out.

Instead of objecting, Harold spread his hands in a magnanimous gesture. "Please, be my guest."

Caron helped Isabella to her feet. The older woman leaned down and pressed a kiss to Harold's weathered cheek. "Be back in a jiffy, my love."

"Take your time."

Isabella giggled like a girl in pigtails and the lady cupped her face, kissing the older woman deeply. Little flutters rocketed around Mattie's belly at the passion on open display for all to see. They broke the kiss, and the Lady took Isabella's hand and Caron's arm. The trio headed out of the bar.

Mattie couldn't help but look at Harold who had just happily handed off his wife to the Lady and her partner.

"Um, would you like anything to drink?"

"Oh, yes, please. I'll have a gin and tonic and bring Isabella's sherry. She'll want it afterwards."

Mattie gave a slow nod, trying to keep the myriad of questions flitting around her brain from showing on her face. "Coming right up."

"How long have you worked at the House?" Harold asked her before she could slip away.

"It's my second night," she admitted with a small smile.

"Well, there's not a better House to work for than Verity, let me tell you. You may not know by looking at her today, but Isabella was the prettiest can-can dancer in all of New Orleans. Spending time with the Lady and Caron makes her feel young again. Desired, you know?"

"It doesn't bother you?" The question popped out before she could stop herself.

The older man shook his head, a smile playing on his lips. "Not at all. I want her to feel good about herself. She deserves that." He looked around before leaning toward Mattie. "Besides, when we go home tonight, we'll make slow, soft love while she tells me every juicy detail." Sitting back with a grin, he spread his hands out. "Everyone wins."

A delighted laugh escaped Mattie. "I'll be right back with your drinks."

As she continued working, the interaction played over and over in her mind. The older couple were married—Caron had asked to borrow his wife. And

Harold not only was okay with his wife heading off for some hanky-panky without him, he encouraged it! She tried to imagine what would have happened if the interaction had taken place with her and Lenny. Well, for one, they never would have gone to a speakeasy, and two, if someone had propositioned her like that, it likely would have ended in a bar fight and Mattie being forbidden from ever stepping foot outside the house again.

The idea that there was another way to do marriages, one where "everyone wins" as Harold put it, appealed to Mattie. Even if she never got married again (once was more than enough, thank you), it pleased her that the option was out there.

She was heading to drop off a Sidecar to a nearby table when the Lady and Caron returned Isabella to Harold. Her shawl was slung over one arm, and her careful coiffure mussed into a white halo around her head. After kissing Caron and the Lady, she dropped into her chair and planted a kiss on Harold that included quite a bit of tongue. When the older couple came up for air, Isabella let out a delighted noise as Harold offered her the glass of sherry. While she was taking a sip, the older gentleman looked up and caught Mattie's eye. He raised his half-drunk glass and gave her a conspiratorial grin, which she returned with one of her own.

The overhead lights flashed, catching her by surprise. Was it already time for the show? She handed off the drink to a man who gave her the briefest of nods, his attention already riveted to the stage. Her tray now empty, she made her way to near the wall where she set it on a side table. Jo had told her that Grace was dancing tonight, and even though she'd already seen Grace's tattoos in all their glory, she was looking forward to seeing them again. The music started up, accompanied by cheers and whoops from the crowd, and Mattie added her own voice to the cacophony. The curtains slid back to reveal Grace dressed in a long black satin gown with a high collar. She held her arms above her head like a dancer's, encased in black evening gloves. Not a single drop of ink showed.

"Evening, bunny."

Mattie jumped and whirled, her heart hammering in her throat.

"I'm sorry. I didn't mean to startle you." Daniel held up his hands in a placating motion, but his lips quirked in that amused smirk of his.

She swatted at his shoulder. "Then don't sneak up on a person like that!"

He grinned, catching her hand and pressing a kiss to her palm. She melted. Her fingers curled along the side of his jaw.

"Did you make it to Clementine's shop today?" There was a hunger behind the words that sent a shiver down Mattie's spine. A warm flame flickered to life in her stomach at the realization that she wasn't the only one looking forward to further exploring their new friendship.

"Yes. Arbor Gifts is the bee's knees."

As his hand curled around her hip, Daniel grinned and drew her to him. Her hands went to his chest, her fingers running under his suspenders.

"I even had my first cup before my shift. For something medical, it's quite tasty. Didn't even need the honey pot Jo shoved at me."

Daniel laughed. "Our crow-girl has a sweet tooth for sure. Though, I can't blame her."

He leaned in and kissed her. His hands cupped her ass, lifting her up on her toes. Her eyes flicked to the occupied tables next to them, but the customers only had eyes for Grace. No one was paying attention to their dark spot against the wall. Her hands pulled on his suspenders, and she kissed him back as hard as she could. Something long and hard pressed against her lower belly, and she grinned, irrationally pleased to have that effect on him. His fingers dug into her rear for a moment before he leaned back, breaking the kiss. His forehead pressed to hers as he let out a deep breath. Dimly, Mattie was aware of the cheers of the crowd.

"Grace's act is not long enough for what I have planned…"

Mattie let out a little mew and tightened her grip on his suspenders. He kissed a line down her jaw before pressing another kiss to her lips.

"Doesn't mean I can't give you a preview."

Before she could ask what he meant, he angled her toward the wall and slid one hand up the front of her dress, his fingers skimming over her underwear. She sucked in a breath as her eyes darted to over his shoulder even as she came up on her toes, spreading her legs and offering him more access.

None of the patrons were paying a bit of attention to them as Daniel pushed aside the edge of cotton and plunged a finger into her. She pressed her mouth against his shoulder to muffle her cry at the glorious stretch as he worked a second finger into her. Slowly enough to make her thighs tremble, he removed his fingers. Little pants escaped her as she watched him bring his fingers up to his mouth and lick them clean.

"Delicious."

The crowd erupted in whoops and cheers. Reluctantly, Mattie glanced to the stage where Grace was taking a bow, every one of her beautiful tattoos on full display.

"You should get back to work, bunny."

Her pussy was aching with need, and her head felt like it was stuffed with a hive of drowsy bumblebees. Work? She had to work? After such a monstrously good-looking man had just done *that*?

Daniel swatted her ass with enough force to make her take a step forward and left a pleasant sting.

"After your shift, bunny." His words were a statement. A promise.

Mattie headed to the bar on wobbly knees, grinning so hard her cheeks hurt.

Chapter Nine

Daniel

With the show over, the dance floor filled back up.
After getting a drink from Francis, Daniel made his way
to where Mac stood at their post.

"Boss."

"Daniel."

The two stood in companionable silence, surveying
the room. Mac was on the lookout for trouble or the
start of trouble. Daniel was trying hard not to stare as
Mattie made her way between the tables, offering
drinks and smiles to the customers. Maybe stopping by
tonight had been a mistake. He should have waited until
closing. Instead, now that he knew for certain what was
on the menu, he was finding it very difficult not to
throw Mattie over his shoulder and take her back up to
his room. Especially with her exquisite taste still on his
tongue and his cock hard as rock in his trousers. As
tempting as the thought was, though, he wouldn't
jeopardize her work. Not if he wanted her to stay in the
House.

"Come to see about changing shifts again?" Mac's
piercing eyes never stopped their sweep of the room.

The thought was temping. Extricating himself from
Mattie's sleep soft body had been a test of his
willpower that morning. "No, not yet."

As delicious as the previous night had been, he wasn't sure he was ready to upend his life for the bunny. No matter how sinfully good she'd looked with her lips wrapped around his cock. It would be good for him to maintain a bit of distance. Especially since she was still so green to New Orleans and fresh from her marriage. The thought of how anyone could stifle the curiosity and fire of that woman made his hands clench at his sides. With effort, he forced himself to relax. Lenny was long gone, and even if he only spent a few nights with Mattie, Daniel would make sure that bastard of an ex-husband never bothered her again.

Mac gave a slight shrug. "Suit yourself. I'm not opposed if you change your mind."

"Much obliged."

The night wore on. Time moved as slowly as a tortoise in a three-legged race. Mostly, Daniel tried to stay out of the way and not get so drunk he'd ruin his plans for the evening. If he wasn't holding a drink, he kept his hands in his pockets so that every time Mattie came within ten feet of him (which she seemed to do more than was strictly necessary), he wouldn't reach out to tuck an errant curl behind her ear or squeeze her pert rear end. With each missed opportunity, the space between his shoulder blades tightened.

When folks finally started to clear out, it took every bit of Daniel's self-control not to help them out by the seat of their britches. He even assisted with cleanup, moving the chairs up on the tables so it was easier to sweep and mop and helping to wash glasses behind the bar. By the time Francis went to give Mattie her nightly take, the need in Daniel had frayed his normal restraint to tatters.

He sidled up to Mattie, entwined his fingers with hers, leaned down, and whispered in her ear, "Come on. Work's over."

The look of hunger she gave him made him think he should just throw her over his shoulder, but then she hesitated, her gaze flicking to Francis.

The barkeep let out a long-suffering sigh. "Get out of here."

"Thanks, Francis," Mattie said, looking like she'd give him a kiss on the cheek but then thought better of it. "See you tomorrow!"

Francis waved them off. This time it was Daniel's turn to lead her through the House and up the stairs to his own room. Not all the members kept rooms in the House, but most of the gargoyles chose to live on the premise. Over time, they had taken up the entire third floor. It gave them easy access to the roof, and whether they were a wing or a climber, they all preferred heights.

Daniel's room was the last one on the right and contained a wooden four-poster bed and comfortable leather furniture. The windows looked out over the Tonique & Lace courtyard, allowing him to keep an eye on things even when he wasn't officially on duty.

As soon as they were through the door, he closed it behind her and pressed her back against the wood. His mouth found hers as his hands cupped her ass, pulling her against him once more. She let out a little moan as she slowly rubbed herself against his already hard length. Her mouth opened wider and invited him to taste her deeper. He ran a hand up her thigh, gathering and pulling the fabric of Jo's dress as he did.

A small bit of his mind wondered if she'd let him

take her shopping. Jo's clothes were top-notch, but they were Jo's. He wanted to see what she'd pick out for herself, and it would be nice not to have to worry about damaging the dresses while getting her out of them. He'd revisit the thought when his hand wasn't lifting her thigh so she could wrap it around his waist, and her hands weren't trying to undo the buttons on his shirt. He kissed his way down her jaw as she tilted her head back to allow him more access to the soft skin of her throat.

"Such an eager bunny."

She stiffened at his words, her hands going still, and once again he mentally cursed that lowlife husband of hers. Ex-husband.

"I love how eager you are," he reassured her.

She melted once more, her hands returning to undo the last of the buttons. Mattie's apprehension aside, the interruption was welcome. It allowed Daniel to get a reign on his runaway libido. With how starved for touch, for pleasure, Mattie had been last night, she deserved better than a quick and rough tumble against the door. Reluctantly, he leaned back to watch her face. She bit her lower lip, looking at him with those big brown eyes. The sight made his dick ache with need.

Before he could give in to his baser nature, he picked her up off the ground, his fingers digging into her perfect ass. He grinned at the squeak of surprise she made as she clung to his shoulders. He couldn't seem to get enough of that adorable sound. In the middle of the room, he paused, weighing his options, before heading to the leather couch. There would be plenty of time for the bed and all its accessories later. He'd make sure of that.

Reluctantly, he set her down on the ground and removed his suspenders and unbuttoned shirt. Her eyes were big and questioning as he sat down on the couch.

"Take off the dress, bunny. Let me see all of you." He undid his pants just enough to let his aching cock spring free. He took it in his fist and stroked down once to let her know just how much he was going to enjoy this show.

Her pink tongue darted out to lick her lips as she stared at his lap. Slowly, her hands went to the hem of her dress, and she gathered up the feathered material. She pulled it up overhead in one motion, almost tangling it around her upper arms. As she removed her plain bra, a small flurry of dollar bills drifted to the floor like leaves, and Daniel suppressed a smile, afraid she would take it as a critique of her performance and not because she was utterly adorable. There were no flourishes or coy looks as she undid her garter belt and slid her stockings and cotton underwear down to her feet, but the eagerness—the naked look of desire that suffused her face was enough to make his cock throb. That and the way her full breasts glowed in the soft light of his bedside lamp. The way her hips curved from her waist to the tops of her thighs. He wanted to sink his teeth into all of her soft places.

When she stood there, naked as the day she was born, he said simply, "Come here."

She crawled onto his lap, her limbs trembling just a little as she straddled his thighs. When he ran his hands up her sides and cupped her breasts, her breath hitched, and her eyes fluttered closed. Little tremors raced down her body as he brushed her nipples with his thumbs, teasing them into stiff peaks.

Gods and monsters. Her body was so responsive to his every touch. The noises she made, the way her body pressed into his hands, wanting more, nearly made his head swim. Better than a glass of Francis' top-shelf whiskey.

Taking her nipple between his thumb and forefinger, he squeezed and received a squirm in response that brought her wet pussy against his cock. A groan escaped him, and Mattie's eyes snapped open. With slow care, she pushed herself up his length, shuddering as her pearl rubbed against his blunt head. Her hands went to his shoulders, her fingers digging into his skin as she slid up and down. He gritted his teeth, desperately wanting to push into her, to feel her close around him, but he forced himself to be still. This time he wanted her to be in control. To take what she needed.

Her pace increased with her breathing, rocking against him over and over. Little shuddering pants escaped her as her gaze locked with his. Her nails bit into his shoulders.

"Please…" A word filled with pleading and need.

"Say the words, bunny. Tell me what you want, and I'll make it happen."

His words stilled her, and she looked at him with those big eyes. "Anything?"

"Anything. That including taking sex off the menu if that's what you want." His dick might have disagreed with that statement, but he needed her to want this as much as he did, not just because of the House rules.

Her eyes went soft even as her hand reached between them to grip his length. A hiss escaped him as he fought the urge to buck his hips.

"I want your cock deep in me." Her words were punctuated with little squeezes from her fist.

She didn't have to tell him twice. His hands went to her hips and lifted her just high enough so she could position his cock at her entrance and held her there. She squirmed in his grip, trying to take him more firmly into herself and failing. At her mew of frustration, he grinned and slowly lowered her. It took all his willpower not to thrust up into her tight, warm pussy. Instead, he let her acclimate as she stretched herself around him. By the time her hips were resting firmly on his, her eyes were closed, and her forehead rested against his as she took deep breaths.

It was pleasurable torture to remain still, surrounded by her intense, wet heat, but he would give her all the time she needed. Her pussy squeezed him. Hard. A moan slipped from him as his fingers dug into her hips. A wicked little grin spread over her face, and he had to kiss it, his hand tangling in her curls as he pulled her to him. His tongue tangled with hers as she started rocking herself up and down his shaft in slow, tentative strokes. Breaking the kiss, she sat up and increased her pace. Her hands flexed on his shoulders, and her eyes drifted closed as she lost herself to the motion. He drank her in. The way she bit her lip, the bounce of her breasts, the slight tremble in her thighs as they lifted her up and plunged her down, impaling herself over and over on his cock.

The fire in his belly flamed higher with each of her long strokes, but he pushed his growing pleasure down. His thumb brushed over her bottom lip, freeing it from her teeth. Gently, he pushed his thumb into her mouth and that eager tongue of hers immediately lapped at it.

He groaned in approval as he pulled it from her mouth and found that place that lit her up with the wet, rough pad. Her head tilted back in a cry as he made circles in time with her rocking.

"Come on my cock, bunny. Let me feel every inch of you."

Warmth radiated from her body as her little panting breaths became ragged. As she clenched around him, he pressed against her pearl, sending her just a little higher. A frantic cry ripped from her throat, and he pressed his mouth to hers, swallowing it down.

His willpower slipped its leash, and he wrapped one arm around her waist, thrusting up into her still trembling pussy. Over and over until pleasure knotted at the base of his spine and the dam inside him burst, spilling himself into her.

Slowly, the world swam back into focus. Mattie had both her hands on his face, stroking his cheeks.

He licked his suddenly dry lips. "I didn't hurt you, did I?"

A smile like a sunrise lit her face as she shook her head. "Quite the opposite."

"Good." He felt like he should be more articulate but settled for wrapping his arms around her and pulling her to his chest. The frantic beats of their hearts slowed in time together. Sometimes that's all the words you needed.

Chapter Ten

Mattie

Mattie rested her head on Daniel's shoulder and listened to the quiet sounds of the French Quarter settling in before the dawn that drifted through his open window. Her limbs were heavy, content to lie draped over Daniel's lap and shoulders.

"Is everyone else asleep?"

"Not all. Some probably are. Why do you ask?"

"Because I can hear a horse cart passing by out on the street, but the rest of the house is quiet."

He shifted slightly and brought a hand up to stroke the back of her arm. "That's because every room in the House is soundproofed. With the range of its members proclivities, the Lady thought it best to invest in some charms. This way those who want to make noise can do so to their heart's content and they won't disturb the other House members or have the coppers called on us."

"That's terribly clever and quite thoughtful of the Lady." It eased her worry about how loud she had been on both occasions. Not that Daniel had complained. The opposite, in fact. Still, something bugged her. "But what about if someone falls or gets hurt? No one would know they need help."

"That's why the Lady sprung for the top-rate

charms. Genuine pain or distress will always be heard and alerts the Lady."

"She thinks of everything, doesn't she?"

They lapsed into a companionable silence as Mattie looked around the room. The furnishings were simple but well cared for, and Daniel's tastes seemed to run toward wood and dark leather. The only decoration on the walls was one painting. She couldn't make out the details in the dim light of the bedside lamp, but she could guess Grace had painted it. It had the bright colors and sensuous lines of the works Mattie had seen in her studio.

Her gaze went to the pile of her clothes on the floor. Several dollar bills were scattered among the fabric. She thought of the rest of her money tucked into the lining of her carpetbag.

"I know it's a shot in the dark, but do you know of a bank where I could open an account?"

"Actually, yes."

She sat up and looked at him. "Really? Without my husband's say so?"

He nodded. "Caron, the Lady's partner, runs a small bank. Caters to those the regular banks turn away for opening accounts or getting loans."

"Like women."

"And Black folk. We've come a long way in the new century. But not nearly far enough."

She settled back against his chest. "How does he run a bank if he can't go out in sunlight?"

"His righthand man is a human named Bossley. Been with Caron as long as long as anyone can remember. He acts as bank teller and lawyer for the House. Keeps a room over on Burgundy, up by

Rampart. Day after next is my day off. If you'd like, I'd be happy to take you."

"I'd like that." The thought of walking through the French Quarter with Daniel set a pleasant glow in her chest. Maybe they could even stop at a cafe for coffee and beignets. It would be worth it to dip into her savings for that, wouldn't it?

She realized she'd been staring at his bed, trying to make out the details in the low light. "What's that hanging from your bed posts?"

"Do you want to find out?"

The words were low and dangerous, making Mattie's heart flutter in her chest. The dark part of her unfurled, sending a hungry spike of curiosity through her. "Yes."

Daniel stood, picking her up in one fluid motion, and strode across the room. With care, he set her down in the middle of the bed before pulling something from the shadowed space between the edge of the mattress and the bedpost.

"Give me your wrist."

Her eyes strained against the low light, but it wasn't until he ran something soft along the inside of her wrist that she fully understood. Her heart hammered in her chest as his deft fingers buckled a fur-lined cuff around her wrist. A chain ran from a ring on the cuff to the bedpost.

"Some rules. If for any reason, you want me to stop, just say the word 'stop.'" He moved over to the other side of the bed and started buckling the other cuff. "Understand, bunny? You can say it at any time. You could say it right now. No harm done."

She nodded and then caught herself. "Yes." She

didn't want to say 'stop'; she wanted to find out what he was going to do with her strapped to his bed. It reminded her of the Spicy Detective stories she'd read in secret in the barn. Several of the women had been tied up and ravaged, and those scenes had always left Mattie breathless and aching.

"Good girl."

He crawled over to her to straddle her waist, his cock standing at attention once more.

"I'm only going to use the wrist ones tonight," he said, his hands trailing down her arms and across her chest. "But, some night, I will use both. Strap you open and get you off until you beg me to let you stop."

The thought of being vulnerable, completely at the mercy of his clever fingers and tongue and massive cock, made her clench her legs and sent shivers down her spine. Daniel smirked at the telltale rattle of the chains at her wrists. He bent down and kissed her as his hard length pressed into her stomach.

He kissed his way along her jaw to her ear and whispered, "And then, maybe, I'll free you. But not until you come on my cock at least one more time."

With a whimper, she squirmed beneath him, trying to press her breasts against his chest. He grinned and nipped her earlobe before kissing his way down her neck. Her chest heaved up and down as he kissed his way down her collarbone and between the mounds of her breasts without even pausing to lick or squeeze her aching nipples. He moved down the bed to lie between her legs.

By the time he'd pulled her thighs over his shoulders, Mattie's need had built to a fever pitch. She needed him to touch her. His thumbs came up to spread open her folds and then he paused, his mouth mere inches from her.

Her head came up off the bed to watch him where he looked up at her from between her legs, that damn smirk on his face.

"Lick me. Please, Daniel!" She didn't care if the words were ragged with need. She didn't care that she was begging.

His tongue darted out and slammed into her wet slit. She screamed at the overwhelming sensation and came off the bed, only for the restraints on her wrists to yank her back down. The shock of it snapped her back to herself. Tentatively, she gave a tug on her wrists, but the leather and chains held fast.

As Daniel explored her depths with his tongue, the steel bands crept back across Mattie's chest. She was trapped. Panic fluttered in her ribcage as she tried to test the cuffs again, gently so that Daniel wouldn't notice. That suffocating feeling that she hadn't experienced since she'd stepped off the bus from Prairieville was back, stealing the air from her lungs. She pushed it down, forcing her arms to still. She slipped into that calm, distant place she would go when Lenny visited her bed or when he would lecture her about not taking care of the household properly.

The world receded. It was still there, but muffled. Like Mattie was wrapped in layers of quilt, warm and safe from the elements. Like there was a delay in the telephone line—she could still hear the words coming through, but they were soft and fuzzy from zipping through the wires.

"Mattie."

Her eyes snapped open at the sharp concern in

Daniel's voice. He'd sat up and had one hand on her cheek, forcing her to look at his face. His mouth pulled into a frown with his eyebrows knit together.

"Daniel?"

He let go of her face and undid one of the cuffs.

"Wait, no!" She tried to tug her wrist away from him to no avail.

"Shush, Mattie. It's ok," he said, letting go of her wrist to caress her face again. "Before you even say it, you haven't mucked anything up. I promise."

She bit her lip and nodded as he went back to undoing the cuff. After he released the other one, she pushed back to sit against his headboard and rubbed her aching wrists. She must have pulled harder than she thought. Daniel sat down with his hip pressed to her thigh so he could face her, but she couldn't bring herself to meet his gaze. Disappointment settled in her chest like a boulder.

Daniel leaned over, braced one of his hands on the other side of her legs, and nudged her chin up to look at him.

His voice was low and soft. "Use your words, bunny. Tell me what happened. Where did you go?"

Tears stung the corner of her eyes. "I swear I do like the idea of it. Being tied up for you. But in the moment, I panicked. Like I couldn't breathe… I'm so sorry."

"Hush. You have nothing to be sorry about. Why didn't you just say the word? I would have stopped."

"I thought I could just endure." She didn't say that she didn't fully trust him to stop—to honor her right to say stop. She liked Daniel. She certainly like being his *friend*, but she didn't really know him, and her experience told her to be wary.

"That ex-husband of yours better pray to all the gods and monsters that I don't get my hands on him," he grumbled under his breath before spearing her with a look. Apparently, she hadn't needed to say the words.

She closed her eyes. It was easier to talk when she couldn't see him looking at her so intently. "You seemed to be enjoying yourself so much, and I didn't want to muck that up. Though, it seems I've done it all the same."

"Horseshit."

Her eyes startled open as his hand shifted to hold her chin in a firm, but not painful grip.

"Listen well, Mattie Logan, there is no pleasure for me if you aren't fully engaged in the experience. You don't have to fucking endure anything. I want you to enjoy it. Enthusiastically. Wholeheartedly. If you can't do that, we can't be this type of friend." He paused. She swallowed hard, her heart a lifeless lump in the pit of her stomach. "I refuse to do that to you, and I won't do it to me. The next time this happens, you say the damn word. You don't hide from me. Ever."

A tear slid down her cheek as she bobbed her head up and down. One rough thumb swiped it from her cheek. The weight on her chest evaporated, and she took a deep, stuttering breath. "I promise."

"I'm sorry too. I shouldn't have teased you so hard. Not when you were trying something new."

She gripped his hand. "But you have to understand, I *want* new. I want to be teased hard. I really did enjoy it. At least until I panicked."

He nodded slowly, the gears in his head turning. With a squeeze of her hand, he got off the bed and opened a small chest of drawers. She stretched upward and tried to see what it contained but could only make out bits of leather and the shine of metal. After rummaging around a bit, he came back with two long lengths of black silk.

Trailing one end along her bare leg, he said, "Next time, we'll use these. I'll only wrap them around your palms so you can let go at any time, for any reason. This is your choice. I want you to choose to be here. You were always in control, but this way, you don't have to even say anything. All you would have to do is let go."

Mattie ran the cloth between her fingers. Her voice was soft and hopeful. "Can next time be now?"

He looked at her for a long moment before taking one of the silks and securing it to the bedpost. Before he could tell her to, she scooted down onto her back and offered him her wrist. Instead of wrapping the material around it, though, he looped it around her palm. Her fingers closed around the silk.

"Show me how you'll get free."

She did what he commanded, opening her fingers and flicking her wrist until the fabric unwound from her hand. Daniel nodded, took her wrist, and pressed a kiss to her palm before re-wrapping the fabric around it. He made quick work of the other side until once more her arms were pinned to the bed. She flexed her fingers but didn't move to unwrap the silks. Not pinned. Choosing to be there. Her fists closed back over the material.

Daniel settled back between her legs. He leaned over and brushed one nipple with his fingers, teasing and caressing. "I'm going to give you what you want. This time. But know this, Mattie Logan, I will earn your trust, and then I'll give you exactly what you need, and you won't be able to do a thing to stop me."

Her sex clenched at his words. At the promise in his voice. The dark part of her reveled in it. Wanted her to beg, to plead for that day to be today, but she kept her lips closed. Today it would be a lie, and he'd know it. But one day.

He pinched her nipple hard enough to send a jolt of pleasure straight to her core. Small whimpers escaped her as he pressed his hand flat against her sex. She rocked her hips up as the palm of his hand circled against her mound. His hand disappeared to grip behind her knees and hauled them up until her heels nearly touched her rear end.

"Look at me, bunny."

She forced her eyes from where Daniel's hard cock was hovering near her entrance. His eyes never left her face as he pushed into her. Her back arched at the delicious invasion, her hands jerking against the silks. But she kept her eyes open and forced herself to breathe. Forced herself to stay in the moment. She could let go if she wanted to.

But she didn't want to.

He growled his approval as she rocked her hips up to meet his next thrust. The world faded once more, but this time, instead of retreating from it, it merely narrowed, and she was fully present to experience it. There was only the feel of Daniel above her. The feel of his long fingers on her hip. The stretch of her pussy around his cock. He shifted and the head of him bumped a place in her that sent sparks cascading down her spine. Over and over, it pressed into that spot until the sparks became an explosion. Despite her best efforts, her eyes closed as she screamed, arching her head back, her arms tugging against the silk ropes. With one last thrust, Daniel followed after her.

The only sound in the room was their ragged breathing. Mattie let go of the silks, extracted her hands, and shook out her wrists. With a grunt, Daniel hauled himself up next to Mattie and pulled her close. She nestled into his chest as his hands stroked down her spine. As her breathing evened out, her curiosity poked its head back up.

"Can I ask what else you keep in that drawer?"

Daniel's laugh rumbled against her ear. "Oh, bunny, I think we are going to be top-rate friends."

Chapter Eleven

Daniel

Even with the back door and all the windows open, the kitchen was hotter than Satan's left tit. Daniel had stripped down to his undershirt and was sauteing andouille sausage. Nothing new about the kitchen being hot, but at least the view was much improved this week. He glanced over to where Mattie sat at the kitchen table in a simple cotton dress, cutting a mound of onion, celery, and green pepper. She'd hiked up the hem, exposing the long line of her legs.

"You really make this much food every week?" Mattie asked as she placed another pepper on her cutting board.

"Every week. Tuesday night dinners are a tradition."

He didn't add that normally he ran anyone who offered to "help" out of the kitchen with a threat of flying wooden spoons. Preparing Tuesday night dinners was meditative. A time for him to let his brain settle and sort out the events of the week. Plus, other people tended to slow him down or offer unwanted opinions on how much butter he was using. In true creole fashion, Daniel believed there was no such thing as too much butter. But when he'd told her his plans for the afternoon, Mattie's face had lit up with that killer smile of hers and he'd been unable to refuse her offer of help. Considering her expert chopping skills and the improved view, he wasn't regretting that choice.

The edges of the sausage were nicely browned. He moved the frying pan off the burner and transferred the contents to the deep bowl with the rest of the finished sausage and already browned chicken.

"But you cook every week?"

"Why do you sound so skeptical?" Daniel pulled the largest pot out of the cabinet and set it on the stove. It was dented and stained, but big enough to boil a small pig. Not that he would boil a pig, it would be a travesty to treat pork in that manner.

The chopping at the table slowed. "I guess I just haven't met many men who have an interest being in the kitchen. Except for eating."

"Fair enough. Mimi, my grandmother, raised me. She was a champ in the kitchen and taught me everything she knew." The chopping had stopped completely. Daniel glanced over to find Mattie staring at him with a slight smile on her face. "Done over there?"

She started and continued chopping the pepper. "Almost finished."

"When I came to New Orleans, I started as a cook before I found my way to the House." He adjusted the burner, poured olive oil into the bottom of the pot, and added the minced garlic.

"Do you miss it?" There was the sound of metal on wood as Mattie scraped the chopped vegetables into another bowl.

"Being a cook? No, not full time. It's hard, sweaty work with long hours. I tip my hat to chefs everywhere.

These days, Tuesday dinners satisfy my need to feed people massive quantities of food." He accepted the bowl from Mattie, pressed a kiss to her sweaty temple, and upended it into heated oil.

"Anything else I can do to help?"

"There's some tomatoes in the cold box—dice 'em up?"

She grinned. "Ab-so-lute-ly."

He found his favorite wooden spoon and gave the trinity a stir so it wouldn't burn. The chopping resumed behind him.

"Can I ask a question?"

"Anything, bunny."

"You know what brought me to New Orleans. What brought you?"

The vegetables began to soften, and the smells of garlic and onion filled the kitchen. "What brings everyone to New Orleans—they're looking for something. There's never been a lot of us. Gargoyles, that is. Humans have a tendency to fear what they don't know. That fear keeps our numbers small. It's easier in bigger cities. Especially ports or places where people from all over the world live. Funny enough, my mother fell in love with a human. Most men would have been mortified to have a wife who could pick them up without a thought, but Father thought it was damn good fun. Took me ages to realize he meant that in a hanky-panky kind of way."

He wiggled his eyebrows, and Mattie suppressed a giggle with her hand.

The smile faded from his lips. "When I was still in short pants, there was a thunderstorm. Lightning struck our house, and I was the only one that made it out."

He didn't say that his mother had gotten him out, setting him by the old plum tree in the yard. Or how he'd cried as he'd watched her rush back into the flames to try to find his father. Neither of them had come back. He wasn't even sure why he'd told her as much as he had. The past wasn't something he liked to think about, let alone talk about. There was just something about Mattie that made him want to spill all his secrets. Maybe it was the sweet curiosity with which she approached the world.

Mattie brought over the tomatoes, set the bowl next to the stove, and wrapped her arms around his shoulders. "I'm so sorry, Daniel."

He shrugged and leaned over to give the side of her head a kiss. "It was a long time ago. Anyway, Mimi took me in, even though she was a wing and not my real grandmother. She still raised me as if she was."

"Are wings and climbers really so different?"

"You are just full of questions, aren't you?" Daniel said with a laugh.

Her smile faltered. "Is that bad?"

"That's also a question." He kissed the end of her nose. "But, no, it's not bad at all. Dump those in." The smile returned as she tipped the chopped tomatoes into the pot. "Honestly, there's not that much difference. Wings think they're superior just because they can fly, but climbers can beat the piss out of them. It evens out in the wash."

He added the rice and chicken stock. After a good stir, he headed to the cabinet containing the spices.

A frown tugged his lips. "Gods and monsters, I love Jo, but she needs to keep her beak out of my spices."

The sound of glass jars clicking together mingled with Mattie's giggle. She hoisted herself up on the counter so she could watch as he dumped cayenne pepper, salt, and other spices into the pot, not bothering to measure anything out. He gave everything a good stir, the handle of the spoon long enough for the large pot and worn smooth until it fit in his palm perfectly. After knocking it against the edge, he set it on the ceramic spoon rest vaguely shaped like a rooster.

"That smells divine."

"Wait until you taste it."

Knocking her knee with his hip, Daniel waited until she opened her legs and then stepped between them, putting his hands on her hips. As she draped her arms over his shoulders, he nestled his nose into the crook of her neck. She smelled of warm skin and tomatoes and peppers. In other words, she smelled delicious. His cock was already straining against his pants, and a small part of him wondered at the intense hunger this woman inspired in him. If he would ever get his fill of her.

Her knees squeezed his sides as she said, "Don't you have to cook?"

"It has to simmer for at about thirty minutes. Plenty of time." His hands kneaded her pert ass.

"Then let's head upstairs."

The eager need in her voice made his dick ache. When she tried to push off the counter, his hands gripped her harder, holding her in place. She looked at him, her eyebrows knit in confusion.

"I need to stay here to keep an eye on things and give the pot an occasional stir."

"Oh." Disappointment filled the word.

He hauled her to the edge of the counter and rocked his hips so that his hard length pressed against the apex of her thighs.

"Oh. *Ohhhhh*. But what about…?" Her eyes flicked to the closed door that led to the rest of the House even as her own hips rocked to maintain the delicious friction.

He started hiking up the hem of her dress. "Everyone knows to stay out of my kitchen on Tuesday afternoons unless they want a frying pan to the head."

She grinned before kissing him hard, her hands going down to the buttons of his trousers. Sure, he'd have to clean the counter thoroughly afterwards, but he couldn't think of a better appetizer before dinner.

****

The smell of warm bread and butter drifted up to tantalize Daniel's nose. He walked behind Mattie, who carried the other basket of French bread. It was so large it took both her arms to carry it. At the door end of the hallway, she paused and looked back at him with large, questioning eyes.

"Are you sure it's all right for me to join y'all for dinner? I'm not a member of the House."

He suppressed a sigh. "Bunny, you work for the House. You live in the House. You get invited to House dinners. Thems the rules." Before she could think too hard about that or decide she might need to look for other accommodations—which did not appeal to him at all—he shifted the basket to one hip and used his free hand to swat her bottom. "Now move."

She gave him a glare that would have been intimidating, if it hadn't been so adorable. Squaring her shoulders, she turned and headed into Tonique & Lace.

He wiped the grin from his face and followed her.

Six of the tables had been grouped together in two rows of three in the middle of the room. Most of the seats were already full. The pleasant buzz of conversation in the air became an excited shout of greeting. Daniel held the basket of bread above his head like a boxer at the end of a prize fight. He glanced to where Mattie was already putting hers at one end of the makeshift dining room table. Twin pink spots stood out on her cheeks, but she was smiling. As he put his basket down at the other end, anyone standing around found a seat.

"Sit with us, Mattie!" Nelly called, waving Mattie over to a chair between her and Jo. A flair of jealousy spiked through Daniel, and he pushed it down. What was wrong with him? He didn't get jealous. They were just friends, and it wasn't like he hadn't had her all to himself for the afternoon. A grin pulled on the corners of his mouth as he thought about the counter and the new memory he'd always associate with it.

He dropped into a free chair with Mac on one side and an open seat on the other. Mac gave him a nod of greeting before turning to where the Lady stood at one end of the table. Her hands were clasped in front of her, and a pleased smile played on her red lips as she looked over the crowd. Her gold eye flashed in the light from the chandelier.

To her left, Francis finished opening a bottle of wine, poured, and held the full glass out to the Lady.

"Thank you, Francis." When she raised her glass, everyone followed suit.

"Welcome House Verity." She let the cheers die down. "Not only has Daniel made another incredible dinner for us," she said with a wave to the covered dishes of jambalaya and black-eyed peas before tipping her head to Daniel. He acknowledged the praise with a nod of his own. "We also have a new guest with us tonight, Miss Mattie Logan."

Down at the other end of the table, Jo gripped a violently blushing Mattie's arm and shook her with a cawing cheer.

"Mattie is our newest waitress, and since she's successfully completed two full shifts without Francis firing her or quitting in tears, she's working out just fine."

The ends of Francis's mustache twitched as he inclined his head in agreement. High praise from him, indeed.

"To feeding our bodies. To feeding our souls. To House Verity. Baise tes Amis!" The Lady finished, her voice warm and affectionate despite the fact that she repeated the words every Tuesday night.

"Baise tes Amis!" Everyone chorused before taking a drink.

The serving dishes were passed around and plates filled. The clink and scrape of forks and knives on china punctuated the murmur of conversation. Daniel kept looking down where Mattie sat with Nelly and Jo. She had her head back, one hand to her chest as she laughed at some story Nelly was telling.

"You sure you don't want to swap shifts?" Mac said, leaning in to block Daniel's view.

"Yes, I'm sure. If that changes, I'll let you know." He'd been a part of the day shift guard ever since Mac had recruited him to the House. He wasn't going to upend that for a dame. Even one as beautiful and curious as Mattie. At least, not yet.

"Suit yourself," Mac replied with a shrug.

Daniel watched as they took a bite out of a flaky round of bread. "Why do you keep asking? You don't want to change shifts, do you?"

Mac didn't pause in their chewing, their face as calm and unreadable as ever.

"Not particularly. If I did, I'd just change the rotation. Thought I'd help a fellow climber out." Mac shrugged one shoulder. "It's in our nature to be protective."

Interesting that they didn't specify what was being protected. Or even who was doing the protecting.

"So my mother always told me." Daniel thought about Mattie's comment about how going back to her old life would kill her. She seemed certain that Lenny was gone for good, but Daniel couldn't believe that any man would let her go easily. If he was on night duty, he'd be there if Lenny did show up looking for trouble. He didn't admit it to himself, but it also meant he could spend the day with Mattie. "Thanks, Boss. I think I'll take you up on that offer."

Mac tilted their head in agreement and had just picked up a spoonful of black-eyed peas when they whipped their head to the Lady. Daniel followed their line of sight to where the Lady sat ramrod straight at the head of the table. One hand covered her House ring as she stared off into the distance. Her gold eye winked, but Daniel didn't think it was from the light of the chandelier. Anticipation tightened his muscles.

The Lady melted into her seat. "Mac." The name was soft, barely audible over the chatter of the rest of the table.

Mac surged from their seat in a fluid movement and knelt next to the Lady's chair. The Lady bent her head toward Mac's, a serene smile pasted onto her face. Her voice was too low to hear what she was telling her head of security, but the tense set of Mac's shoulders was clear even through the dark suit jacket. Daniel looked over to where Leo sat. The other gargoyle was focused on Mac and the Lady as well.

The Lady laid a hand on Mac's upper arm and gave it an affectionate squeeze as Mac nodded. Standing, Mac's eyes flicked to Daniel and then to Leo, their sharp chin gesturing to the back hallway. Daniel stood, deposited his napkin next to his plate, and followed after Mac. Unable to help himself, his gaze found Mattie's. There was a question in the arch of her eyebrows. He gave her a little shake of his head and flashed a smile that he hoped she'd take as *Don't go anywhere; I have plans for you later*. Even if he didn't know exactly what kind of trouble they were headed into, he didn't want it to spoil her first House dinner. She gave him a slow, brilliant smile and turned back to Jo and Nelly.

Squaring his shoulders, he followed Mac down the hallway. They may have been a couple inches shorter than Daniel, but he had to hurry to catch up with them.

"Boss?"

Mac didn't slow their strides as they moved through the House to the garage. Well, it used to be the carriage house, but these days they used it for storing the House automobiles.

"Jimmy's on his way," Mac explained over their shoulder.

"I thought he wasn't supposed to be back from the

supply run until tomorrow?" Leo asked.

"He wasn't. Something must have gone wrong. Not only is he early, but there's a surprise party waiting for him down the block." Mac shrugged out of their jacket and hung it on a hook in the garage without breaking their stride. They paused with their hand on the back doorknob. "We're going to even the odds."

"Aces." Daniel's grin was just as sharp and vicious as Mac's. "Teeth and claws?"

"Not tonight. The Lady didn't know who set up the ambush, so we're going to play at humans for this one."

Daniel shrugged as he followed Mac and Leo out onto the street. Not shifting didn't bother him none. Besides, it had been far too long since he'd had a good old-fashioned brawl.

****

"Amateurs," Mac murmured.

Tucked into the shadows next to the stoop of a house, they surveyed the scene unfolding further down the street. A delivery truck and an automobile were blocking the street, their front bumpers touching, as if they'd been in a collision. But instead of trying to clear the crash, the drivers were leaning against their vehicles, smoking and shooting the shit. Two men stood directing traffic around the blocked street.

"Eight in total," Mac said in a low voice, nodding to another group of men lounging on a stoop. The way they watched the street was too intense for casual observers.

"Eight against three. I like those odds," Leo replied with a flash of teeth.

"Against four," Mac corrected. "Jimmy might be human, but he fights dirty as all hell. Now, let's see if we can't get around these fools and cut Jimmy off before it comes down to a fight—Damn!"

Mabel, Jimmy's modified Ford, pulled up into the intersection. The lookout directing traffic had retreated to the sidewalk, letting Jimmy ease into the clogged street. The change was immediate. The two drivers shouted at each other, both pointing blame at the other party.

"Don't fall for it, Jimmy. Just turn around, you bastard."

Contrary to Mac's whispered instructions, Jimmy stopped Mabel and opened the door. At least he didn't turn off the engine and kept one hand on the door as he stepped out to better see what was going on. He looked road worn and disheveled, as if he hadn't slept in days. Considering how early he was, that might have been the case. Fatigue would certainly explain how the usually cautious Irishman failed to notice the obvious trap he'd stumbled into. He didn't even seem to notice the "bystanders" closing in around him.

"Come on," Mac hissed. They strolled down the sidewalk with their hands in their pockets, as if they'd no better place to be. Daniel and Leo followed.

"Oi! Quit your bitching and move your arses!" Jimmy's voice was loud as always but tinged with a weary impatience.

The motorists stopped their bickering and turned to Jimmy. One of the other members of the ambush had snuck up behind him and raised what looked like a club over their head.

"Watch it!" Mac called loudly, breaking into a run.

Instinctively Jimmy ducked, and the club missed his skull by inches, putting a dent into Mabel's roof.

Mac's shout might have saved Jimmy's thick skull, but it also alerted the others to the gargoyles' presence. Several of the thugs pulled out knives, short clubs, and one even sported a weighted blackjack that he smacked menacingly against his palm. That's the one Daniel headed for. The man's beard was scruffy, and his lips were pulled back into a sneer that revealed tobacco-stained teeth.

"Oi, bastard, that's my bloody car," Jimmy shouted. The thug's knee buckled with a sickening crunch, accompanied by a pained scream.

A grin split Daniel's face. He almost pitied the fool who dare to lay a hand on Jimmy's precious automobile. He brought his full attention back to his own fight as the blackjack swung toward the side of his head. Raising his forearm, Daniel blocked the man's swing. The thug's eyes went wide as oysters when Daniel latched onto the man's arm and dragged him forward, straight into Daniel's swinging fist. The collision made a satisfying crunch as the man's nose flattened in a spray of blood. The blackjack tumbled to the pavement, followed by its unconscious wielder.

Daniel scanned the fight, looking for his next target. Mac had fought their way to Jimmy, and the two were currently fighting back-to-back. To Daniel's left, Leo grunted in pain as a blade slashed along his forearm. A thug in a pair of ugly yellow suspenders held a wicked-looking blade with blood dripping from its edge. A murderous expression clouded Leo's face as he lunged at Yellow Suspenders, tackling him to the ground. Yellow Suspenders' friend dashed forward, his fist raised to deliver a blow to the back of Leo's unprotected skull. Before the sucker punch could land, though, Daniel drove his fist into the man's stomach. The thug let out a pained "oof" but retaliated with a jab to Daniel's face. Dodging the flying fist, Daniel leaned in to deliver two rapid punches into the man's exposed side.

"Coppers!"

Every head that was still conscious popped up at the cry. The thug in front of Daniel turned tail and ran, leaving his buddy on the ground. Shaking his head, Daniel looked to where Mac was shoving Jimmy into Mabel and pointing back down the street. Good. They couldn't afford to have the law poke around and find the hidden compartment in Mabel's backseat.

The harsh trill of a police whistle cut through the chaotic noise over the sound of fleeing fighters and Mabel's V6 engine roaring away.

"Come on, you winged bastard. We got to go!" Daniel cried, hauling Leo off the bruised and bleeding body of Yellow Suspenders.

The two headed away from the vehicles still blocking the road. Apparently, the ambushers were less worried about leaving their own vehicles behind. Two coppers in blue uniforms rounded the corner ahead of them. When they spotted Leo and Daniel, they raised their batons, the whistles in their mouth screeching.

"This way," Mac cried behind them as they darted into a small alley.

Daniel and Leo followed, hot on their heels. Once they were out of sight of the street, Mac raced for the alley wall and leapt. Their hands were replaced with lion's paws, and razor-sharp claws anchored them into the side of the building.

Daniel shifted his fingers into talons. Partial shifts

were harder and required more concentration to maintain the shift. Besides, a full shift would ruin his shirt and he liked this shirt. Next to him, Leo ripped his own shirt off and unfurled his large bat-like wings. As Daniel followed Mac up the wall, Leo shoved off the alley floor. Wind from his flapping wings rushed across Daniel's face as the other gargoyle passed him. Reaching the top of the building, Daniel hauled himself over the edge and let his hands return to their human form. He joined Leo and Mac where they peered into the alley below.

The two policemen were arguing about where they could have gone. One of them poked at the bloody shreds of Leo's shirt with his baton. Mac shot an accusatory glance over to Leo.

"What? It was ruined already," the wing whispered in response.

In the alley below, the coppers finally gave up and headed back out to the street. Mac stood up and frowned at the dirt marring their pants. They halfheartedly swiped at the mess before heaving a sigh and straightening. "Come on. Jimmy should be back by now. Unless the idiot got himself caught."

The group took off across the New Orleans' rooftops, heading back to the House.

Chapter Twelve

Mattie

It turned out that Nelly was quite the storyteller. Mattie sat rapt with her excellent dinner forgotten as Nelly spun the tale of a patron becoming so drunk and enamored with one of the dancers that he had gotten up on a table and did his own burlesque show like a drunken peacock mating dance.

Nelly raised her hand upright. "Hand on heart, Mac let him get down to his striped skivvies before they hauled him off the table and threw him out of the club. It was raining that night and he looked like a waterlogged nutria in his underpants and sock garters."

"Stop. Stop. Not while I'm drinking!" Mattie cried, setting her half-full wineglass on the table.

"The worst part, for him at least, was that Mac refused to give him his clothes back. Instead, they tossed out one of the silk robes—you know, the ones Jo keeps behind the bar? Can you imagine the looks he got stumbling home in a lady's rose-covered robe?"

"I wondered where that robe had gone. It was one of my favorites," Jo lamented with a pursed mouth. "Oh, well. At least it went to a good story." She gave the others a grin.

Warmth suffused Mattie, a combination of excellent food (Daniel really was a top rate chef), good wine, and the company. She couldn't remember the last time she'd had dinner with anyone besides Lenny, and Lenny's disappointment with her inability to be the perfect wife had always hung over the table like an uninvited guest. Either she'd bought the wrong cut of meat or cooked the carrots for too long or not cooked them enough. Try as she might, she'd never seemed to please him. Right before she'd left, she'd begun to suspect his disapproval had nothing to do with her cooking ability at all.

Mattie let the friendly banter around her push the sour taste of Lenny's disappointment down where it belonged. It was rowdy and jovial in a way that only came from years of easy camaraderie or the weathering of tough times together. At the head of the table, the Lady presided over the meal like a queen at a banquet or an indulgent mother watching her rambunctious brood. Maybe the wine was getting to her, but Mattie couldn't help but think the Lady was a bit of both.

She looked around. Daniel and Mac still hadn't returned. A part of her wanted to worry, but she remembered the smile he'd given as he left. The one that set her stomach aflutter. She didn't think she'd get used to having someone smile at her like that, like she was the brightest star in the sky. That smile was also a promise. A promise of filthy things to come. A little shiver went down her spine as her pussy ached with the memory of him taking her on the counter, the smell of spices and sex filling the kitchen.

"Mattie, you still with us?" Nelly teased next to her.

"Huh? Oh, yes. Yes, I am."

Jo elbowed her gently and rolled her eyes.

That promise would have to wait, but it just meant that it would be all the sweeter when it was fulfilled. Still, she hoped he would return soon.

After dinner ended, everyone pitched in to clear the tables and rearrange the furniture back to its normal configuration. Several folks disappeared into the depths of the House to wash dishes. Mattie had tried to help but was told firmly that the cooks didn't not do cleanup. Her protests that she'd only chopped vegetables were brushed aside. Instead, Mattie found an unobtrusive corner to stay out of the way.

The band arrived and began setting up their instruments in their corner. Someone pulled the front curtains closed, and a gargoyle named Nigel stood watch. Every once in a while, the drapes would part, and the newcomer would be greeted with shouts from around the room.

Nelly sidled up to Mattie and bumped her with her hip before wrapping an arm around Mattie's waist.

"You aren't hiding, are you?"

"No, not hiding," Mattie replied, snaking her own arm around Nelly. The girls of the House greeted each other with a casual affection that they'd extended to Mattie, to her utter delight. "Just observing. Is it like this every Tuesday?"

"What do you mean?"

"It seems everyone knows the folks coming in."

"Oh, did no one explain Tuesday nights?" Nelly said as she waved at the two women who had entered. They were decked out to the nines. The blonde's dress cascaded down in waves of pink silk to the floor. Her companion's massive bosom was encased in silver beaded dress. Mattie realized with a start that she recognized that bosom. BeeBee and Darlene had arrived.

The ladies waved at Nelly and broke into grins when they noticed Mattie. She raised her own hand in greeting as the ladies headed over to them but were waylaid by other House members who wanted to say hello.

"No. It just seemed like everyone's favorite night?"

Nelly laughed. "Well, it's definitely that, but Tonique & Lace isn't officially open on Tuesdays. You need to be a friend of the House to attend, and we don't have to sling drinks for anyone but ourselves! What's not to love?"

Mattie glanced to where Grace was making drinks behind the bar. It was strange to see anyone except Francis reigning over the bottles and glasses. Considering that he was chatting with other guests, the barkeep must have the night off as well.

"Any particular reason it's held on Tuesdays?"

"Well, Wednesdays means the week is half over! Thursdays are the day before Friday and should be celebrated with booze and dancing. Fridays are the end of the week, obviously. Saturday nights are when the French Quarter shines brightest and Sundays are made for prepping to survive the week ahead. Mondays mean the start of the week, and doesn't everyone need a drink after that? Then there's Tuesdays. Tuesdays are the lull in the week which means those of us who work in the French Quarter can get together."

"Makes perfect sense," Mattie replied with a grin.

"Speaking of drinks, why don't we go get one? Grace makes a mean Manhattan."

Mattie raised her eyebrows. "What's a

Manhattan?"

Keeping her arm around Mattie's waist, Nelly pulled her toward the bar. "Let's go find out!"

****

After trying Nelly's Manhattan, Mattie made a face that had Nelly and Grace laughing.

"I'll stick to the sweeter cocktails, thank you!" Mattie said, pushing the highball glass into Nelly's eager hands.

Grace snapped her tattooed fingers. "I have just the thing."

She turned around to grab ingredients. Her dark hair was piled on her in head in a mess of curls, showing off the heart pierced by an arrow tattooed onto the back of her neck. With a few deft motions, she prepared the new cocktail and pushed the pale gold drink across the bar to Mattie.

She took a sip. "So much better!" The comment earned her a truly impressive eyeroll from Nelly. "What's it called?"

"A Bee's Knees. It's gin, lemon, and, of course, honey. 'Cus, you are just so sweet!" Grace finished with a wink.

A delighted laugh escaped Mattie as Nelly gave another eyeroll before tugging on Mattie's arm.

"Come on, you. Let's say hello to the gals."

With Nelly leading the way, Mattie headed to a table where BeeBee, Darlene, and Jo sat with their drinks. There were greetings all around as Mattie and Nelly slid into open seats.

"I had a feeling you'd be sticking around," Darlene said in a way of a greeting.

"You always have a feeling," BeeBee teased.

"Pleasure to see you again, Mattie."

"Likewise. Your dress is stunning."

As BeeBee preened, Clementine swooped in over one of her shoulders to give BeeBee a hug.

"Heya, dolls." She handed BeeBee a bar of soap. "Be back in a bit."

"Oh, you're a peach, Clementine!" BeeBee cried as Clementine gave her a grin before heading toward the bar. BeeBee held up the soap and took a big sniff. Her eyes rolled back in pleasure as she heaved a contented sigh and then stuffed the soap into her bosom. Mattie's eyes went round as saucers.

"Impressive, isn't it?" Nelly said with a giggle and an elbow to Mattie's side.

"You can't even tell there's a whole bar of soap in there," Mattie said, her voice soft with wonder.

The rest of girls cackled as Mattie turned bright red. "BeeBee, I'm so sorry. I didn't—"

The woman cut her off with a wave of one red-nailed hand and a smile. "No sweat, doll face. You'd be amazed at what I've hidden down these girls over the years."

"I once saw her pull a cigarette case, two decorative lighters, a coin purse, and a good-sized tin of crackers out of those glorious knockers." Darlene reached over and gave BeeBee's breasts an affectionate squeeze.

"So, Mattie, have you had a chance to further examine our Daniel's credentials?" Clementine asked as she sat her cocktail on the table and plopped into the remaining open chair.

Darlene and BeeBee whipped their heads to Mattie who had her glass halfway to her mouth. Her first instinct was to deflect or minimize the accusation, but why should she? No one had purposely tried to make her feel ashamed, not even one bit, since she'd gotten here. And really, what did she have to be ashamed of?

"Let's just say it was a hair-curling experience," Mattie commented as she sipped her drink, a wicked smile on her lips.

The table erupted in cheers and claps.

"So good in fact, I think I'll repeat the experience again tonight."

Instead of more cheers, the statement earned her raised eyebrows from several of the ladies.

"What? I thought the House motto was 'Baise tes Amis.' Daniel and I are being friends." Despite her best effort, concern crept into Mattie's voice. Had she said something wrong?

"Daniel is friends with lots of folks," Clementine explained gently. "He's rarely *friends* with anyone more than once. Especially not several nights in a row. Unless it's with the Lady and Caron."

"Or if he stops by House LeBlanc," BeeBee said. "Though that man is such a delight in bed, you almost feel bad charging him."

Darlene raised her glass and nodded. "Amen."

"We're just friends," Mattie protested. "Well, *friends*. That's all."

"Sure, sweetheart," Nelly said with a smile.

As the conversation drifted to other topics, Mattie thought about what they had said about Daniel. She'd known he wasn't virginal, that much was very clear given his skills and that drawer with its objects made of lace and leather and metal, but he'd been to see Darlene and BeeBee? He'd paid to see them?

She worried the idea around in her head. Lenny and Pastor Michals, for sure, would say it was shameful and wicked. But that was their opinion. What was hers? She thought about her first conversation with the Lady and her admiration for what she called "the oldest profession." By all accounts, Daniel had been a courteous and respectful to the ladies he visited. Examining her own feelings, Mattie found no jealousy or disgust at the idea. In fact, there was something very appealing about the thought of Daniel's long fingers squeezing BeeBee's luscious breasts. Did that make her wicked?

As if her thoughts had conjured him, Daniel laid a hand on her shoulder.

"Ladies," Daniel said. "May I steal Mattie for a dance?"

The others gave their consent as Daniel pulled her to her feet and dragged to her to the dance floor where several other couples were already jitterbugging to the sounds of The Crawfish Brothers. She wanted to ask him where he'd run off to, but he spun her around and pressed her close to his chest, driving the question from her head with the solid warmth of him. As the music swelled, the tempo wormed its way into the dancers' bloodstreams, and Daniel started to move. Mattie immediately strode all over his toes.

"Oh! Sorry. I'm so sorry." With a strained laugh, she admitted, "I don't really know how to dance."

"No harm. Just follow my lead, bunny. I've got you."

Letting out a long breath, Mattie forced her muscles to relax, forced herself to relax in Daniel's arms. It allowed her body to listen for the small movements of Daniel's that told her to step back or sway to the side. Joy filled her chest until it felt like her feet were barely touching the ground.

One dance turned into two. After the third dance, Daniel asked if she wanted to keep going.

"Ab-so-lute-ly!"

He grinned and kissed her before spinning her in a circle. Around them, other couples jitterbugged and Charleston-ed, coming together, splitting apart, and clashing against each other once more.

Through the moving bodies, Mattie spied Mac, looking sleek in wide-legged trousers and a cream silk blouse that made their skin glow. A beaded headband with a ruby feather adorned their dark hair. They were dancing with a short man Mattie hadn't seen before. He had his head against Mac's chest, a grin stretching his face. From Mattie's limited experience with the stoic enforcer, she was surprised Mac allowed the contact, but there was an amused expression on the gargoyle's face.

The couple next to them pulled Mattie's gaze. Their movements slow and sensual. Then again, Mattie wasn't sure if the Lady could ever be anything other than graceful. Her mouth was locked with Caron's, the two of them devouring each other as they danced. Mattie swallowed hard, her gaze tracking down to where Caron's hand gripped the Lady's ass through her dress in a possessive caress.

A third hand pressed into her lower back, interrupting Mattie's voyeurism. Jo had shimmied up to them, the beads on her white and blue dress shaking with the music. Daniel took one of Mattie's hands and spun her, so she faced the crow-girl.

Daniel's hands remained on her hips as Jo's arms encircled her shoulders, her own hands coming up to grip Jo's slim waist. The three of them moved together with the music. Sweat poured off Mattie, dripping down between her shoulder blades, but she couldn't bring herself to care enough to stop dancing within the arms of those two beautiful creatures. Not when the music still wrapped around the dancers, making hips sway, toes tap, and heads nod.

Jo leaned forward until her lips brushed Mattie's ear, the edge of the crow-girl's bob teasing her jaw. "Is it later now?"

"Later?" It took a moment for Mattie's brain to process the question. "Oh. Oh!" She licked her lips and became very aware of Daniel's hands on her hips and the feeling of his chest pressing against her back. She tilted her head up to look at him.

He leaned down. "Don't look at me, bunny. That's a question for you."

"But I thought we were… you know, going to be friends this evening?"

Mattie let out a little gasp as he sucked her earlobe into his mouth and sank his teeth in before letting go.

"We are, but that doesn't stop Jo from joining us. I think you deserve to have all the friends you can get and to enjoy them over and over." He reached to brush Jo's hair behind her ear, cupping her cheek. "That is assuming Jo doesn't mind?"

The crow-girl tilted her head, leaning into Daniel's palm. "Why would I mind?"

Mattie's heart beat against her ribs, faster even than the beat of the band's drum. Her fingers found Daniel's as they cupped Jo's face and trapped them there. With his help, she pulled the crow-girl to her and brushed Jo's lips with her own. They were just as soft as she remembered them. Jo kissed her back with feather light kisses until Mattie's head nearly spun with need. Her tongue darted out to tentatively taste Jo's lower lip. The crow-girl's mouth opened and kissed Mattie deeply.

Between kisses, Mattie savored the feeling of Daniel pressed against her back and his hard cock nestled between the mounds of her rear end. His hand was still trapped between hers and Jo's cheek, but his thumb made slow circles under Mattie's chin.

"Ladies. As much as I'm as enjoying the view— and believe me, I'm not the only one. Let's take this dance back to my room." Daniel's voice was low and rough.

"What?" Mattie pulled back enough to look around and was mildly surprised to find that they were still on the dance floor. Several of the surrounding couples were watching them with large, approving smiles.

"Baise tes Amis!" Nelly cried from where she leaned back in the arms of her dance partner. A huge grin spilt her face.

Mattie grinned back at her, grabbed Jo and Daniel's hands, and dragged them off the dance floor.

****

Away from the music, Mattie's nervousness settled, becoming a flutter in her stomach. She didn't have the first clue how to go about—well, something like this. She wasn't even sure she knew the proper term for what they were about to do. As Daniel closed his door, she stood next to Jo, shifting from foot to foot and trying not to squeeze Jo's hand too hard. Why was it that when she needed her confidence the most, it flew out the window?

"Ladies." Daniel came up to them, his mouth serious, but his eyes had that glint that made Mattie's lower stomach clench in sweet anticipation. His hands came up and sank into both of their hair. "You two will follow directions, won't you?"

Relief washed through Mattie as she nodded, his hold on her hair causing little sparks of pain that sizzled down her neck. She should have known he would take the reins. There was something freeing about giving control to him, allowing herself to just feel and experience without the need to think or over analyze her every move.

Next to her, Jo nodded as well. The hand at the back of her head guided her forward, and he met her in a kiss that curled her toes in her shoes. When his teeth sunk into her bottom lip, she let out a low whimper. He soothed the bite with his tongue before his hand pulled her back.

"That's a good bunny," Daniel murmured before pulling Jo to him and kissing her thoroughly. The sight of two such gorgeous creatures softly devouring each other made Mattie's knees weak. Only Daniel's restraining hand in her hair kept her from leaning forward and to try and lick the place where their mouths met.

Daniel broke the kiss and regarded the two of them seriously before extracting his hands from their hair. "Let's get you out of these clothes."

Jo's hand gave hers a squeeze before letting it go. The crow-girl turned her, so she was facing Daniel, and stepped behind her. She planted little fluttering kisses along Mattie's shoulder. Between the soft feel of Jo's hands along her arms and Daniel's intense, hungry stare, Mattie shivered as desire curled in her belly. Jo's clever fingers made quick work of her buttons and before long, the dress pooled on the floor. As Jo removed her bra, Daniel knelt down to unbuckle and remove her shoes. Still kneeling, he unclipped her stockings and rolled them down her legs as Jo's fingers brushed along her newly exposed skin, skimming between her breasts, fluttering along her stomach, smoothing over her hips and thighs. Soon her garter belt and underwear joined the growing pile of clothing.

Mattie's own hands itched to return the favor. She undid the tie for Jo's wrap dress and let her hands enjoy the soft skin of the girl's shoulders as she slid the fabric down her arms. A little groan escaped her when she realized the crow-girl wasn't wearing any undergarments.

Daniel looked up from where he was removing Jo's shoe, one hand holding her calf to help her balance. He gave a low chuckle. "Our Jo prefers to remain unhampered by things like panties and bras."

"Brassieres are torture devices for tits. Why would I ever do that to my beautiful breasts?" Jo replied with a tilt of her head.

While she didn't necessarily agree about with Jo's view on undergarments, Mattie did agree that Jo's breasts were beautiful. Even though she'd seen Jo naked before when she'd first arrived at the House, this time Mattie took the time to savor the view. Her perky little breasts, the lean lines of her stomach, and the dark triangle of fluff above Joe's thighs that reminded Mattie of baby bird fuzz.

With her lips buzzing from the memory of their

kisses on the dance floor, Mattie leaned forward and pressed her mouth to Jo's, savoring the flick of Jo's eager tongue against her own.

"Bunny."

The word was sharp and mildly disproving. Cheeks aflame, Mattie stepped away from the crow-girl. Her eyes darted to where Daniel rose from the floor. His face was stern, but she was pleased to note the stiff tent of his pants.

"Did I say you could taste?"

More heat flooded her cheeks. "No. You didn't."

That mischievous glint was back in his eyes. "Jo, I'm afraid we must punish her for not following directions. Won't we?"

Mattie's heart sped up at his words. Next to her, the crow-girl grinned and threw an arm around Mattie's shoulder.

"I think we'll have to."

Daniel crossed over to the couch, sat down, and patted his thigh. "Put her on my lap. Facing out."

With surprising strength, Jo steered Mattie over to him, spun her around, and pushed her down until she perched on Daniel's lap. His stiff cock, still trapped in his trousers, pressed against her ass. His hands slid up and down her arms as he instructed Jo to get a pillow from the bed and put it on the floor in front of them. Anticipation and curiosity sparked along Mattie's nerves, but she held her tongue.

"Such a good little crow. Now kneel." He waited until Jo had slid to her knees on the pillow, her large dark eyes eager. "In order to teach Mattie her lesson, you are going to kiss and lick and suck her tight little pussy."

Mattie let out a strangled, pleading sound. Jo only grinned.

"Do you remember what I told you the other night? Promise you'll say the word if you need to," Daniel whispered into her ear, his hot breath sending little shivers down his spine. Even now he was looking out for her, making sure she was comfortable. That she knew she was in control of the situation.

"Yes. Promise."

He pressed a kiss to the side of her neck as his strong fingers wrapped around the tops of her thighs and forced her legs open. On reflex, she tried to close them, which earned her a stinging slap to the top of her thigh. He pulled her legs back open, draping her knees over his to keep her pinned.

One of his hands came up to grip her chin.

"Look at her, bunny. See how eager she is to taste you. That's because she knows you will be delicious."

Jo kneeled between her knees, a chittering noise of impatience escaping her as her hands clenched and unclenched by her sides.

"Taste her, Jo."

Mattie could only watch as Jo slid her hands up Mattie's thighs and her thumbs rubbed little circles where they met her hips. Leaning forward, Jo pressed gentle kisses to Mattie's sex that only made Mattie want more, more friction, more contact, but she knew if arched or squirmed at all, there would be a corrective smack from Daniel. So she sat there and let Jo explore her wet folds.

Just when she thought it might be worth the price to find relief for her aching, needy pussy, Jo sealed her lips around Mattie and sucked. The feeling exploded up

Mattie's stomach, and she let out a cry. With efficient little sips and licks, Jo brought her right to the brink and sent her spinning over it.

When Mattie's entire body began quivering, the crow-girl pulled back and stared up at Daniel expectantly.

She couldn't help it. Mattie let out a desperate little whimper.

With a low chuckle, Daniel reached around and stroked Jo's chin, still glistening with Mattie's wetness. "Absolutely perfect. Again."

Eager as ever, Jo resumed her licked and sucking, working a rhythm that brought Mattie back to the edge faster than she thought possible. Soon she was panting and squirming, her hips rocking to meet Jo's tongue, and then the orgasm gripped her, bending her back into Daniel as she cried out.

"I think she's learned her lesson, don't you, Jo?" Daniel said, trailing his hands along her heaving sides. Every muscle felt as limp and wrung out as a dishrag.

Looking from where she was resting her head on Mattie's thigh, Jo nodded. "But I think she needs one more." The crow-girl's eyes gleamed and her smile was wicked. "Just to make sure."

Between the look on Jo's face and Daniel's answering chuckle, Mattie's heart resumed its frantic beating. A part of her wanted to plead with them for a break, and another part of her wanted more. Everything they'd give her, even if her poor body couldn't take it.

"I think you are right. This time, though, use two fingers."

"Yes, sir!" Jo cried as she leaned forward once more.

Her tongue lapped at Mattie's swollen and sensitive button, sending pleasure so sharp it was almost pain zipping back up Mattie's spine. Soft fingers worked her entrance, petting and parting her folds. When Jo slipped two fingers into her aching pussy, Mattie cried out, little pleas falling from her lips. Whether they were to Jo or Daniel, she couldn't be sure.

Every nerve sparked and sputtered like firecrackers as Jo's lips and tongue teased and kissed and licked and her fingers stretched and pressed within her. Mattie arched and wiggled, loving the hot, wet press of Jo's mouth in front of her and Daniel's hard cock behind her. His fingers came up to cup and knead her breasts, making her squirm even more.

When she thought her heart would burst out of her chest with its wild beating, when her muscles were screaming from the tension, Daniel pinched her aching nipples, sending a zing of pleasure straight down to where Jo's face was buried between her legs.

"Come for us, bunny."

As if she was waiting for his explicit permission, Mattie didn't just tip over the edge, she exploded. Over and over, waves of pleasure crashed through her until she wasn't sure which way was up. Moments or maybe years later, she floated back to herself.

"Still with us?" Daniel asked as he rubbed her arms.

"Hmm?"

Daniel laughed, and the feeling was a comforting rumble against her back.

"Give her a minute," Jo said with a grin. "She nearly flew to the moon there."

Mattie scrounged up enough brain power to whisper, "Ab-so-lute-ly."

To be honest, it still felt like most of her was floating among the stars. But that seemed like too much trouble to actually say out loud.

Chapter Thirteen

Daniel

Mattie still felt mostly liquid in the protective circle of his arms, but between Daniel's feet, Jo shifted on her pillow. Rest time was over.

"Since Jo did such an excellent job, bunny, I think you should return the favor. Don't hold back, though—let's see if we can't ruffle her feathers."

"Yes, please!" The eagerness of her words made his dick twitch against her plump ass.

"Go get on the bed, Jo."

Jo got to her feet and headed to the bed with more enthusiasm than seduction, and it made Daniel smile.

"Up you go." Daniel lifted Mattie and set her on her feet. Thankfully, he kept his hands on her hips, because her legs wobbled alarmingly.

After steadying herself, she reassured him, "I've got it."

A smack to her bottom accompanied his answering smirk. Rubbing the pink cheek, she padded over to the bed where Jo was already laid out like a feast. It wasn't Daniel's fault Mattie's ass was perfectly spankable.

He stood up and stripped off his shirt, his eyes riveted to the bed where Mattie crawled up and kissed the crow-girl before licking her own sticky sweetness from her lips. As he watched the two gorgeous women exchange sweet kisses, he made quick work of the rest of his clothes.

Starting at Jo's collarbone, Mattie worked her way down, pressing kisses and little licks to Jo's skin. She seemed especially delighted with the soft mounds of Jo's tits and their small, dark nipples that tightened into peaks under Mattie's attention. She was kissing her way down the soft plane of Jo's stomach when Daniel placed a possessive hand on her ass.

"Jo, I think our bunny deserves something sparkly. Don't you?"

The crow-girl nodded enthusiastically. "She would look lovely with a shiny."

Mattie gave him a curious look over her shoulder. He could feel her gaze tracking his movements as he went over to the dresser. After a bit of rummaging, he found what he was looking for, grabbed a bottle of oil, and headed back to the bed.

"Eyes forward, bunny."

Reluctantly she stopped trying to see what was in his hand and turned back around.

"Continue what you were doing."

He held up the metal teardrop with the enameled rose decorating its flared base. Jo nodded her approval before falling back against the pillows with a little cry of pleasure.

Mattie had reached Jo's pussy and was taking her time exploring with her lips and tongue, but the tension in her hips and ass betrayed her nervous excitement. He knelt behind her on the bed and poured some oil into his palm. With one hand, he spread her glorious cheeks and used the other to drip the slick liquid onto her tight ring of muscle.

Using only the tip of his finger, he made gentle circles against her. "Is this something you want, Mattie?"

"Yes," came the breathless answer as her hips shifted backward, pressing into his hand.

Mattie's head popped up with a little gasp of pleasure, her back arching, as he gently slid one finger into her.

"If you stop, I'll stop. Because that wouldn't be fair to Jo and you wouldn't want that, would you, bunny?"

Her black curls shook. "No, I don't want that. I won't stop. Promise."

"And you have to relax," he commanded, his other hand stroking along her hip.

With a little nod, she bent back down, and the muscles in her hips relaxed slightly. Daniel worked his finger into her over and over before adding a second finger, carefully stretching her open. When he removed his hand, Mattie never stopped enthusiastic pearl-diving, but her body nearly hummed with anticipation. Daniel's face split with a grin as he positioned the blunted tip of the teardrop. With gentle pressure, he worked it into her until only the engraved rose was visible. Mattie's breath was coming hard and fast, and her thighs quivered.

Gods and monsters, she was gorgeous with her face eagerly buried in Jo's cunt with her luscious ass in the air. From his angle, he could see how wet she was, how it dripped down her thighs. He'd meant only to watch the show, but he couldn't help himself. His cock was so hard it hurt. He positioned his prick, already slick with precum, at her entrance and gently massaged the globes of her ass.

"Remember what I said, bunny. You stop and I stop."

That was all the warning she got before he slowly buried himself into her. To her credit, she let out a small cry but didn't raise her head. He slid in and out of her in long, controlled strokes despite his desire to drive into her hard and fast. With the toy in her, anything more would be too much, overwhelming her.

"Suck her pearl, Mattie. But be gentle and use that clever tongue of yours, as well."

Mattie repositioned her mouth, and Jo let out a little keening noise in response.

"Perfect. Now take one finger and slide it into her. See how wet you've made her."

Both Mattie and Jo groaned in tandem as Mattie complied with his instructions. There was something so appealing about debauching this little country bunny, especially since she was so eager and willing to be debauched.

Jo's hands were making little fluttery movements as they clutched Mattie's curls. With a strangled caw, the crow-girl bucked and came before flopping back on the bed.

He stroked Mattie's side. "Beautiful, bunny. Make her do it again. But this time use two fingers."

She threw a grin over her shoulder at him that made his balls tighten before diving back into her task. Keeping a tight rein on his own pleasure, he kept fucking her as she finger fucked Jo. Mattie was a quick learner, and soon Jo was panting and quivering once more. This time as she climaxed, feathers sprung out of her hair, sticking up at all angles.

"Seems you've ruffled her feathers after all,"

Daniel said with a grin as he pulled Mattie's chin up so she could admire her handiwork.

The crow-girl gave them a grumpy little pout as she smoothed her feathers back into hair. The pout dissolved into a cheeky grin as Jo wiggled her way down until she could kiss Mattie, her hands coming up to tweak her nipples, making Mattie arch hard, driving back on his dick.

"Tell me how it feels, bunny," Daniel asked, his voice rough and low. His control was fraying with each warm clench of her pussy.

"So good. Like I was empty before, but now…now, I'm so full."

His control snapped, and he thrust hard into her, using her hips to pull her back on to him. He lost himself in the sweet friction of her body, the sounds of his hips hitting her ass, the little breathless pleas that he wasn't sure she was conscious of making. The tightness of the orgasm building in his lower back and hips. When she came, Jo kissed her, smothering her cries with her mouth. Two hard strokes later, Daniel followed her, leaning over her back, one arm braced on the bed, the other clutching her hip as if it was the only thing keeping him attached to the earth.

For a long moment, he just stayed there, panting with both Mattie and Jo underneath him before he rolled onto the bed with a groan.

Mattie was still on her hands and knees. "Um, what about?" Her eyes flicked over her shoulder.

"I'll get the shiny," Jo offered as she wiggled out from under her.

Daniel ran a hand along her sweat-slicked back and marveled at how gorgeous she looked with her sex-tousled hair and satisfied smile. She let out a soft little mew as Jo slipped the silver plug out of her. He scooted up to the pillows and pulled her with him. She snuggled into his chest and raised her head, her eyelids already half-closed with sleep. He bent down and pressed a kiss to her lips.

"Come on, Jo. Bedtime," he said, patting the bed on Mattie's other side.

The crow-girl curled up behind Mattie, resting one arm around her hip. Before Daniel could even get the covers pulled up over the girls, they were both fast asleep.

****

"Penny for your thoughts?"

Daniel dragged his mind back to the present and smiled at Mattie walking next to him.

"Shame on me for neglecting a beautiful woman," he said, bringing her hand up and kissing the base of her palm. "Especially over something as dull as business."

Mattie cocked her head to the side, and he surpassed a grin at her unconscious mimicking of Jo's mannerisms. "Is that why you and the other gargoyles left dinner? To take care of business? I meant to ask about it last night, but you and Jo distracted me."

A grin broke out on Daniel's face as he thought about how the previous evening had ended. "We did a pretty good job of it."

"That you did!"

They crossed over Esplanade near Grace's tattoo parlor. The day was warm against the back of his neck, but a breeze caught the Spanish moss in the trees, making it sway above their heads, and provided a needed relief.

"Last night, there was a bit of a dustup. Jimmy, the Irishman dancing with Mac last night, he's our runner."

At Mattie's confused look, he elaborated, "Rum runner. He keeps the bar stocked by ferrying booze from our sources to the House."

"Isn't that dangerous?"

"Very. The stills still in operation are hidden in swamps and forests away from prying eyes. He has to deal with the revenue agents, the highway patrol, and sometimes the local sheriffs, but he's aces behind the wheel."

"I guess I never thought about where all the bottles in Francis's bar came from. But you said there was a dustup?"

"Such a curious bunny," Daniel said, bopping her gently on the nose.

She scrunched her face. "Is that a bad thing?"

"Not at all. It's one of things I like best about you. Apparently, the family who supplies most of our gin started acting shifty during the handoff. Jimmy got a grim feeling and hightailed it out of there. Turns out they'd ratted us out to save their own skins. The only thing that saved him was Mabel's modified V-6 engine and his superior driving skills. Normally, he'd break the trip in two and stop off in Baton Rouge but instead drove straight through rather than risk it. Unfortunately, that wasn't the only double-cross. An ambush was set up down the street from the House, looking to relieve Jimmy of the hooch stashed in his backseat. Mac, Leo, and I made sure they weren't successful."

Mattie stopped in her tracks. "You got in a fight? Were you hurt?"

"No, I wasn't hurt at all." He pushed a curl behind her ear, trailing a finger along her jaw. "The only one who go hurt was Leo and it was only a minor cut. I'm half convinced he allowed it to happen so Hazel would fuss over him."

Her grin faded. "What is the House going to do?"

"The coppers showed up before we could figure out who was trying to steal our booze, but we'll look into it. What are we going to do about the double-crossing bootleggers? Not much."

"But they ratted out Jimmy!"

Daniel smiled at the indignation in her voice and gave a shrug. "But nothing came of it in the end, and that's what happens with illegal dealings—not much recourse when things go sideways. The Lady can be ruthless when she needs to be, but the family in question is outside of Shreveport. She does what she can to keep Tonique & Lace from being raided, but she won't overextend the House without good reason."

"That makes sense," Mattie admitted reluctantly. "What about the gin then?"

"We have the last shipment which will tide us over while we find another supplier. Both the Lady and Jimmy will send out feelers. Something will turn up."

Daniel stopped. "Here we are."

"This is a bank?" Mattie said incredulously as she took in the pale blue home with its darker blue trim and the white wrought-iron fence that separated it from the sidewalk.

"You should know by now not to judge a place by its exterior." Daniel opened the gate and extended an arm. "After you."

Mattie didn't budge.

"Problem, bunny?"

She looked up at him with those big eyes of hers. Her teeth worried at her bottom lip. "Bossley works for Caron. You said he's a…you know."

Daniel leaned forward and whispered dramatically, "A vampire. Yes. Is that the holdup?"

"Well, are you sure it's safe?"

"I'm not sure what kind of horror stories you've read, but I promise there's nothing to worry about. Do you trust me?"

"Yes."

The lack of hesitation shouldn't have felt like a shot of whiskey warming his insides, but it did. "Do you trust the Lady?"

Her mouth quirked into a smile. "Yes, I do."

"Then trust us. You have nothing to fear from either Caron or Bossley. Now get."

He motioned his head toward the house. With an adorable pout, Mattie stepped through the gate and up to the front porch where she waited for him. With one hand, he knocked on the door and with the other he squeezed her bottom. Even in the shapeless day dress she was wearing, he couldn't keep his hands to himself. She swatted his arm away and straightened the hem of her dress.

The door swung open to reveal a tall man in a dark pin-striped suit. His sandy hair was carefully slicked back from his face, and delicate gold-rimmed glasses made him look like a farmhand turned scholar. Which, in a way, he was.

"Hello, Bossley."

"Daniel!" The man cried, shaking Daniel's hand vigorously. "How ya been?"

"Pretty good. We missed you last night."

"Yes, bit of business cropped up, but I'll be there next week for sure. And who might this fine young lady be?"

"Mattie Logan, may I introduce you to Bossley? Bossley, this is the newest waitress at T&L."

It took Mattie a moment before she extended a hand to Bossley. "Pleased to meet you." Daniel couldn't blame her. Bossley was a bit of a contradiction in his own right. A low country boy who'd paid his way through college by sheer determination and oyster fishing, Bossley had never lost his accent, even after somehow becoming a Vampire's right-hand man. The tales about how that particular partnership came about were as varied as the men themselves.

Bossley took her hand and bent over to brush his lips along her knuckles, his broad shoulders straining the fabric of his well-tailored suit. The angle allowed a better view of the scars peeking out from his starched white collar, pale and stark against his tanned skin.

"The pleasure is most certainly mine."

When Bossley didn't immediately release Mattie's hand, Daniel cleared his throat. "Mattie has a bit of business with you."

"Oh, yes. Come in. Come in."

Placing a possessive hand on the small of Mattie's back, Daniel steered her into the house. Bossley led them through the front room that was set up like a standard parlor, complete with lace doilies covering the back and arms of the floral couch, and into the second room. This one dropped the pretense of being a normal house. A compact waiting room contained several chairs and a secretary's desk.

Bossley waived a hand toward the empty desk chair as he opened the door leading further into the house. "You just missed Mrs. Felix. She had to pop out for an errand."

"If we don't see her, please give her my best," Daniel said as they entered Bossley's office.

A simple wooden desk dominated the space, with one wall dedicated to bookshelves and the other to wooden filing drawers. Two leather backed chairs faced the desk, and Bossley gestured to them as he went around to the other side. With a practiced hand, he unbuttoned his suit jacket and sat down.

"Would either of you like some iced tea? Coffee? I might even have a Coca-Cola in the icebox."

Mattie arranged herself in a chair and politely declined.

"Thank you, but we're ok," Daniel said as he sat in the other one.

"Let me know if y'all change your mind. Now, Miss Mattie, what kind of business can Caron and Associates take care of for you today?" Bossley picked up a fountain pen and held it poised over a clean sheet of paper. The instrument looked delicate and too small in his hand.

"As Daniel mentioned, I've recently taken up a waitressing position at Tonique & Lace and I'd like to open a bank account. Though, I must admit, I have little to deposit at the moment."

"No trouble at all. We handle accounts of all sizes," Bossley said with a dismissive wave of his hand as his other began taking notes.

Mattie's eyes darted around the room, and her lips pressed together. Bossley paused his scribbling to look at her through his gold-rimmed glasses.

"What is it, Miss Mattie?"

"Well, I'm very sorry. It's just a regular house doesn't seem very secure for holding valuables."

Daniel suppressed a chuckle as Bossley carefully set his pen down and entwined his fingers on the desk.

"I can assure you that this is no ordinary home, and your assets will be as safe here as they would be in any of the marbled halls of the major banking establishments. More secure, in fact, since its protected by both magical and non-magical means. We take the security of our clients very seriously." He leaned forward on the desk. "Besides, only a right fool would try to steal from a vampire."

Mattie shook her head and gave him a grin. "Daniel tried to warn me about appearances. I should have listened."

"It happens all the time," he said with a dismissive wave. "Now, in order to open your account, I'll need some information, including your identification if you have any, otherwise, Daniel will have to vouch for you as a House member." Bossley picked up his pen once more.

"Oh, of course." She opened her pocketbook and pulled out a sheet of paper but didn't hand it over. "Actually, that was the second thing I wanted to talk to you about."

Daniel shifted in his seat. What else could she want from Bossley?

After handing over her identification, she said, "As you can see, my legal name is Mrs. Mattie Stumps. I was hoping you could advise me on how to go about returning to plain old Mattie Logan."

Warmth flooded Daniel. He'd been telling her the truth when he said he didn't give a shit if she was still married, but the idea of her formally severing that tie was appealing. Objectively, he knew this decision had nothing to do with him—it had probably been in her brain since before she got on the bus to New Orleans— but with everything he knew of Lenny, Daniel wanted him as far from her as possible.

"I see," Bossley intoned. "I must warn you that the courts are not kind to women in these situations. You likely would receive no lands or funds as part of the settlement."

Mattie shook her head. "I don't want his money or the farm. I just no longer want to be his wife."

"That makes things easier. On what grounds would you be seeking this divorce?"

"On the grounds he's an insufferable jackass?" Daniel muttered.

Mattie shot him a look that clearly said while the statement was true, it also wasn't helpful.

"I'm guessing my not wanting to be married to him any more isn't good enough?"

"Believe me, Miss, I wish it were. It would save a lot of folks a lot of heartache. As it stands, not only does one party have to be at fault, if the court thinks the couple colluded together, they can bar the divorce."

"You mean force them to stay married? That's barbaric!"

"That's the law," Bossley said with a tilt of his head. "To secure a divorce, a spouse must prove either extreme cruelty, mental illness, or adultery. But that last one only sticks if there is physical proof—usually photographs or the like."

Mattie winced and then straightened her shoulders. "While I'm not ashamed of what I've done, I'd rather not provide photographic evidence of it."

Daniel wasn't sure what he could say to that. While the idea of her in scandalous photographs was appealing, he wanted them for his own enjoyment, not submitted as evidence to the court. He reached over and snaked his fingers through hers and gave them a gentle squeeze. To his relief, not only did she not pull away, but squeezed him back.

"Another option is, of course, abandonment."

"Oh. That probably doesn't work since I was the one who left," Mattie said, a frown pulling her eyebrows into a V-shape.

"But if he applied for the divorce, abandonment would be appropriate, wouldn't it?" Daniel couldn't stop himself from interjecting. He knew this was Mattie's fight, but he couldn't bring himself to sit quietly on the sidelines. That was not the gargoyle way.

Bossley tapped the end of his pen against the desk. "That might work. Yes."

Mattie squeezed Daniel's fingers as she leaned forward, her eyes large and hopeful. "How would we go about this?"

"As my client, I could write to your husband to let him know your wish for the dissolution of your marriage. That you have no designs on his property or assets and will provide whatever evidence necessary to support his claim of abandonment in the courts."

"Yes, yes, please." She was nearly vibrating with excitement, and Daniel couldn't help but smile with her.

With any luck, in a few weeks, his bunny would be

Mattie Logan again. His bunny? Now where had that thought come from?

Chapter Fourteen

Mattie

After squaring everything away with Bossley, Mattie and Daniel headed back to the French Quarter. Joy suffused her until she thought her chest would burst. The only thing keeping her feet on the ground was the feeling of Daniel's bicep under her fingers.

Not only did she have a bank account in her own name, but Bossley promised to send the letter to Lenny this week. She had no delusions about how he would react when he read the letter—she'd been on the receiving end of Lenny's temper too many times to hope he'd be happy at her request for a divorce—but he was also a logical man. Once he calmed down, she was sure he'd see the benefit in separating and finding a wife that better suited his strict beliefs. He had to.

Daniel brought her to the French Market, and they walked between the stalls of vegetables and fruit. The sides were open, which allowed a welcome breeze to snake its way between shoppers and stands, while the roof overhead kept the sun and rain at bay. The warm air smelled of growing things, cut flowers, and spices. Several cafes made their home around the market, and Daniel picked one with a bright red and white striped awning. At a little wrought-iron table in the shade, they drank chicory coffee and ate beignets.

The sweet fried squares of dough reminded Mattie of the decorative pillows that had lined Granny Marie's sofa and tasted like sugared heaven. The thick nutty coffee was the perfect balance for the powdered sugar-covered treats. When they were done, the only thing left on the plates were white drifts of sugar.

As they walked back out into the afternoon heat, Mattie stopped Daniel with a hand on his arm. "Hold still," she fussed as she brushed powdered sugar from his dark locks.

"How on earth did you get it in your hair?" she asked with a laugh.

"Don't question how I eat beignets." He grabbed her hand and kissed the sugar from her fingers. His eyes flicked to the row of shops opposite the Market. "I have a request."

She tilted her head. "What's the request? Should I be concerned?"

"I don't believe there's any reason to be concerned." The serious expression on his face didn't put Mattie at ease. "Let me buy you a dress and take you to dinner tonight."

"You don't have to do that. While I'd love to go to dinner with you, I could always borrow a dress with Jo…" She thought of her new bank account and its tiny balance. Jo was very kind to share her wardrobe, but if she was honest, Mattie couldn't wait until she could purchase her own glad rags.

"You're right, Jo would be more than happy to share, but it would make me happy to buy you your own dress." He leaned in and brushed a curl behind her ear. "This is entirely selfish of me as I want to show off the House's hottest new tomato, and I think you deserve a proper celebration."

The side of her mouth quirked up in a smile. It would be very unfriendly of her to refuse his kind offer. And they were friends, weren't they?

"Well, in that case, I'd be delighted."

****

When Daniel had said he wanted to take her to dinner, he'd actually meant they were going to one of New Orleans mainstays of culinary cuisine—Antoine's.

Mattie had been a bit in awe, having only heard of the restaurant by reputation and reading food guides' glowing write-ups in various magazines. When they entered the double French doors of the Saint Louis Street restaurant, Daniel greeted the maître d' as an old friend. Though, really, she shouldn't have been surprised. It seemed as if everyone who lived and worked in the French Quarter had been family for years. It was only Mattie who was the newcomer.

The tuxedoed maître d' led them to the dining room with its tables draped in blindingly white cloths with high-backed chairs. Polished wooden beams arched overhead with chandeliers providing soft light for the diners. The maître d' led them to a table in the corner, and Daniel insisted on holding her chair for her.

As he sat in his own chair, he said, "Have I told you how incredible you look tonight?"

"Yes," she said with a smile. "Or maybe I just interpreted your needing to scrape your jaw off the floor as approval."

"It certainly was approval. You are stunning."

Mattie's hand came up to touch the neckline of her new dress. It was emerald silk with a drop waist and a black satin belt. Jet beads decorated the neckline.

Shopping with Daniel had been surprisingly delightful. She'd had to put her foot down when he'd tried to buy her more than the agreed upon one dress.

She picked up the menu and let out a laugh. "It's all in French!"

The side of his mouth quirked. "What did you expect with a name like Antoine's? Don't worry, there isn't a bad dish on the whole thing."

"Well, since this evening is all your doing, I'll trust you to order for me," she said as she folded the menu.

"Challenge accepted. Though, it is a shame that prohibition means we can't enjoy the meal the way it should be enjoyed—with at least one bottle of wine. Possibly two."

"We'll manage."

Manage they did. Daniel ordered Oysters Rockefeller, baked oysters in butter, parsley, and breadcrumbs, cups of gumbo, delicately fried sole Florentine, and filet de boeuf Robespierre. Between the two of them, they cleaned the plates; Daniel even used some of the French bread to sop up the last of the demi-glacc from the beef dish.

During the meal, they traded stories from their childhood, relaying tales of adventure, or misadventure, and happy anecdotes. When Daniel told her the story of how, on a dare, he'd climbed to the very top of an old oak tree, gotten stuck, and had to be rescued by his mother like a wayward cat, Mattie laughed so hard her sides hurt. In return, Mattie recalled the time she'd pretended the fence was a tightrope after her Granny Marie had taken her to see the circus. It had gone very well, right up to the point she tipped over and ended up covered from head to toe with stinking mud. She could still hear her mother's outraged shriek when she'd found Mattie trying to wash up in the kitchen sink, a trail of mud marking her path from the back door to the kitchen.

After the dishes had been cleared away and coffee served in delicate white cups, Mattie sat back in her chair with a sigh. "That may be the best meal I've had in my life."

"The company was certainly top rate. Cigarette?" He held out the packet he'd ordered with the coffee. Mattie waved him off, and he lit one, taking a long drag.

"Horrid things, but there is something appealing about having one after a particularly good meal, especially with a particularly good-looking woman."

She raised her coffee cup up in cheers. As they had lingered over their meal, the dining room had slowly emptied of patrons until they were one of the few who remained.

"Shopping for a beautiful frock. An incredible meal. I'm not sure today could be any more perfect."

Daniel took a moment to tap the ash into a crystal dish. "Do you trust me?"

Mattie's heart sped up as much at his words as at the mischievous glint in his eye. "Yes," she breathed. It was the second time he'd asked her that, and the answer still surprised her. She did trust him.

"Then let me pay the bill and we'll get out of here."

Chapter Fifteen

Daniel

The night air was warm and thick as they headed toward the waterfront and turned onto Royal Street. It was late enough that they only passed a few couples heading home. That would suit his purposes just fine. When they got to Pere Antoine Alley, he swung them down the cobblestone lined way.

"Where are we going?" Mattie asked.

He pulled her to a stop. "Right here."

"Here?" She looked around with a quizzical expression.

Instead of answering, he pointed up to where the St. Louis Cathedral loomed in the dark. After following the line of his finger, she turned back to him with large, wide eyes.

"You can't be serious."

He stripped off his suit jacket and hung it from a spike of the wrought-iron fence that encircled the Cathedral's small back garden. His vest followed along with his favorite hat. "You said you trusted me."

She gave him a wary nod, watching him closely as he undid the buttons of his shirt at his wrists and neck. No point in ruining a perfectly good shirt. His pant legs were loose enough that he wasn't worried about them. After kicking off his shoes, he pulled off his socks and stuffed them into the shoes.

Cupping the side of her face, he kissed softly. "I want to show you something. When the times comes, hold tight and remember, you can always say what?"

"Stop," she replied with a smile.

The shadows of the alley weren't thick enough to obscure the curiosity and confusion that shone on her face. His heart hammered in his chest as he stepped back. He shook out his hands and double checked that they were alone in the alleyway. Mentally, he kicked himself. What did he have to be nervous about? It wasn't as if he didn't do this every day, and it sure as hell wouldn't be the first time he'd shifted in front of a human. Sure, normally it was with other gargoyles or long time House members or the occasional drunk palooka who needed to be taught a lesson, but this was Mattie.

Besides, if she was going to be skittish about the other side of him, he'd rather know now. While his heart was still safe. It was still safe? Wasn't it?

Taking a deep breath, he pushed that question aside and settled into the change like slipping into a favorite suit. Talons extended from his fingers and toes. The muscles in his arms, legs, and chest strengthening their attachments and bulking up. When he had first learned to shift, the pain had been so excruciating he'd almost passed out. But after years of practice, it had dulled down to a familiar deep ache.

The biggest change happened last. His ears lengthened to points, the sounds of the nightlife in the French Quarter becoming sharper, more defined. The bones in his face rearranged to form a hound's snout, his teeth elongating to sharp points. As his eyes shifted, the world brightened until he could see as clear as day.

Consequently, he heard Mattie's heart speed up, and he saw her eyes widened, and she smelled…well, she smelled like desire.

Her hand came up and paused. "May I?" she asked breathlessly.

In this form, he couldn't speak. Not human words anyway, so he nodded. Her fingers tentatively stroked the edge of his muzzle. It took everything in him to hold perfectly still and not nuzzle her hand as she continued her explorations. She ran a finger up the outside of his long ear, and he suppressed a shiver.

As her hands explored the planes of his chest, she said, "It is monstrously unfair for you to be so gorgeous in not one form but two."

He grinned. At the sight of his sharp teeth, she sucked in a breath. Instead of the stink of fear, though, he smelled desire roll off her, hot and wet.

In a single fluid motion, he took one of her arms and slung her across his back. She let out that adorable little squeak and instinctively wrapped her other arm around his neck.

"Daniel, what are you doing?" she asked, her breath warm against the back of his neck.

With a reassuring pat, he headed for the stone wall of the Cathedral. The arms around his neck tightened.

"Daniel." Mattie's voice had gone up several octaves.

He reached up with his right hand, found a niche in the rock, and pulled himself up. As he used the talons on his feet to find footholds, he wrapped his left hand behind to press Mattie's back more securely to him. Using only one arm slowed him down and forced him to rely on his feet more than he usually did, but it was a minor inconvenience. Higher and higher he climbed, taking pains to avoid the darkened windows set into the side of the church. After the first couple of feet, Mattie had buried her head into the crook of Daniel's neck and hung on tighter.

With a little maneuvering, Daniel pulled himself up onto the square roof that formed the base of the Cathedrals middle and largest spire. As gently as he could, he set her down on the flat roof and pried her hands from their death grip around his neck.

"Oh," she said as she finally looked around, one hand clamped onto his forearm. "You can see the whole French Quarter from here. It's beautiful."

Keeping her closest to the spire, he pulled her around the platform so she could see St. Charles Street with its towering oaks and streetcar, meandering its way between the opulent Garden District homes. When he brought them to the riverside of the Cathedral, he paused.

For a moment, they stood and watched the lights of riverboats winking up down the darkened surface of the Mississippi. This was his favorite view of all New Orleans. Whenever something was bothering him or he just needed a quiet moment alone, he would sit on the edge and watch the river drift by.

Mattie heaved a sigh. "This is utterly, completely incredible. Thank you."

Taking care with his talons, he guided Mattie until her back was against the tiles of the spire.

"Daniel?"

He dropped to his knees in front of her and looked up at her with a grin.

"Oh, you cannot be serious."

He pushed up the hem of her dress with one hand and nuzzled his way up the inside of her leg. The smell of her flooded his senses, the sweet tang going straight to his core and making him painfully hard. One hand kept her dress pinned to her stomach while the other slid her panties to the side. A rumble of approval escaped him at the dampness of the fabric.

"Da...Daniel." Her voice was breathless, and her heart fluttered in her chest.

He opened his mouth and extended his long tongue to drag up her pussy in a slow lick. A full body shudder went through her, and he pressed his hand harder against her stomach to keep her still. He repeated the long lick and marveled that in this form, she tasted even better.

With little tongue rolls, he lapped at her, slowly at first, but quicker and quicker. When her breath was coming in little gasps and he knew she was close to that sweet peak, he stopped and pulled away.

Mattie's head whipped down. When he didn't resume his attentions, she let out a frustrated cry.

"Please, Daniel. Please lick me."

He let the tip of his tongue snake out of his mouth as he kept his gaze on her face. Her eyes locked onto its long, pink length as her own tongue darted out to wet her lips. But instead of returning to licking her pearl, he explored the wet folds of her pussy.

"Ah, thank you!" she gasped as she widened her stance, allowing him even more access.

He paused at her entrance for just a moment before thrusting the entire length of his tongue up into her.

"OH SWEET BABY JESUS!"

He let out a rumbling chuckle as he retreated before licking back into her. Her thighs trembled next to his muzzle as he took his time fucking her with every inch of his considerable tongue. One of her hands found his ear and grabbed hold. He wasn't even sure if she realized that she was clenching it, pulling his head toward her, and he had never experienced anything sexier.

The smell of her changed subtlety, and he knew she was close once more. Working his tongue into her even further, he pressed his broad nose against her pearl. With a breathless cry, her entire body stiffened around him, and her pussy clenched around his tongue. He held on to her hip and stomach, holding her in place as she shuddered through wave after wave of climax. Eventually, she slumped against the spire with an indulgent sigh.

He extracted himself from her depths, stood, and spun her so that her back pressed against his chest. A rough growl escaped him as his aching, hard dick nestled between the globes of her ass. He didn't need to say anything—the obedient little bunny just pulled up her dress around her waist, stood on her tiptoes, and shifted her panties to the side, open and ready for him.

Daniel undid his trousers, not caring if his talons ripped the fabric. Wrapping one arm around her breasts, careful not to pierce her skin, and the other around her stomach, he stroked up into her dripping warmth. His arms held her in place, speared on his cock as she trembled around him.

A little pleading sound escaped her as she rocked up and down on her toes, trying to get the delicious friction she craved. Unable to hold back any longer,

Daniel lifted her up his length and then fucked hard into her.

He thrust into her with hard, slow strokes, savoring the impossibly warm clench of her pussy around him. Her head fell back against his shoulder, one hand holding her dress up, the other coming up to clutch his neck.

Before them, Jackson Square with its white footpaths and lush greenery shone in the moonlight. Beyond that stretched the powerful Mississippi, a black ribbon of water stretching off as far as the eyes could see in both directions. The crescent moon slid from behind a cloud, shining like a polished oyster shell hung from the heavens. A few late-night pedestrians strolled along Decatur in ones and twos, but none of them looked to the top of the Cathedral.

There was something wonderfully possessive about taking her like this with the Mississippi rolling before them and all the city able to see Mattie in her sex-softened glory if only they bothered to look up. A part of him wanted them to. To claim this trusting, curious, fabulous creature for his own. Maybe that was the gargoyle in him, but right then he had no desire to fight it.

Fire built low in his stomach, stoked higher with each thrust. Her fingers clenched into the side of his neck, her panting breaths driving his own pleasure even higher. He changed the angle slightly, looking for that spot deep within her that would send her over the edge. When her breathing hitched and her nails dug into his neck so hard that they would leave marks if shifting didn't mean accelerated healing, he knew he'd found it.

He growled his encouragement against her ear,

hoping that the sound translated. "Let go for me. Show the moon and the Mississippi how pretty you are when you come."

Maybe he didn't need the words, because she shuddered and clenched around him, her hand leaving his neck to smother the screams of pleasure that were spilling from her mouth. With a low moan and one final thrust, he followed after her, the pulses of her orgasms wringing him dry.

For a long moment, the two of them stood there, breathing hard, watching the lights of the city play on the river's muddy waters, a poor but still lovely imitation of the stars in the dark sky above.

"Um. Daniel?"

He gave an acknowledging noise deep in his throat as he savored the smell of sex and sweat that rolled off of her.

"How are we going to get down?"

Chapter Sixteen

Officer Boudreaux

Night patrol was not Officer Boudreaux's favorite shift. Still, every man had to do their part and that meant occasionally picking up extra shifts when fellow Officers came down with the sniffles. Or had it been a stomach bug? Either way, it meant Officer Boudreaux was walking the lamp-lit streets of the quarter with his trusty nightstick and lantern.

He was just passing the St. Louis Cathedral when his razor-sharp hearing picked the sounds of feet on cobblestones and a woman's giggle.

Heaving a sigh, he turned down the side street next to the church. The light of his lantern pierced the deep shadows in the narrow space, illuminating a couple in romantic embrace. A man in a black suit with a shirt that looked as if it was in the process of being unbuttoned by the hands of his companion.

"Now I know you two weren't planning on desecrating our great cathedral by getting up to some hanky-panky in its sacred shadow."

"We would never dream of it, Officer," the man said as he shaded his eyes with one hand. With the other, he moved his companion around behind him. Officer Boudreaux didn't get a good look at her face, but she was wearing one of those flapper dresses—

indecently short and fringed, of all things.

"Hrmf," Officer Boudreaux replied, keeping his light on the man's face, letting him know he couldn't pull one over on New Orleans Police's finest.

"My beautiful companion here is new to the city." The man tucked his companion's hand into the crook of his arm and gave it an affectionate squeeze. The woman kept her head ducked, looking properly deferential. "She has a love of architecture and ghost stories. How could I not bring her to one of the most exquisite and haunted buildings in New Orleans?"

The man offered a charming smile and recognition clicked in Officer Boudreaux's brain. This was one of Lady Lorna's young men. She hired them to drive her about, take care of her business, things like that. Proper Lady, Lady Lorna. Beautiful, even with the missing eye. Royalty from Belgium or Peru, somewhere across the pond. Try as he might though, Officer Boudreaux couldn't remember the young man's name.

Officer Boudreaux lowered his light so it no longer showed in the man's face and hitched up his belt with his other hand. "That is true on both accounts. Though, I'm not sure a dark alley is the proper place for young folk. Not at this time of night."

"What better place than the dark to whisper ghost stories? Especially if they cause a lady to shiver and tremble and give me an excuse to be a gallant gentleman." This last part was said with a flourish of his unoccupied arm.

"Ah. Not many chances for a man to be a gentleman these days. What with the state of the world being what it is. Still, probably best if you two headed on home." He used his Stern Policeman Voice. The one that told folks he meant business.

"Will do, Officer. You have a good evening." The Lady's man—his name was on the tip of Officer Boudreaux's tongue… Darren? Donald—tipped his hat and steered his lady companion in the opposite direction out toward Jackson Square.

"Be safe, ya hear?" Officer Boudreaux called, still using his Stern Policeman Voice.

"Yes, sir!" came the young man's reply.

Exiting the alleyway, Officer Boudreaux continued his beat, pleased he had once again done his sworn duty of keeping the citizens of his fair city safe. Who knows what kind of trouble two young folk could have run into in the dark if he hadn't been there?

Chapter Seventeen

Mattie

It had turned out that climbing down the church had been similar to climbing up—just backwards, and somehow, even more terrifying. When he'd finally set her down on the bricks of the alleyway, her legs wobbled like her grandmother's famous apple jelly. Though, whether that had been from the heart-stopping descent or Daniel's thorough fucking with nothing but his powerful arms keeping her from tumbling to her death, she couldn't have said.

The run in with the police officer hadn't helped the state of her nerves at all. At least Daniel had been human-shaped and mostly dressed when the officer had found them.

Walking arm-in-arm back to the House, Mattie asked, "Is it true what you said about the church? About how folks think it's haunted?"

"This is New Orleans. Pretty much everything is haunted." The tension had dropped from his shoulders, and he gave her one of his mischievous grins.

"What do you mean?"

"When the French first landed here in the late 1600s, this whole area wasn't much more than a disease-infested swamp. Any sane person would have taken one look around and rowed all the way back home. But they didn't. It's always been a hard place to live. Damn near everything tries to kill you. Mother Nature tries the hardest of all. Between the swamp, the wildlife, the hurricanes, the floods, and the fires, it's a miracle there's still a city here. To say nothing of the atrocities that humans have inflicted on each other. Especially in the name of maintaining the white status quo.

"Folks had to be mighty hard to kill to keep the city alive. Even then, most of what you see has been rebuilt at least once. Turns out when you fight that hard to live, sometimes you keep fighting even after your body is dead and gone."

"You mean ghosts are real?" She couldn't help the skepticism that creeped into her voice.

Daniel turned his head and raised an eyebrow at her. "Your friend turns into a crow. You work for a succubus, and you just had sex at the top of a church tower with a gargoyle."

"Fair enough," Mattie conceded with a laugh. "Though, considering what you told that officer, I think it's only fair to actually tell me those oh so scary stories."

He puffed out his chest and put on an air of authority. "I am a gentleman of my word. Even though it's hard in this day and age, what with the state of the world—you know those flappers with their short, tempting skirts showing God knows how much tasty leg and doing manly things like voting and learning to read—"

He was laying it on thicker than a bowl of grits and Mattie swatted at his shoulder until he held up his hand in defeat.

"Uncle. Uncle. All right then, the story of Pere Dagobert de Longuory and the miracle he performed one rainy night."

As they walked, he told her about how in 1796 the French Creoles rebelled against their Spanish governor and ran him out of town. Spain, not taking too kindly to this, sent Alejandro "Bloody" O'Reilly to become the military governor. O'Reilly then executed the ringleaders of the rebellion and had their bodies displayed on the levee opposite the church. To add insult to injury, he set two thousand Spanish soldiers to guard the bodies, refusing to allow them a proper Christian burial. This greatly upset their families, and they turned to Pere Dagobert, a much beloved monk and priest of St. Louis Cathedral. One rainy night, Pere Dagobert led several assistants up on the levee where they took the bodies right from under the soldiers' noses and brought them back to the Cathedral for burial mass. The entire way back to the church, Dagobert belted out the traditional hymn "Kyrie". The legend goes that on rain-soaked nights, the funeral procession can be seen heading down the alleyway they had just left, with Pere Dagobert leading the way, still singing his hymns.

When Daniel finished, Mattie couldn't help but shiver at the thought of ghostly singing during a rainstorm. It was also how he told the story that affected her. His voice took on a low, serious quality, as if every word he spoke was weighed down with history and absolute truth.

"But that's only one of the ghosts of St. Louis Cathedral. Do you want to hear about the rest?"

"Ab-so-lute-ly."

He regaled her with other ghostly tales, and Mattie drank up every one of them like wine. Even though she was thoroughly caught up in the stories, a part of her mind kept tumbling over the events of the evening. From dinner at Antoine's, to making love at the top of the Cathedral, to being nearly caught by the police, and ghost stories on the way home. She knew this was a night she'd keep with her always. That she'd revisit in her memories like a loved photograph.

A realization struck her so suddenly, her foot caught on the sidewalk, and she stumbled.

Daniel caught her elbow and righted her. "All right, bunny?"

"Yes, fine. Just wasn't paying attention. Please go on." Heat tinged her cheeks, and she hoped he chalked it up to embarrassment at being clumsy and not the actual reason—she might deeply care for this man.

As he continued to tell her about another of St. Louis's singing ghosts, Pere Antoine, her mind furiously examined this new revelation.

She couldn't possibly love Daniel. They had only been together for a brief time, and this wasn't supposed to be anything serious. He was just being friendly. It's what members of House Verity did, after all. They were friends. Just because he was handsome and created amazing food and told her stories from New Orleans history and showed her all the ways her body had been missing another human's touch did not mean that there was anything more to their relationship.

They were half a block from the House when he asked again, "Are you sure everything is all right?"

"Yes, sorry. I'm just tired." She gave him an apologetic smile, not having to fake the way her eyelids drooped.

"Come on, let's get you into bed."

As they made their way up to Daniel's room, Mattie came to a decision. Of course, she cared about him. That's what friends do. They cared for one another. But she wouldn't be ditzy enough to mistake it for love. Not when Clementine and the others had told her that Daniel doesn't do relationships. Why risk him pitying the poor country bunny who thought herself in love with the gargoyle and ending it? Better to enjoy what he was offering and keep all thoughts of deeper feelings nonsense buried deep. Maybe if she did that for long enough, she'd believe it was true.

****

The night was in full swing at Tonique & Lace. The band had the dance floor packed into a glittering swirl of bodies. The air pulsed with jazz, laughter, and heat.

"Look at you all dolled up. Love the rags, Mattie!" Nelly declared over the noise.

"Thanks, doll." Mattie bobbed a careful curtesy as Nelly gave her an appreciative once over, a tray of drinks balanced on one hand.

Not only was she wearing the dress Daniel had bought her, but she'd gone shopping with Jo in the afternoon for "new lacy things" as Jo had put it. The white silk slip with its delicate pink lace and matching underpants had been expensive, but worth it. She could definitely get used to the feeling of silk versus the scratchy roughness of over-washed cotton. Besides, knowing what was hidden under her dress made her feel powerful, like she had a delicious secret or hidden armor. It would be even better when she got to show them off to Daniel later that night.

She couldn't help the satisfied smile as she headed to her table. She still needed two hands to hold her tray with confidence, but she was determined to build up the strength and grace to dance through the unpredictable patrons with her tray poised securely above her head like Nelly.

"I've got two Gin Rickys." Mattie deposited the full highball glasses. "Can I get you folks anything else?"

A man wearing a fedora that was more feather than hat asked for a Sidecar.

"Coming right up."

Mattie made her way to the bar and leaned against the end. Down the way, Francis was in his element, mixing drinks so fast his hands were a blur. She tapped her foot and waited for him to acknowledge her—Nelly had warned her on the first night that yelling orders at him would result in no drinks being made and a grumpy barkeep. And a grumpy barkeep was a quick way to being jobless. Better for the patrons to wait a bit longer and to keep the man slinging the drinks happy.

"I don't think we've had the pleasure."

With a little jolt, she turned to find the Lady's partner, Caron, leaning next to her on the bar. Had he been there the whole time, or had she just not been paying attention when he walked up? She couldn't have said. His gaze snagged hers and held it. His irises were so dark they looked black, as if his eyes were all pupils, but that would be silly. No one's eyes were all pupil.

He had prominent cheekbones and a pointed chin that gave his face a sharp, cutting beauty. His long honey-colored hair was pulled back into a low ponytail with a black ribbon. It would have seemed old-fashioned except that his dark charcoal suit and vest were as modern as they got. The man really was dressed to the nines, including a dark red satin pocket square.

Mattie swallowed hard and remembered her manners. "I'm Mattie Logan. Pleasure to meet you."

An amused grin tugged on the corner of his mouth. "The pleasure is all mine. I believe you met my associate, Bossley, the other day." His words were softly accented, the r's rolling off his tongue. Mattie would have bet her boots it was true French and not the Creole French spoken in southern Louisiana. His accent hinted at outdoor cafes and glittering lights, not crawfish boils and Spanish moss.

"Yes, he was incredibly helpful. He got my account all set up and even helped me with a little legal matter."

"Ah, speaking of legal matters. It seems your Daniel is in the process of playing judge, jury, and executioner of Lorna's fine establishment."

Mattie turned her head to scan the room. There, near the back of the House, Daniel loomed over a table, his shoulders and arms tense. A man sat back in his chair, arguing with him, his arm gesturing wildly as he spoke. There was no way for Mattie to make out what he was saying over the din of the music, especially at this distance, but if she had to guess by how red the man's face was, it wasn't a friendly chat.

"Apparently that particular gentleman is taking umbrage with who is allowed to frequent our establishment," Caron said, as if reading her thoughts. "Even if he apologizes, which it doesn't look like he has any intention to, your Daniel won't let that kind of talk stand."

A part of her wanted to correct Caron that he wasn't "her Daniel", but she didn't. Not when she liked the sound of it so much. Even if she didn't think it was true.

"You can hear them from there?"

"Heavens, no. My hearing is better than humans, but even mine can't compete with The Crawfish Brothers. I read lips. When you've been as alive as long as I have, it behooves one to cultivate the skills necessary to stay alive."

Curiosity forced Mattie to blurt, "Vampires aren't immortal?"

"Sadly not." He gave her a grin. "We can be killed like any creature. Though, we are tougher than most. Much like your cockroaches."

She desperately wanted to ask him how old he really was, since at least physically, he looked no older than his early forties. Before she could ask further impertinent questions, though, her attention was drawn back across the room. The red-faced man had stood from his chair and squared off against Daniel.

Concern flickered through Mattie. The man was at least six inches taller than Daniel. There was a roughness around him that spoke of years of hard labor. The muscles of his neck, shoulders and arms bulged under his shirt, reminding Mattie of overstuffed sausages ready to split.

A hand the size of a Sunday ham swung at Daniel's face. With an annoyed grimace, Daniel ducked under the swing and smashed his own fist into the man's nose. The man stumbled back a few steps and shook his head before locking his eyes on where Daniel stood watching him, perfectly still. He let out a bellow that could be heard over the music and charged. Now, every head in the place turned to watch the fight, even the band had trailed off playing. The red-faced man tackled Daniel around the middle, and Mattie was sure he'd smash them both to the ground. But all Daniel did was take a step or two backwards before he retaliated with two rapid-fire hits to the man's kidneys and then drove his elbow into the back of the man's head.

The man crumbled to the ground at Daniel's feet. The band had got quiet, the whole room focused on the back corner. Daniel dusted himself off, reached down, grabbed the man by the waist of his pants and the back of his neck, and hauled him toward the front door. The sight reminded Mattie of her father dealing with an unruly farm puppy who had piddled on her mother's clean kitchen floors. Despite the man's colossal size, Daniel made the move look effortless. Sweet baby Jesus, the man was strong.

As Daniel and his cargo ducked behind the curtains to the entrance, applause rang out in the House. Mattie joined in the clapping as the band started back up.

"What will it be, Mattie?"

Francis looked at her expectantly.

"A… Sidecar. Yes." Between Caron and the fight, she had nearly forgotten the order.

"Coming right up." Francis slid a drink to Caron with a nod before turning on his heels.

Mattie's gaze went to where Caron's hand wrapped around a coupe glass of amber liquid garnished with a twist of lemon. No rings adorned his pale fingers. She knew he wasn't a member of the House but had wondered if maybe he was a member of another one.

Caron caught her staring and raised one eyebrow.

"I'm trying to learn all the cocktails," Mattie blurted out, her brain scrambling for a better explanation. "But I don't think I recognize that one?" She knew it wasn't an Old Fashioned because Francis always garnished those with orange, not lemon, and sometimes a cherry if he had them in stock.

"A joke from our resident barkeep."

Francis made jokes?

Caron must have seen the confusion on her face because he continued, "It's dry gin, Lillet blanc, lemon juice, and just a dash of the green fairy. In other words, a Corpse Reviver No. 2."

"Oh." Mattie wondered at the bravery it would take to make a vampire that particular drink, and her already high estimation of Francis went up a few notches.

If he could be brave enough to tease a vampire… "May I ask a question?"

A small smile played on his too perfect lips. "Hardly anyone these days is brave enough to indulge their curiosity around me. So yes, please ask."

"You're the Lady's main partner, but you aren't a member of the House. Why is that?"

Caron took a long sip, and Mattie wondered if she'd overstepped her bounds.

"Vampires, for the most part, are clan creatures. We've survived this long by supporting one another. Did you know that there is an entirely vampiric House in New Orleans?"

Mattie shook her head. "No, I didn't, but I'm still learning about all the Houses." The thought of an entire House made up of vampires, the creatures from old gothic novels and scary stories sent a little shiver up her spine.

"House Ambrosio. They run all the gambling parlors in the city. Much like Tonique & Lace, these parlors are run in secret. Poker games, roulette, and the like. I was a member of their House for many years, until we had a falling out. It's not often a vampire leaves their clan, but it does happen. However, no matter my feelings for Lorna, it would be in poor taste to join House Verity. There is no need to cause further tension between the Houses."

Mattie guessed that his relationship with the Lady was a factor in his leaving House Ambrosio. While she burned to confirm this, she noted the bitter sadness in his words and left it alone.

"May I ask another question?"

One eyebrow quirked up in amusement. "I think we are past the point of asking to ask a question stage."

"Sorry, the Lady told me I should just ask, but it's a hard habit to break. You said House Ambrosio runs gambling parlors and you run a bank. Do all vampires deal with money?"

He gave her an amused smile and some of the sadness left his too black eyes. "Clever, but not quite. Vampires love numbers, not money. It's a weakness of ours."

Love of numbers was a weakness? Before she could ask about it further, Francis deposited the Sidecar on her tray and leaned over the bar.

"No more gin drinks. We're all out." The look on Francis's face told her how much that fact annoyed the barkeep.

"Jimmy and the Lady couldn't find another

supplier?"

"Not yet, but they better soon if they know what's good for them," Francis huffed before hurrying off to mix more orders.

Mattie looked down at the cocktail on her tray. "Well, I should probably get a wiggle on."

Caron's honey-colored head tilted toward her, his peculiar eyes never leaving her face as he held one hand out to her.

"Oh." Mattie placed her hand in his and was surprised by the intense warmth of it. Weren't vampires undead creatures? Shouldn't they be cold as the grave? Instead of a handshake, Caron lifted her hand to his mouth and pressed those perfect lips to the soft skin of her wrist. She was intensely aware that she was allowing a vampire, a creature that drinks human blood, to kiss the veins of her wrist, but she couldn't seem to muster any fear, just a delicious fascination.

"Pleasure talking with you."

"You as well," Mattie said a little breathlessly. He let go of her hand. Giving him her best smile, she headed back into the fray with the feeling of his stare on her back.

After depositing the Sidecar, she made her way around the tables, checking on folks and the level of their drinks. She found herself circling around to the front entrance where Daniel was back at his post with not a hair out of place. The little flicker of concern that had been fluttering around her chest since the fight dissipated.

He crossed his arms over his chest, his voice warm and mocking. "Checking on me, bunny?"

"No," Mattie replied as casually as she could.

"Maybe I just wanted to make sure that big palooka didn't put you out of commission for what I have planned later."

"Oh really, now? And what plans would those be?" With a grin, he snagged one of her wrists and pulled her to him.

She leaned back enough to tap a finger against his chest. "You will just have to wait and see."

"Does it have anything to do with all the boxes and bags you and Jo came home with?" His cheeky grin was back.

"Maybe." She went up on her toes to press a kiss to the corner of his mouth before sauntering away, enjoying the feeling of silk and Daniel's stare on her swaying backside.

Chapter Eighteen

Mattie

Life had settled into a comfortable but busy rhythm for Mattie. During the day, she explored New Orleans with Daniel, went shopping with Jo and Clementine, and stopped by for iced tea and gossip with the girls of House LeBlanc on Bourbon Street. At night, she waitressed at Tonique & Lace. She laughed hard, drank enough cocktails to have a preference, and learned to dance reasonably well—at least her dance partners never seemed to complain. Then, in the early mornings, she would stumble up to Daniel's room to continue to explore their friendship.

One Wednesday morning, Mattie found herself sitting in Darlene's bedroom on a chair facing the best-stocked vanity she'd ever seen in her life. The whole surface of the white marble top was covered in jars, bottles, lotions, hair tonics, and various pots and tubes of cosmetics. She wasn't even sure what parts of the body some of the items were intended for.

"Are you sure, sugar? Once it's cut, even with a charm, it will take weeks to grow back to this length." Darlene stifled a yawn with one hand and ran her other one through Mattie's long curls.

"You've already asked me that three times. I'm sure."

The decision had been a long time coming, even before she'd moved to New Orleans. Whenever she'd gone into the drugstore back in Prairieville to pick up talcum powder or Ingram's shaving cream (Lenny had been particular about making sure he had a smooth shave for Sunday morning services), she had always spent a few minutes lingering over the magazine rack. She'd been fascinated by the daring flappers that graced the covers of Photoplay and Movie Reel with their short bobs and spit curls. Only once did she make the mistake of purchasing such a magazine. She'd hidden it under the sink behind the borax and read it over and over in secret. However, when Lenny had gone over the monthly expenses, he'd seen the line item for the magazine. He'd given her a lecture that had lasted half the evening about wasting money and the temptation and sins that such rags peddle as their bread and butter before he'd burned it in the fireplace. Well, Lenny wasn't here to lecture her now or ever again.

At Tonique & Lace the previous evening, Darlene had mentioned she routinely gave haircuts to the ladies of LeBlanc House and even maintained Jo's signature straight bob. With the boldness of two French 75's in her veins, she'd pounced on the knowledge and made Darlene promise to cut her hair first thing in the morning. The liquid courage was long gone, but the conviction remained.

"I just don't know why you want to cut off all these lovely curls. I have to sleep in curlers to get waves like this, and I always end up with a kink in my neck."

"If you like it so much, you could make a wig out of what you cut off," Mattie said with a laugh.

"Don't tempt me. If you're really sure, I'll do it.

Just let me finish this cup of coffee so I'm awake enough to cut straight." She held out the large ceramic coffee pot decorated with soft pink roses. "Would you like a warmup?"

Mattie held out her rose-patterned cup for her to refill with thick, chicory coffee. After stirring in a good bit of cream and a little sugar, she took a long, appreciative sip, using the motion to look surreptitiously around the room. The large French windows were open, letting the early morning breeze in and giving a view of her plant-covered balcony. Her love of roses was further present in the pink satin bedding that covered the large four poster that dominated the room and the rose-patterned brocade fainting couch where Darlene sat, nursing her coffee.

Darlene's bed-messed blond hair, and the way her dressing gown hung off one slender shoulder, gave her a delightfully disheveled look. She drained the last of the coffee from her cup, stood, and stepped behind Mattie.

"Right, last chance." Darlene gripped Mattie's shoulders and grinned at her in the mirror.

"Get a wiggle on, woman!"

"All right! All right, bossy!" Darlene picked up a silver-handled set of scissors and a matching comb. "At least we're doing a long bob and not an Eaton crop. With your curls, you'd end up looking more like a dandelion puff than a flapper."

Mattie's heart sped up in her chest as Darlene combed out her hair. There was a long moment where she held her breath until a loud "snick" rang out in the room. She blew out the breath in a joyful whoosh as Darlene held up a long brown handful of hair.

"You are going to look aces and eights after this," Darlene said as she snipped more hair.

Mattie knitted her eyebrows together but kept her head perfectly still. "Wait, you think this is a good idea? Then why did you ask me four times if I was sure?"

"Oh, I just like to triple and, sometimes, quadruple check. This way, if you get a bee in your bonnet later, you can't get mad at me since I tried to warn you." She kept working her way around and with each snip of the scissors, Mattie's head and spirit felt lighter and lighter. "It's a dramatic change and sometimes it's too much for folks."

"I think I'm ready for change."

She'd uprooted her life, moved to New Orleans, rescued a Crow-girl, got work in a speakeasy, started an intense…friendship with a gargoyle, and had her first threesome. She thought she was handling change pretty darn well.

****

"Well, what do you think?" Mattie asked as she turned her head this way and that, reveling in the lightness, in the feel of the breeze on the back of her neck.

"You are one hot tomato," Daniel said as he ran a hand along the ends of her curly bob. "It really suits you."

A pleased smile played on her lips. "Thank you. Darlene did a top-rate job."

"That she did. Buy you a beignet before our shift?" He held out his elbow in over-the-top gallantry.

"Ab-so-lute-ly!" she replied with a laugh and tucked her hand onto his forearm. It was hard to say no to the deep-fried sugary treats, especially when it was Daniel doing the offering.

"Mrs. Mattie Stumps."

The name froze Mattie in her tracks as fear crawled down her spine and nestled like a rattlesnake in her belly. Instinct caused her to jerk her hand away from Daniel's arm as she turned around slowly. Wild hope said that if she was slow enough, the person who had angrily, disdainfully, shouted her name would no longer be there. Her luck wasn't that good.

"Um. Hello, Lenny."

There was her ex-husband, standing in the middle of the French Quarter sidewalk. He was wearing his best Sunday suit and his wide-brimmed hat. His sweet farm boy features that had so charmed her before they were married were now twisted and contorted, one side of his lip raised in an ugly sneer. A vein like a Cyprus tree root stood out on his forehead.

"What in the name of all is that is holy have you done with your hair?"

Her hand flew to her newly cut locks. The years of bending to his will made the apology spring to her lips, but she forced it down before it could burst forth.

"It's my hair. And I like it."

"You've lopped it off like a painted sheila and look at how you're dressed. No self-respecting Christian woman would dare show that much leg." Lenny made a disgusted flick toward her stripped cotton dress that ended just below her knees. "How dare you shame me like this? You. Hussy." Each word was spat at her like a poisonous sunflower seed.

Before she could reply, Daniel stepped forward with a placating hand. "Hey now, pal. I can see you're upset, but that's no way to talk to a lady."

Lenny's fists curled at his sides. Hands turned hard and strong from plowing fields and hauling hay bales. "She is my wife. Nothing can change that. Certainly not this." He held up his left fist. The large gold ring that had been his father's glinted in the afternoon sun. Mattie's heart sank at the sight of the crumpled piece of paper he held. It could only be the letter from Bossley. He must have tracked the letter to New Orleans.

Why had she thought it was a good idea to try and amicably dissolve the marriage? Why hadn't she just left well enough alone? Because she didn't just want the illusion of freedom. She wanted freedom itself.

Fear wrapped around her insides and squeezed. Would he try to drag her home by her newly shorn hair? She gave herself a mental shake. She was no longer the weak-willed housewife he'd married. If he tried anything of the sort, he'd find out that Mattie had grown teeth. Sharp ones.

"We're still married in the eyes of the Lord, and I'll talk to my wife as a damn well please." Hard eyes flicked to Daniel. "And we are not pals or friends or any such thing. Don't think I don't see how you look at my wife, the little jezebel."

Mattie grabbed Daniel's arm as he lunged for Lenny. He could've shaken her off as easy as pie, but, instead, he stilled. Though, the muscles in his arm were tensed and coiled.

"Don't."

"Why not, Mattie?" It didn't seem possible, but Lenny's sneer became every uglier. "Afraid I'll mess up his city boy face?"

"Oh, I don't think you would stand a chance with

him in a fair fight," Mattie replied, her hand still locked around Daniel's bicep. She flicked her chin over Lenny's shoulder. "But it seems we've attracted some attention."

At the end of the street, the policeman stood in his long, belted coat and shiny brass buttons despite the heat. The man's flat-topped hat turned toward them, and he fingered his baton in a way that made Mattie nervous.

Lenny glanced over his shoulder. "I'm not afraid of no lawman."

"Unlike the policemen in Prairieville, the New Orleans coppers don't care who starts the fight, everyone gets arrested, and they let the judge sort it out later," Daniel supplied.

The policeman in question strutted up to the trio. He had a weathered face and a small potbelly that strained over his belt. His old-fashioned mutton chops were streaked with grey and gave him the look of an elderly basset hound.

"Good afternoon, officer," Daniel said, his voice once again taking that on polite deference he'd used in the alley of the St. Louis Cathedral.

"Gentlemen. Lady," he said with a nod to each of them. "Everything all right here?"

Mattie made her voice as bright and chipper as possible. "Everything's just dandy. Isn't it, Lenny?"

There was a long, tense moment before Lenny bit out the words, "Yes sir, officer. We're all just dandy."

"You have a good day, Lenny. Officer." Mattie rearranged her hand on Daniel's arm and started pulling him toward the closest side street.

"I'll be seeing you, Mattie." The words were said

in a light enough manner, but the look that accompanied them sent little shivers of fear down her spine.

She had no doubt to the truth in her husband's words. That's what terrified her.

Chapter Nineteen

Daniel

Anger simmered under Daniel's skin. The ends of his fingers itched with the need to extend his talons and disembowel that worthless ex-husband of Mattie's. He almost didn't care that it was broad daylight. Or that a copper had been down the street. Or that it would have put the House in jeopardy. The only thing that had stopped him was Mattie's hand on his arm.

The entire way back to the House she had jumped at every noise, convinced that Lenny would ambush them from around a corner or down an alleyway. Daniel had almost wished the son of a bitch had tried. He hated the tension in her shoulders and the worry lines around her eyes.

Her shoulders only dropped from around her ears when they'd entered the House courtyard and were greeted with a terse nod from Mac, who was standing guard from the perch over the door. He returned the nod and hurried Mattie inside. He'd have to debrief Mac at some point soon, there was no way they hadn't noticed the tension in both of them, but his priority was Mattie. The room was blessedly empty, though Francis would probably show up to prep for the night ahead soon.

With a hand at the small of her back, he steered her to a table and set her in a chair. The blank look was back in her eyes, and it was all Daniel could do to leash his temper. After pulling another chair close, he sat and took a hold of her limp hands, trying to rub some gentle warmth back into them.

"Talk to me, Mattie."

She turned her head toward him with all the liveliness of an automaton. The sight made Daniel's heart seize in his chest.

"Do you want me to bump him off?"

Slowly Mattie's eyebrows came together. "Bump off?"

"Deal with. Just say the word and I'll get rid of him. He'll never bother you again." It would be a pleasure to make sure that one could never pop back into her life.

"No!" She cried, gripping his hands tight. "That's not what I want at all."

"What do you want then?" Fear gripped his insides. What if New Orleans was no longer what she wanted? What if he was no longer what she wanted? "You don't want to go back with him, do you?"

She slumped back into her chair. "No. Of course I don't want to go back with him. But just because I no longer want to be married to the man, doesn't mean he deserves to die though."

Relief flooded through him even as he pondered her response. While technically she was correct, Daniel thought back to the entitled, angry man standing on the sidewalk, waving his wedding ring like it was a magical talisman that gave him absolute control over Mattie. He doubted that the man would tuck his tail and quietly go home.

"All right, death is off the table, but that still leaves

a wide range of options."

A wry smile played on her lips as she leaned forward and kissed his cheek. "That's very sweet, but Lenny is my problem. I'll take care of it."

"Mattie. You don't have to take care of it. Please, let me do this for you."

She shook her head. "This is something I need to take care of. I made this mess and I'll be the one to deal with it."

When Daniel didn't say anything, she must have taken it for agreement because she smiled like they'd settled the matter and stood. "I need to get ready for my shift."

He watched her walk to the House entry as his mouth twisted like he'd just ate a bad oyster. The need to protect her was a physical thing inside his chest, a demanding roar that left no room for other words or feelings. Of course, the gargoyle protective drive would choose now to kick in, when the object of that instinct wanted him to do nothing of the sort.

Mimi was probably watching from Heaven and laughing herself sick. He'd never really understood it before, but she'd always sworn that one day, he would. The old bat just had to be right, even in death. God, he missed her. Mimi would have liked Mattie, would have said she had spunk. Mimi would have known exactly what to say to convince Mattie of the severity of the situation. To convince her to accept the help that was being offered.

Mattie's blank expression flashed through his mind again. The same one that she'd hidden behind when she panicked in the cuffs. The one he knew she'd learned to retreat behind in order to survive her marriage. When she got that look, it was like a storm cloud eclipsing the sun. It made Daniel want to beg and plead and promise anything and everything just to wipe that look from her face. It made him want to tear and punch and eviscerate anything that caused that expression.

He took a deep breath and let it out into the silent speakeasy. Since Mimi's ghost was silent on the matter, he'd just have to find another way to make sure Lenny never harmed her again. Never again caused her to retreat to that blank, cold place. Despite what Mattie thought they'd agreed to, there was no way Daniel was going to stand by and do nothing. No, he wasn't going to lose her like he'd lost so many others.

Chapter Twenty

Mattie

Never had a shift at Tonique & Lace been so long. Usually the nights flew by in a haze of happy customers and drink orders, but that night seemed to drag on as slow as a heat wave of an August day. Mattie was so sure that Lenny would show up at any moment, making trouble, that she not only got several orders mixed up, but she also spilled an entire glass of champagne over a gentleman. Thankfully, he'd been drunk enough to find the whole thing a lark, but still too many mistakes like that and Francis would show her the door.

It also didn't help that Daniel was on door duty and kept watching her with that concerned look on his face. At least he'd agreed to let her handle the Lenny problem, but a part of her knew that if Lenny showed up and threatened the House, Daniel wouldn't hesitate to "take care of the problem" despite their agreement. Not that she would blame him in that case.

Eventually the crowd cleared out, and Mattie went about her closing duties. Once everything was swept and put away, she sank down into a chair at an empty table, her hands flat on the surface, her gaze not really seeing the House's early morning wind-down ritual.

Thoughts flew through her head like mosquitos, buzzing and biting for her attention, but never being caught. Lenny obviously wasn't going to just divorce her. He'd made that painfully clear. So what was she going to do about him?

Slowly, she realized she was no longer alone at the table. Turning her head to the left, she gave a little start. "Oh, Lady, I'm sorry. I didn't see you sit down."

The Lady's red lips quirked into a smile. "I'm not surprised. Daniel said you were having a rough day."

Shame burned up Mattie's neck and cheeks. "He shouldn't have bothered you with that. It was a minor thing, I swear."

"I would have been more bothered if he hadn't told me. Anything that could affect the House is my concern."

Mattie thought of her worry around Lenny tracking her back to the House and winced. The Lady was right. As much as Mattie hated to admit it, the Lady needed to know that Mattie's husband was in New Orleans and looking for her.

Mattie's gaze went to where her fingers curled against the polished wood of the table. "I can find other lodgings." She couldn't bring herself to add "and new employment." The thought of giving up her little room made her stomach turn, but not nearly as much as leaving Tonique & Lace all together.

"Why would you do that?"

Mattie's head snapped to where the Lady was regarding her with amusement. "Because I don't want to bring trouble to the House."

The Lady's laugh was bright as moonbeams. "One little ex-husband is the least of the House's problems. This is your home, and we will not let him drive you from it." She reached out a hand and laid it over

Mattie's curled one.

"Thank you, Lady. I can't tell you how much that means to me." Warmth like golden honey dripped down Mattie's spine and pooled in her belly. She appreciated the Lady referring to Lenny as her ex-husband. Even if it wasn't true yet.

"The other thing Daniel mentioned was that you could use some distraction." The Lady had the same look in her eye as when she and Caron had "borrowed" Isabella from her husband.

Mattie swallowed. "Oh, he did?"

With liquid grace, the Lady stood up, pulled Mattie to her feet, and tucked Mattie's left hand into her elbow. She motioned to where Daniel and Caron stood next to the House entrance. Daniel had his hands in his pockets and that smug glint in his eye.

As they made their way to the waiting pair, the Lady leaned her head toward Mattie. The light smell of magnolias filled Mattie's nose.

"You are under no obligation to say yes. If you'd rather spend the evening only with Daniel or just on your own, I'll make it happen."

She had a choice. A choice that would be respected. But being alone was the very last thing Mattie wanted. Her eyes flicked between the regal beauty of the Lady and Caron's sharp good looks. Her mind brought up memories of the Lady taking her to see Grace on her first day, the fluttering desire that had consumed her while she watched the Lady's skillful hands.

Her tongue darted out to wet her lips. "I think I could use some friends tonight."

"Wonderful to hear, cherie."

The men stepped aside so that Mattie and the Lady led the way into the back hallway. Instead of going up the stairs, they turned the opposite direction. On this side of the House, there was only a single door.

The Lady opened it and ushered Mattie inside before turning on a couple of lamps with dark red shades that bathed the room in a soft glow. With wide eyes, Mattie looked around. The room was larger than she thought possible, but she should have been used to the peculiar physics of the House by now. There were large French windows covered by thick purple velvet drapes. The four-poster bed was the biggest she had ever seen. It could have easily fit at least four people comfortably and six or seven if they liked to cuddle.

One silver door probably led to the Lady's washroom since a set of double doors stood open, giving Mattie a glimpse of bookcases and the corner of a wooden desk—the Lady's office. A large armoire sat near the bed as well as a vanity, mirror, and small stool. The surface of the vanity held cosmetics, silver-backed brushes, and cut crystal perfume bottles. A couch and two armchairs formed a small sitting room. Near one chair was a large, round footrest, but the legs had metal rings fitted into them, reminding Mattie of the posts on Daniel's bed and sending a pleasant shiver down her spine.

Strong arms snaked around her, pulling her back to Daniel's chest. His hands pressed flat to her stomach, grounding her.

Across the room, Caron headed for a glass and silver bar cart filled with crystal decanters and various styles of glasses. He moved with a grace that reminded Mattie of the lean, sleek farm cats that stalked the mice in the barn back home. After selecting a decanter, he pulled the stopper and poured a couple of fingers of liquid.

Glass in hand, he headed to where the Lady stood and offered her the drink. As the Lady took a long sip, Caron nuzzled her neck. A fizzle of unease raced through Mattie as the memory of Bossley's scarred neck flashed in her mind. She chided herself. The Lady didn't have any scars, and even if Caron did feed on her, there was no way he would do it without her permission. Not when consent was such an integral part of the House.

One of Caron's hands stroked the Lady's hip as his eyes locked on Mattie and Daniel. "Lorna love, why don't you help Mattie get more comfortable?"

After pressing a long kiss to his mouth, the Lady handed the drink back to him and stalked toward Mattie.

With a question in her eyes, Mattie looked between the approaching Lady and Caron, who had sat back against the headboard on the bed.

The Lady noticed the question in Mattie's eyes. "I may be head of House Verity, but in this room, Caron is the boss. Even I follow his orders here."

"Now that's not the full truth, is it, love?" Caron asked, raising his glass. "Sometimes our Lady likes to defy me just so she'll be punished."

The Lady's answering grin was fierce and delighted. "You can't expect me to good all the time, cherie."

Punishments could be something that you wanted? At least in terms of bedroom play?

But wasn't that exactly what had happened when

she'd kissed Jo without Daniel's permission? It hadn't been on purpose, but Daniel had still "punished" her all the same. Now that she knew the kind of consequences that could come from disobeying, maybe she'd defy Daniel on purpose in the future. Just to see what would happen.

The bigger question was, though, did she trust Caron? True, he was good-looking but in a scary, predator way. She didn't know him, not really. She'd only had the one conversation with him.

Mattie looked up at Daniel, her lower lip pulled between her teeth.

He leaned down and whispered in her ear. "I trust Caron to make sure everyone is safe and taken care of. If you can't trust him, trust me. I won't let him do or request anything of you I don't think you can handle. Let us take care of you tonight. Let us make you feel good." When she nodded, he pressed a kiss to the skin under her ear.

Louder, he said, "She'll be a good bunny and do everything asked of her."

The Lady placed her hands on either side of Mattie's face and leaned in to press those red, red lips to hers in a kiss that had Mattie melting in Daniel's arms. It was one thing to watch the Lady kiss Grace and another to experience it for herself. To feel the press of her perfect lips against her own. To feel the Lady's tongue darting out to thoroughly taste Mattie's own lips and tongue and mouth. When the Lady finally pulled away, Mattie swayed in Daniel's arms, her head swimming from a single kiss! She took comfort in the hard press of Daniel's erection against her buttocks. At least she wasn't the only one enjoying themselves.

A satisfied smile graced the Lady's face as she started undressing Mattie with Daniel's help. With each layer they stripped away, the two pressed kisses and little nips of teeth into her newly exposed skin until she was stark naked, every inch of her rosy from their attention.

"What a beautiful sight."

Mattie looked up to where Caron lounged on the bed, having completely forgotten about their audience. The way his black eyes roamed over her in appreciation brought a pleased blush to her cheeks. Where once she would have tried to hide, now she held herself open, allowed herself to be appreciated fully.

"I think such gorgeous tits could use some decoration. Don't you, love?" Caron asked.

The Lady's hands came up to cup Mattie's breasts. "Right as always, cherie." Using her thumbs, she teased Mattie's nipples until they pebbled into hard peaks. Little shivers of pleasure raced down her spine. Without warning, the Lady pinched hard, forcing a little moan from Mattie before leaning down to sooth them with her tongue, one after the other.

"Keep these warm for me," the Lady said with a fond pat to the underside of Mattie's breasts before she sauntered to the armoire in the corner.

"You know your favorite drawer in my room?"

Mattie was so focused on the way Daniel's hands were squeezing and kneading her breasts, she almost didn't catch his question. "Um…yes?"

"It's nothing compared to the Lady's collection."

The breath caught in Mattie's throat as the Lady opened the doors wide, revealing shelves covered in leather cuffs, shiny silver toys, and other items that

Mattie could only guess at their purpose. Hooks hung from the inside of the doors, sporting a variety of leather floggers, paddles, and whips. The Lady's brown and golden gaze flicked between Mattie and one of the shelves where she was pulling out a long, shallow drawer.

"The purple, cherie?"

Caron tilted his head as he regarded Mattie for a long moment before nodding. "Excellent choice. A little weight without overwhelming her."

After grabbing something from the drawer, the Lady shut it and headed back to Mattie and Daniel, leaving the doors of the armoire open. She held up a tiny metal clothespin, the type with a spring used to hang laundry on a line to dry. From the end, a string of purple cut glass beads dangled.

"They're beautiful," Mattie breathed. "But what are they are they for?"

A wicked gleam glinted in the Lady's eye. "Allow me to show you."

Daniel's hand cupped the underside of Mattie's breasts and lifted to present them to the Lady. As the Lady's long fingers rolled Mattie's nipple gently between her thumb and forefinger, understanding slowly dawned on Mattie. Her tongue darted out to wet her lips in anticipation.

The Lady pinched the legs of the clothespin, and the other end opened. She fitted the end around Mattie's peaked nipple and let the metal tip close slowly around it. Pleasure bordering on pain burst through Mattie and made her breath fast and quick. With each heave of her chest, the purple beads danced and swung, sending fresh shocks of sensation through her.

Daniel's hands gently squeezed her. "Deep breaths, bunny."

She forced herself to take a deep breath and let it out. The sensation quieted to a low buzz—still there, but less overwhelming. With deft hands, the Lady fastened the other clothespin. She stepped back to allow Caron to examine her handiwork.

"Absolutely beautiful," he purred.

"Isn't she?" the Lady replied as she leaned her head down to run her tongue over one of Mattie's trapped, aching nipples. Mattie cried out, arching hard against Daniel's chest. Liquid heat pooled between her thighs as if there was an electric wire connecting the two.

"I think she deserves a little orgasm for being such a good sport. Can you come standing up, Mattie?"

Mattie took a deep breath before answering Caron's question, "Um…" Her mind drifted to the night that Daniel had taken her up St. Louis Cathedral. The terror and rush of the world opening before her with nothing keeping her upright but Daniel's powerful arms as she orgasmed around him. "Yes, I think so. At least, I'll try my best."

"You were right, Daniel," Caron said with a grin that made Mattie's knees weak. "So very eager. I could drink it like wine."

The Lady nuzzled the edge of Mattie's jaw. "Tongue or fingers?"

"Fingers for this one, I think. If you're very good, I'll let you taste that eager little pussy of hers later."

The Lady gave a little moan and stepped to Mattie's right side so that Caron had an unobstructed view, and the Lady could keep her non-gold eye on her partner. Gold-tipped fingers trailed down Mattie's stomach to the apex of her thighs. Using just her fingertip, the Lady traced the soft folds of her and circled around her aching pearl.

Her eyes locked on where Caron watched with singular intensity, that dark gaze of his watching every movement of the Lady's hand and Mattie's answering quivers and sighs. It was exciting but also made her feel a little like a butterfly, pinned and dissected by an avid collector.

Mattie's legs trembled, and she bit her lip as the Lady's finger dipped into her, working into and out of her.

"Use your words, bunny. Let Caron hear you," Daniel chided before nipping the lobe of her ear.

She released her lower lip from her teeth and let the little moans and gasps spill from her mouth. Next to her, the Lady took a deep breath, pulling the air through her parted lips. The pleasure built and built within her until she was a tight string that quivered between the Lady's delving fingers and Daniel's hands on her breasts. When she was sure she'd snap, Daniel tugged gently on the dangling beads.

Pleasure shot down Mattie's spine, and she cried out, her orgasm sweeping through her. It was only Daniel and the Lady's arms that kept her suddenly liquid legs from depositing her straight onto the Lady's plush grey rug.

"Absolutely perfect," Caron mused as he set his empty glass on the bedside table.

Standing with that fluid grace, he stripped off his jacket and laid it over the back of the chair. His shirt, pants, and undergarments swiftly followed. There was no self-consciousness in his movements. Rather, he undressed with the confidence of a man completely at ease in his own body. It helped that with each article of clothing more of his beautiful, well-muscled body was revealed. An impressive erection stood at attention as he finished disrobing.

Shifting back to the bed, he extended his hand. "Come here, Mattie."

Before Mattie could check with Daniel—her head was fuzzy and not obeying her quite as it should—he gave her a pat on her rear end, gently pushing her toward the bed. On wobbly legs, she came to the side next to Caron. Every step caused the jewelry to sway, sending little tingles down to her stomach. When she laid her hand in Caron's, she was once again surprised at the heat of it.

Caron pulled her onto the bed, turning her so she sat in-between his legs, her back against his chest. The heat of his chest was a pleasant blaze that she relaxed into. The last of her nerves melted away. His hands ran up and down her arms in long, soothing strokes.

"You two are wearing too many clothes. Help each other remedy that."

A little shiver went down Mattie's spine at the sensual steel that laced Caron's words. The quiet command and power of that voice. Daniel spun the Lady around so that her back was to the bed and slowly, ever so slowly, undid the buttons down the back of her dress, exposing a long sliver of her silken skin. Slipping a strap of her dress down, he pressed his mouth to the spot where her neck met her throat, and the Lady tilted her head with a little pleased noise, allowing him more access.

"Beautiful, aren't they?" Caron breathed into Mattie's ear.

She could only nod, her eyes riveted on Daniel and the Lady as they undressed each other. A private burlesque show just for herself and Caron. As the layers peeled away, Mattie's banked desire roared back to life. A part of her couldn't believe that life had brought her to this place, where she was lounging naked against a vampire, watching a succubus and a gargoyle strip just for them. A gargoyle that made her heart race every time his eyes locked with hers as the Lady's elegant fingers removed his shirt or slid his pants down the slopes of his hips. There was heat in that gaze, a promise of what was to come.

Once the last of the clothing was discarded, the Lady led Daniel to the bed in all their naked glory. The Lady was exquisite. Long-limbed and regal. Shapely breasts tipped in darker brown nipples. The most surprising thing, though, was the brilliant gold tattoo that took up one side of the Lady's taut stomach.

Against her dark skin, the lines of the tattoo shimmered like liquid metal. Up close, Mattie realized it was a filigree fleur-de-lis, and that the band in the middle was stylized after the Lady's House ring. The same ring which was currently the only thing she was wearing.

"I've never seen a gold tattoo before," Mattie whispered. "It's beautiful."

Caron reached out a hand and traced a finger down along one of the gold whorls as the Lady said, "And you probably won't again. Grace wouldn't even tell me how it was done, and I was there when she did it."

Following Caron's finger, Mattie realized that there

were details hidden in the tattoo's filigree. Hearts, a feather, the moon in various phases, faces of gargoyles, and other creatures that she couldn't even name. She had the feeling that every time you looked at it, you'd find new elements and details.

"I think our Mattie has recovered sufficiently. Let's see if we can't make her fly." Caron's words made Mattie's heart race with anticipation as he pulled the Lady onto her knees next to them on the bed.

The Lady kissed her, nipping and sucking on her lower lip until Mattie let out of a tiny sigh of need. After pressing a last kiss that left heat pooling between Mattie's legs, the Lady shifted to Caron, affording Mattie a beautiful view of the Lady's breasts. She ran her thumbs over the Lady's nipples until they hardened into peaks. When she pinched them lightly, the Lady's hips twitched and swayed in response. The sight was so lovely, Mattie immediately did it again.

Strong fingers clamped around Mattie's wrists and pulled her hands away. Frustrated, Mattie looked up at Caron, who had stopped kissing the Lady and was looking down at her in fond annoyance.

"Did I say you could touch?"

"No, sir," Mattie murmured, lowering her eyes.

But Caron didn't let go of her wrists, instead he brought them up to lace her fingers around the back of his neck.

"If you remove your hands, we stop. If you say the word, we stop. Do you understand?"

Mattie's eyes found Daniel, who had climbed on the end of the bed and was kneeling near her feet. He gave her that mischievous smile of his and nodded once. He'd arranged this. Let Caron and the Lady know that she both wanted to be restrained, to be at their mercy, but that normal restraints made her feel trapped. This way there were still rules—she could still surrender completely to them—but she could end it at any moment if she needed to. That he cared so much about her desires, her wants, made her heart ache in her chest.

She settled her hands, lacing them tighter around Caron's neck. The fall of his long hair felt like silk on the back of her fingers. "Yes, I understand."

"So eager to please," Caron said. He drifted one hand down Mattie's cheek and she leaned into the heat of it. "Daniel, use your tongue. Let's see how long you can keep her right on the edge."

Mattie froze, a little whimper escaping her, but she kept her hands firmly around Caron.

At her feet, Daniel chuckled low and dark. The sound made her pulse race. "My pleasure."

He nudged Mattie's legs open and then kissed and nipped his way up her calf and thigh. For a long moment, he merely breathed on her trembling sex. When she didn't think she could stand the warm teasing from him a moment longer, his mouth sealed around her aching pearl. The combined sensation made Mattie cry out and arch her head and shoulders into Caron's chest.

"Let's remove these for now," Caron said as he unclipped the jewelry. Blood flooded back into her poor nipples, bringing with it a fierce prickling, almost a burning sensation that was both maddening and delightful.

"Allow me." The Lady leaned down and kissed the red tip of Mattie's breast. After she had soothed the abused flesh with her tongue, the Lady shifted over to lap at the other one.

As Daniel's lips and tongue alternated between lapping at her and delving into her wet folds, Caron's hand stroked up her side to pinch the nipple not occupied by the Lady's mouth.

His other hand came up to grasp her wrist. At first, she didn't understand and clung to his neck, not wanting to call an end to the pleasure that was cascading over her in waves.

"Let go, Mattie," Caron whispered into her ear. "I want to taste Lorna's sweetness on your fingers."

She let go, and he moved her hand to between the Lady's thighs. Eagerly, she caressed the Lady's sex, diving in and out until her fingers were slick and the Lady's breath was hot and fast against her breast. Pulling her hand back, Mattie presented it to Caron. If anything, his mouth was even hotter, his tongue nearly singing her fingers as it licked every drop from them. Then he maneuvered her hand back.

"She makes the most adorable little purrs when she comes. Use two fingers and keep a firm pressure here," Caron said in a low voice as he positioned the heel of her hand.

With Caron's guidance, she moved her fingers in time with the circling of her palm. Instead of her attention being split between Daniel's careful administrations and the way the Lady quivered and gasped under her hand, bringing the Lady pleasure only seemed to heighten Mattie's own.

"Keep going just like that. You'll know she's close when those luscious buttocks quiver and tense."

The pleased note in Caron's voice spurred Mattie

on. She wanted to please him, wanted to please the Lady. When the Lady's body tensed and pulsed around Mattie's fingers, Mattie nearly came with her, but Daniel, sensing how close she was getting, backed off, keeping true to his word. The Lady melted against Mattie's chest, little low rumblings coming from the back of her throat.

The moment slowed and hung in the air. The four of them paused to catch their breath.

Then Caron gently took Mattie's wrist and once more cleaned each of her fingers before settling it back against his neck, and the moment of respite was over.

Sensation burst through Mattie from all angles, consuming her, overwhelming her. Caught between the press of hands and legs and mouths. She was a butterfly pinned and helpless as they dissected her sweetly, finding all her nooks and crannies. All the ways she could burn and be consumed.

Over and over she came to the crest of her pleasure only for Daniel to slow down, ease back, never leaving her completely, but also not allowing her release. Each time the loss became more acute. More unbearable. Every nerve in her body thrummed and ached. She turned this way and that, trying to get enough pressure or friction, and was continually denied. Her need was all-consuming, her body aching with frustration.

Through it all, her fingers remained locked on Caron.

"Please. Please Caron," she finally said, her words spilling from her mouth. She pleaded, her voice a rush of need, barely sensible.

Daniel paused and looked at up her, his mouth slick with her desire. "Use your words, bunny. Tell

Caron what you want."

Chest heaving, she forced herself to take several deep breaths. "Please, Caron. Please let me come. I'm so empty. I ache. I want… I need Daniel's cock in me."

His burning fingers came back up to stroke her face. "Give her what she wants."

Her eyes locked onto Daniel as he rose to his knees, lifted her hips, and fitted his stiff cock at her entrance. For a moment, he paused, his gaze holding hers, before he surged forward into her.

"Thank you! Thank you!" Mattie cried, her fingers digging into Caron's neck, her body finally, deliciously, full.

Friction built as Daniel rocked within her, stretching and bumping up against that place that sent sparks shivering down her spine. The hum in her veins grew as the Lady snaked one hand down her body and pressed her fingers over Mattie's pearl, making small quick circles in time with Daniel's thrusts. Anticipation sang through her, knowing that she'd be allowed to finish this time and finish with Daniel deep in her.

Dimly, she was aware of the little pleading noises that fell from her with each ragged breath as her body wound itself tighter and tighter under their care. Just when she thought she would fly to pieces, the Lady locked her lips around Mattie's mouth, devouring her ragged scream as she orgasmed over and over, her entire body tensing and shaking with each new wave that crashed over her.

"Gods and monsters," Daniel cursed as his body stiffened, pulsed within her. The loss of his control sent her spiraling up once more, and for a wild moment, Mattie was sure it would never end. Her mind seemed to explode from her body, rising to the slowly fading stars, her poor overwrought body a shell that could no longer hold it.

The Lady's gentle kisses brought Mattie back to herself as Caron's hand caressed down the other side of her torso, his burning fingers gentle and soothing. She realized that she'd let go of him at some point, but he didn't seem to mind.

"You taste sublime, cherie."

Mattie didn't have the energy to kiss her back, let alone answer. It took every bit of her to just breathe, to keep herself present.

"Come on, bunny." Gently, Daniel gathered her up and pulled her free from Caron's lap, rolling them both to a clear bit of bed. He positioned them on their sides, facing Caron and the Lady with Daniel curled around her protectively.

With half-lidded eyes, Mattie watched as the Lady climbed onto Caron's lap, straddling his long, hard erection.

"Oh. I should help," Mattie mumbled, reaching out to run a hand along the Lady's smooth hip. "You two were so good to me. I should return the favor."

The Lady's laugh was low and sweet as she leaned over and pressed a kiss to Mattie's sweat-damp forehead. "Next time, cherie. Tonight was about you. Now, just rest and watch."

A smile played on Mattie's lips as she sank back against Daniel's chest, her body heavy and contented.

Despite the beauty of the Lady and Caron's lovemaking—the lithe way she moved her hips, milking up and down his length, the way Caron seemed to devour her with that intense gaze of his, his sculpted body moving in deference to her pleasure—Mattie found it impossible to keep her eyes open.

With Daniel's arm draped protectively around her stomach, his thighs pressing into the back of her legs, a sense of security, of surety that everything would turn out all right, settled over Mattie like a heavy blanket on a chilly winter's night. Lenny was still out there, lurking like one of the villains in her papa's penny novels, but he was a problem for tomorrow, well, later that day.

Chapter Twenty-One

Mattie

Mattie awoke to the low murmur of voices. It took her a moment to realize where she was. Except, she was the only one in the Lady's enormous bed. Her eyes fell to the partially opened armoire, and a smile curled her lips at the memories of the previous night.

After extracting herself from the sea of blankets and pillows, she found a silk robe draped over the foot of the bed and figured the Lady had left it for her. Her legs and arms had that pleasant ache of strenuous activity as she slipped on the robe. She tied the belt as she crossed to the office doors, her feet silent on the thick rugs. The voices beyond the cracked doors resolved as she got closer. The Lady and Daniel's. Absently, she wondered where Caron had gone. Maybe back to his house in the Bywater?

As she was about to push open the door, her feet faltered at the words coming from inside.

"—I'm worried about her."

Daniel was worried about her? It could only be regarding Lenny's abrupt reappearance in her life. But they'd talked, and he'd agreed to let her handle it. Hadn't he already briefed the Lady about this last night? Why was he bringing it up again? Lenny was Mattie's responsibility.

"Understandable. What do you propose to do about it?"

Mattie held her breath as she waited for him to tell the Lady that she would take care of it herself. That there was no risk to the House.

"I'd like permission to make the problem disappear."

The air left Mattie's lungs in a painful whoosh as his words drove a knife into her heart and twisted. He didn't trust her to take care of the problem? Did he really think her so weak and incapable?

"Honey Island?"

"Yes."

The sharp pain of betrayal morphed into hot fury. Not waiting to hear the rest of the plan, Mattie shoved the door open. The Lady sat at her desk, dressed in a robe, her hair covered with a silk wrap while Daniel lounged shirtless in a chair in front of her. At the sound of the door bouncing off the wall, Daniel started and turned to her.

Her eyes narrowed as she pointed a shaking finger at his bare chest. "We had an agreement."

Daniel held up his hands in a placating manner that only made Mattie want to find the nearest heavy object and chuck it at his head.

"I never actually agreed to anything, Mattie. That man is dangerous. I won't let anything happen to you."

She folded her arms across her chest. "Your job is to protect the House. I'm not a member of the House, so protecting me is not your job."

"Maybe I want it to be my job!" Daniel nearly shouted. "Because from where I'm standing, you're doing a piss-poor job of it."

The steel bands clamped back around her chest, strangling her fury, burying it deep down in her chest. A part of her wanted to retreat into herself. To clam up, to roll over, to give in, and allow him to deal with Lenny.

That other part of her though, the one that helped her escape the farm, escape Lenny, roared to life. It refused to let her hide or bend to another man's will. The bands snapped.

"You are not my bodyguard. Or my husband. Or my beau. You are a *friend*. And considering how little you respect my wishes, I don't think we can be that anymore."

Daniel reeled back as if she had hit him with the carved jade statue that sat on the corner of the Lady's desk.

In the resulting silence, the Lady cleared her throat gently. "Am I to understand that you have already expressed your wishes on this matter, Mattie?"

Not trusting her voice, she merely nodded.

"And your preference is to deal with your ex-husband on your own, without House assistance?"

"Yes," Mattie said firmly.

"Lady, please—"

The Lady cut Daniel off with a sharp look and a raised hand. Her eyes, one dark, one golden, flicked back to Mattie.

"Does your ex-husband pose a threat to the House?"

"No. He's not a threat to the House. He's barely a threat to me." Her gaze went to where Daniel was tense but silent. He wouldn't disobey the Lady by contradicting her, no matter how much he wanted to.

"All right. So long as he continues to be harmless, you may deal with the situation as you like. However, if that changes and the House is in danger, I will not hesitate to eliminate the threat in any matter that I deem fit. Are we clear?"

"Yes, Lady. Thank you very much."

Daniel remained silent.

"Daniel. Are we clear?" The Lady's voice was hard and sharp as a knife.

"We are clear, Lady," Daniel said through clenched teeth.

At least he wouldn't try to go behind the Lady's back. It was a small bitter comfort.

"Thank you for the wonderful evening, Lady. If you'll excuse me, I have things I need to take care of."

"Of course, cherie," the Lady said with a wave of one hand. "Please, close the door on your way out. Daniel, sit down."

The words were sweet enough, but the steel that ran beneath them left no room for argument. Mattie closed the door softly behind her as she retreated to the Lady's bedroom and found her dress in one of the piles of clothing on the floor. She changed into it quickly before draping the robe over the back of a chair, all the while refusing to look back over her shoulder at the closed office door or acknowledge the low buzz of angry voices coming from behind it.

Once more, gratitude surged through her for having stumbled upon Jo in that alley and subsequently meeting the Lady Lorna. The Lady would keep Daniel in line, and he wouldn't dare defy the Lady by interfering with Lenny now. Not wanting to take the time to deal with stockings or shoes, she gathered them into her arms and let herself out of the Lady's sumptuous rooms.

At the bottom of the stairs, Mattie paused. The steps seemed to stretch up forever. She forced one foot up, shifting her bundle to one arm so she could help haul herself up with the handrail. Eventually, she reached the top and headed toward her rooms. Halfway down the hallway, she stopped. Cursing herself, she turned around, away from Daniel's room, and headed the opposite direction.

Once inside her own room, she dropped her shoes and stockings into a pile on the table and climbed onto the bed, not even bothering to take off her dress. Despite the heat of the day, she pulled the quilt around her shoulders and finally let herself fall apart.

Hours later, Mattie dragged herself from the bed and forced herself into the bathroom. Turning on the tap on the clawfoot tub, she waited for the water to heat. Her mind tried to work on the problem of how to deal with Lenny, but despite her best efforts, her thoughts kept circling back to Daniel. To all the nights they'd spent together. The feel of his hands on her. The gentle way he both pushed her and respected her limits. His face as he said she couldn't take care of herself.

Wet heat assaulted her, pulling her back into the bathroom.

"You complete ninny!" Mattie cried as she lunged to turn off the tap, the steaming water nearly to the rim of the tub.

After letting some of the water drain out, Mattie climbed in and leaned her head back. It would have been easy to spend the entire evening wallowing in the bath, but she had to get ready for her shift.

Reluctantly, she pulled out the last sliver of the sample soap Clementine had given her and took a long inhale of the calming scent. Using it to wash the smell of sex and Daniel, in particular, from her skin, she decided she'd visit Clementine in the morning and buy herself at least two new soaps. Maybe a lotion as well.

She ended up spending too long in the tub and had to rush through the rest of her evening routine. At least with her new haircut, there was less time needed to dress it. Leaving her curls damp, she used one of Jo's sparkly hairpins to pull one side away from her face. She was bending down to buckle her shoe when her bedroom door flew open, the shock nearly causing her to fall back on her rear end.

"What are y'all doing here?" she asked the two women standing in her doorway.

Jo held up a box of chocolates. "We've brought presents!"

Next to her, Clementine had a small, covered basket in one hand and in the other, she held up a bottle of "the good" sherry.

Mattie's heart ached in her chest. She shouldn't have been surprised that the news was already spreading through the House. Nothing could stay secret for long when people lived and worked in close quarters. Still, it felt nice to have the gals come to the rescue. Ever since Samantha had moved away, Mattie hadn't had any female friends. Though, now that she thought about, Lenny hadn't exactly encouraged her to have friends of any kind. She shoved that sour thought down.

"Thank you so much. Really, y'all don't know how much I appreciate it, but I have to get down to the bar. I don't want Francis to be cross because I'm late."

Clementine just shook her head and barged into the room. "Nonsense. The Lady gave you the night off."

"She did?"

Jo pressed a kiss to Mattie's cheek and then joined Clementine at the table, flopping onto a chair.

"Are you just going to stand there? Or are you going to join us?" Clementine asked.

Mattie closed her gaping mouth, shut her door, and drifted over to the table where she sat down in a bit of a daze.

"Do you have glasses?" Clementine had pulled a corkscrew with a wooden handle from her dress pocket and was screwing it into the top of the sherry.

Mattie shook her head. "Afraid not."

"I've got it," Jo cried, jumping to her feet and rushing out of the room.

"Did you nick that from Francis?"

With an adorable grunt of effort, Clementine pulled the cork from the bottle, accompanied by a satisfying pop. "Not this time. Francis actually donated this particular bottle."

Mattie's mouth nearly dropped open again. "He did?"

"I know Francis can seem gruff and aloof, but that hard exterior hides soft squishiness."

One of Mattie's eyebrows quirked up.

"I swear!"

"If you say so. Can I ask if the two of you are friends?"

"No," Clementine said a bit wistfully. "Francis is not really interested in bedroom games. With anyone, as far as I can tell. And as much as I adore our banter,

I'm the kind of gal who needs a good tumble every once in a while, you know?"

Mattie thought back to her interactions with Francis. He had never engaged in the casual affection that was a staple of the other House members. Nor did he ever seem to watch the shows, instead using the time to tidy up the bar or prep for the after-show wave of drink orders. Yet there was no denying that he was a full member of the House.

"Everyone really can just be who are they are here? Can't they?"

Clementine smiled at the wonder in Mattie's words. "Yes."

"Victory!" Jo cried as she burst back in the room, three glasses clutched to her chest.

While Jo got situated at the table, Clementine filled the three glasses nearly to the top and passed them around.

"Cheers y'all," Mattie said, carefully raising her glass.

"Cheers!" The other two chorused, and all three took long sips from their drinks.

"Oh, you really did get a bottle of the good stuff," Mattie commented, taking another sip. Bursts of sweet raisins and nutty undertones danced along her tongue.

"I never lie about the good stuff." Clementine shoved the small basket at her. "This is also for you."

Mattie removed the cloth covering to find several bars of soap, a bottle of lotion, and a small vial of perfume nestled in the bottom. Tears stung her eyes as she looked up.

"Clementine, I can't accept this. It's too much!"

"Nonsense. It's a gift and you can't refuse a gift

from a friend. Besides, I think you're going to have a couple hard days ahead. The least I can do is make sure you smell good for the battle to come."

A startled laugh burst from Mattie's lips. "Thank you. Thank you for the basket. Thank you for the sherry, and mostly, thank you for being here."

Jo scooted her chair closer to Mattie and laid her head on her shoulder. "Where else would we be?"

Mattie pressed a kiss to the crow-girl's hair.

"Do you want to tell us about it?" Clementine's voice was gentle.

The choice was Mattie's. She could tell them about the disastrous last couple of days or she could just enjoy their companionship. Taking a deep breath, she decided getting their opinion on the whole thing wouldn't be a bad idea.

The girls were an excellent audience, letting Mattie tell the tale at her own pace and giving her the space she needed to formulate her thoughts. By the time she neared the end, the bottle of sherry was half empty and Jo had taken one of Mattie's hands, entwining their fingers together.

"Afterwards, I wallowed for a good bit. Then you guys showed up like the beautiful alcohol-wielding angels that you are," Mattie concluded, giving Jo's hand a squeeze.

"That's quite the pickle. Who would have thought our Daniel would turn into such a chest-pounding brute?" Clementine commented with a shake of her head.

Mattie slowly spun her half-full glass by the stem. "You don't think I was too harsh on him? He did just want to keep me safe after all."

Jo shook her head, her bobbed hair swinging back and forth. "I know you care about Daniel. But if he doesn't respect your needs or listen when you express how you want him to support you—how you want to handle your own life and problems—you need to respect yourself enough to walk away."

Clementine raised her glass. "Top shelf advice, Jo. As much as I hate to say it, our Daniel acted an awful lot like your ex-husband in this case. That's not acceptable."

"You're right. You're both right. But it still hurts." Mattie reached up to dash a tear from her cheek.

"Of course, it hurts," Clementine said, moving her chair closer and wrapping her arms around Mattie's shoulders. "And who knows, maybe Daniel will realize the error of his ways and come crawling back to you, but you can't bank on that."

"No, I can't," Mattie whispered from the circle of Clementine's arms. The pain was still there, but the world looked a lot less bleak sandwiched between two women who cared so much for her. Friends, even. She had genuine friends again, and dear sweet baby Jesus, she had missed it.

"What are you doing to do about the other palooka? Lenny?" Jo asked.

"I'm going to try to find him. See if we can't have a conversation about this like adults. He's not violent… normally. I really think he was just taken off guard and hurt. I did leave him without any warning."

"Was there really no warning or did you try to talk to him about how you felt, and he shut the conversation down?"

"I…" Mattie thought back to all the times she tried

to tell Lenny how lonely she was, or suggest she visit her mother for a few days, and how Lenny would counter her with a response that seemed logical on the surface, one that seemed to leave no room for her to argue. Till eventually she had stopped trying, because there was never any discussion, just lectures that left Mattie feeling worse than before. "I guess I did try."

She could feel Clementine's nod against her shoulder. "What makes you think he'll listen now?"

Oof. That was a good point. The three sat in silence for a long moment as Mattie pondered what to do. "I think I need an intermediary. Someone who can speak for me if I get too flustered or turned around by Lenny. Someone impartial but authoritative."

"Bossley," the two said in unison.

"Bossley," she agreed. It only seemed right. After all, engaging the lawyer had started this whole mess in the first place. He'd know how to handle Lenny and help her push for the best outcome. Considering Lenny's tirade on the sidewalk, she wasn't hopeful for the divorce going through, but maybe Bossley could convince him to at least go back to the farm and leave her in peace. She'd stay legally married to him so long as he left her alone. That wouldn't be the end of the world, would it?

"If you want us there too, just let us know."

Mattie patted Clementine's arm as Jo nodded next to her. "I will definitely consider it. Thank you both for your excellent advice."

Clementine waved her off. "What are friends for? Besides, Jo did most of the heavy lifting. I just brought the booze."

The crow-girl lifted one shoulder. "Just because I

like shiny things doesn't mean I'm a complete fluff-brain."

The defensive note in Jo's voice made Mattie wonder how often people underestimated Jo. With her sweet outlook and joy for life, it would be easy to do. Mattie reached over and ruffled Jo's black hair.

"No, not even a little bit of a fluff-brain."

Jo batted her away before grinning widely.

"And anyone who says otherwise will have to deal with us," Clementine added.

"Ab-so-lute-ly!"

Giving Mattie one last squeeze, Clementine let her hand go and reached for the bottle. "Now that that's settled, who wants more sherry?" Not waiting for an answer, she began topping up the glasses. "Jo, why don't you open that box of chocolates?"

The crow-girl did just that. The three of them ate and drank until late in the night. When the two gals finally left, all the chocolate was gone, and there was only a couple of fingers of sherry still in the bottle.

Pleasantly drunk, Mattie climbed into bed. The glow from an evening spent laughing faded as she realized it was the first time she'd gone to sleep alone in a long time. For several hours, she stared at the ceiling, both missing, and hating that she missed, the warmth of Daniel's arms around her. The bed felt achingly empty, but it was something she'd just have to get used to.

Chapter Twenty-Two

Daniel

Mac's fist collided with Daniel's stomach. He let out a huff of breath but was able to stay on his feet despite feeling like he'd been hit by a brick. Backing up a bit, he bought some time to convince his lungs to refill with air. Sweat soaked his undershirt and dripped into his eyes.

"We're not pulling punches today, are we?" he wheezed, using the back of his arm to swipe at his eyes.

"When do I ever?" Mac's lips pulled into a rare smile as they circled Daniel. Considering that they didn't immediately press the advantage, Mac was, in fact, going easy on him.

That pissed him off. Considering how close to the surface his temper had been the past couple of days, it wasn't really a surprise.

He launched himself at his boss, aiming a haymaker at their head. Mac's mouth twitched in a frown as they ducked under his arm, swung their leg behind him, and using his own momentum, sent him tumbling onto his ass.

A cloudless blue sky stretched over his head. For a long moment, he lay on his back, feeling the warm, rough ticking of their sparring mat digging into his back as the sun beat down. A shadow fell on his face as Mac leaned over him.

"All right?"

With a sigh, he pulled himself up to sitting. "Yeah."

When he didn't get to his feet, Mac folded themselves down next to him on the roof. As always, their movements were powerful and effortlessly graceful. All around them the sounds of the Quarter floated up from the street below, blending into the familiar, comforting background noise of the city. Always there, but not intrusive.

"How much did she tell you before she sent you to find me?" Daniel winced at the memory of the Lady's sharp disappointment.

"Enough," Mac said with a slow nod of their head. "Though, considering how you were growling at the customers last night when Mattie didn't show up for her shift, I would have known there was trouble either way."

"I guess I was a bit of a thug."

"We've all been there."

Daniel looked over to where Mac sat crossed legged on the mat, looking out over the city. He had a feeling they weren't talking about the growling—he'd seen Mac take on hulking drunks with a fierceness that bordered on manic joy. Still, there were some things that Mac kept close to the vest.

"You were the one that said being protective is in our nature. What was I supposed to do? Allow that jackass to emotionally beat her down? Drag her back and chain her to a farm? Punish her for wanting to be touched, wanting sex? Let her be miserable for the rest of her life!"

"Definitely not saying that." Mac shook their head with a wry smile. "But you could have been less of a bastard about it."

He let out a startled bark of a laugh.

"Just because we were born to protect others, doesn't mean we can run roughshod over the very people we're trying to safeguard. Otherwise, we end up being the monsters that humans think we are. Let me ask you something, if you asked Lenny—"

"Why would I waste my breath talking that piece of pond scum?"

"Let me finish." Mac speared him with a look that had him biting his tongue and motioning for them to continue. "If you asked Lenny why he treated Mattie the way he did. Why he followed her down here, against her expressed wishes, what do you think he'd say?"

Understanding arched through him like electricity. Grudgingly, he admitted, "Probably, that he was just trying to keep her safe."

Mac merely nodded.

The memory of Mattie's hurt and anger stabbed through him. The way she'd stood in the Lady's office with her hair disheveled from sex and sleep, wearing a robe too large for her so that the hem brushed the ground. The look of hard determination as she told him they were no longer friends.

It wasn't that fact that tore up his insides. Though those things made him want to put his fist through the wall or let Mac beat him until the memory of the Lady's study was pounded out of his skull. The thing he was most ashamed of, the thing that Mac's damnable logic forced him to face, was that she'd looked at him with the same mistrust and fear that she'd looked at Lenny with when he'd found them in the Quarter. And she had every damn right to look at him that way.

"You really care about her, don't you?" Mac's voice was surprisingly gentle.

"Yeah. Yeah, I do. She burrowed under my skin with those sharp little teeth of hers."

Mac let out a soft snort of a laugh before their face went back to its usual placid expression. "I'm taking your shift tonight."

A part of him wanted to protest, to claim that he would be fine, but he'd proven last night that he wasn't fine, not really. "Much obliged."

Mac stood and extended a hand down to him. "Come on, let's go another couple of rounds."

With their help, he hauled himself to his feet. He shook out his sun-warmed muscles and dropped into his fighting stance. Across the mat, Mac took up their own stance, their eyes tracking his every motion. Even on his best days, he was no match for Mac, but that's what made them such a good sparring partner.

"Why don't we shift for this one? Make it interesting?"

Daniel glanced at the side of the roof. "Think it's safe?"

"Safe enough. No one ever bothers to look up." Their hands were already shifting into powerful lion's paws.

The words hit him like a knife to the heart. Mac was right; nobody looked up. Except for Mattie. She had on the first day she'd come to the House. Daniel stood up. With a quirk of their eyebrow, Mac followed suit, their hands melting back into their human configuration.

"Will you look out for her tonight?"

"Of course. You don't even have to ask. She may not wear the ring, but she's still one of us." Mac dropped back into her fighting stance. "Now, less talking. More punching."

That was a sentiment he could get behind.

Chapter Twenty-Three

Mattie

When Mattie saw that Mac was on door duty the following night, she gave up a silent blessing for small favors. Despite the cathartic evening with Clementine and Jo, she wasn't quite ready to face Daniel and his lack of belief in her.

When Jo took the stage for the evening's performance, she walked onto center stage in a pair of sparkly heels and a smile. A large ball that shimmered like a pearl in her hands hid most of her torso. As the crow-girl started a peek-a-boo dance, using the ball to hide and show her assets, Jo found Mattie in the audience and gave her a cheeky wink.

The band hit the end of the song with a joyful wail of saxophone, and Jo tossed the ball high into the air, striking a pose in all her naked glory for a brief moment before catching the ball in front of her once more. Mattie cheered and clapped as hard as she could. With a little kick of her heel, Jo pranced off the stage to deafening applause.

The real triumph was that Mattie got through the entire evening and didn't spill a drink on a patron. Or mix up a single order.

At the end of the night, after all the guests had wandered home, and the glasses cleaned and dried,

Mattie begged off a nightcap with Jo and Francis and headed to her room. Her steps were heavy, both from exhaustion and the thought of her errand she'd need to run after some sleep. Only this time when she went to see Bossley, Daniel wouldn't be going with her. Hopefully, Bossley would be able to help her.

She opened the door to her room, not bothering to flip the light on—she just wanted to change and crawl into bed. After removing her nightly wages, she tucked them into the wooden box on her dresser, making a mental note to take some of the cash with her to deposit with Bossley or to pay him for his services. His rate had been reasonable for writing the letter to Lenny, but mediating a discussion would be more expensive, wouldn't it?

"Hello, Mattie."

Mattie whirled around, her heart slamming into her rib cage. Dim moonlight streamed through the window, illuminating Lenny's ominous form as he leaned in her doorway.

"Lenny. What are you doing here?"

"What does it look like?" He stepped into the room and carefully shut the door behind him. Fear spiked in Mattie's blood as he turned the key in the lock. "I'm having a conversation with my wife. Have a seat."

Without taking her eyes off Lenny, she sat down at the table. He took his time joining her, first turning on the lamp. His eyes swept around the room. The sides of his mouth twisted down at the sight of the almost empty sherry bottle sitting out on the dresser. Mattie suppressed the urge to jump up and hide the bottle in the trash. To apologize. But there wasn't anything to be ashamed of. Not of the sherry, nor her short hair, or her flapper dress.

There wasn't.

The frown was gone by the time he pulled out a chair and sat down across from her. Instead, a timid smile played on his lips.

"You look good, Mattie. I like your new haircut."

The switch in his mood made her flinch. She raised a hand to her hair. "Um…thank you. I thought you didn't like it?"

"It was a shock. But now, I see how much it suits your face." The smile faded. "Mattie, I apologize for how I acted the other day. It was out of line." His head tilted in contrition, his eyes soft.

"I… It's all right, Lenny. Understandable, in a way. It is a rather drastic change and on top of how I surprised you with leaving."

"It was out of the blue," he said, nodding his head slowly. "Your mother has been worried sick about you."

"You talked to Momma?" Surprise and guilt warred in her. As far as she could remember, Lenny hadn't voluntarily spoken with her parents since the wedding. To be honest, it hadn't even crossed her mind to reach out to them, to let them know she was leaving or even that she was safe in New Orleans. The only person she would have thought to tell was Granny Marie, and she was dead. Not that she didn't love her parents anymore, but that they had drifted apart. Or been forced apart by Lenny.

"After I read your note, I called her to see if you had gone to visit them. She had to have a sit down after I told her you had taken off."

Guilt won, twisting her gut into knots. "I'll give her

a ring. Or maybe send a telegram. Let her know that I'm perfectly all right."

"Wouldn't you rather tell her in person? Once you're home?"

The knotted ball in her stomach tightened further and sunk lower. "Lenny…"

"Wait, just wait."

He reached out and took one of her hands. As much as she wanted to, she couldn't bring herself to pull it away. There was such a look of sweet hope on his face. He didn't rub the back of her hand with his thumb the way Daniel would have, or even gently squeezed it like Jo would. Instead, he just held hers in his large hand, callused from working the farm. A part of her wondered when was the last time he'd held her hand?

Maybe it was him making the effort, following her letter to New Orleans, finding her in the middle of this massive city, and literally reaching out to her, but she felt she owed him at least that much. She could hold his hand and listen to what he had to say.

"I've failed you as a husband."

The frankness of statement startled her. "Lenny—"

"Let me finish, please." The plea was anguished in its urgency, in its need. When she didn't say anything else, he went on, "I've failed you as a husband. When we stood before God and joined hands in holy matrimony, I promised to protect you. To always have your best interest at heart."

Mattie squeezed his hand, her heart heavy in her chest.

"If I had done my duty, this never would have happened. You would never have come to this den of sin and filth." The sneer flickered across his face as he looked around the room, but it was gone by the time his eyes found hers again. "I know it wasn't your fault, Mattie." He gripped her so hard the bones in her hand ached.

"It's not?" she whispered, frozen by the intensity of his stare.

"No. You were lured away by the Devil. By the evils of modern society, booze, and women of loose morals. But don't fret, I forgive you for going astray. It was my job as your husband to protect your vulnerable female soul from such evils and I failed you. I won't do it again, I'm taking you home tonight, Mattie. I'm going to take you away from all of this."

With each of Lenny's fevered words, Mattie's heart sank further and further until she it was located somewhere in her shoes.

"Lenny, I'm not bewitched or anything like that. You didn't fail at all, I swear. I'm just not the kind of girl who's happy working on a farm where the biggest event of the week is going to church on Sunday. I'm the one that failed. I thought I could make it work, but it was killing me."

Lenny shook his sandy-colored head. "You only say that because you are still under these evil influences. As soon as you come home and talk to Father Michal, you'll be as right as rain."

"I'm sorry, Lenny, but I'm happy here and can't go home with you. This is my home now." She tried to gently pull her hands out of his grip, but he only held on tighter.

"Don't say such things, Mattie. Your home is with me on the farm."

"Not anymore, Lenny. I wish I hadn't hurt you—I wish to God there had been any other way. If only I'd never listened to my parents and rejected your proposal. At the time, I didn't think I had another option. I do regret that I hurt you, but I don't regret leaving." Her words had stunned him enough that she was able to pull her hand free, tucking it into her lap where she could rub it without Lenny seeing.

His eyes locked on his empty hands on the table, his gold wedding ring looking sad and out of place on his work-worn hands. "What about your vows to God, Mattie? In His eyes, you are still my wife."

"That's between me and God, but I have to say any god who would rather a person to be miserable in a marriage rather than amicably divorce, isn't really a god I want to worship. You deserve to be happy, too."

His hands curled into fists on the table, but he kept silent. The same table that Daniel had spread her on and devoured her so completely that first night. She pushed the thought down into that dark place, irrationally certain that Lenny could see the memory playing out behind her eyes.

Mattie took a deep breath and forced herself to continue, wanting desperately for this conversation to be over. "As the letter said, I'll happily provide whatever you need to prove abandonment. This will give you a chance to find someone else."

"Divorce is a sin." His voice was hard and flat as his eyes swung up to pierce her once more. "And what about me, Mattie? What will I tell Father Michal? Our friends in church? They'll offer words of sympathy, but behind my back they will snicker and judge. I'll be a laughingstock."

Fear crept down Mattie's spine. "It's the 1920s, not the 1820s. No one will laugh at you." If anything, she would be the one that people made mean jokes about, but what did she care what the upstanding folks of Prairieville thought about her?

He didn't say anything, but the daggers in his eyes told her he wasn't buying her argument. It was time to change tactics. Mattie stood up from the table, feeling the mask she had worn for him so many times slip into place.

With calm, reasonable detachment, she said, "If you don't want to get a divorce, that's fine as well. We can stay married, and you can save face with the church. Tell them I'm taking care of a sick relative or better yet, that I've fallen into a coma." The mask was cracking, the desperation threatening to slip through. She knew he would use that emotion against her. Argue that she was not in her right mind. Hysterical. She wouldn't give him that ammunition.

She forced her voice to be hard and flat. "Either way, I'm not going back with you, Lenny. It's getting late and I think you should leave."

She stepped around the table toward the door, but before she could make it halfway, he was out of his chair and blocking her path. Her heart threw itself against her rib cage so frantically she worried it would burst through her chest.

Desperately, she tried to keep her fear from her voice, but it trembled all the same. "Lenny, let me pass."

"No. We are going home. Right now."

Her throat was as dry as a teetotaler's liquor cabinet. It took all her courage to push the words out from her parched mouth. "I'm not."

There was a hard, mean light in his eyes. Movement near his side drew Mattie's gaze to his hand and the open switchblade clutched in it. She took a stumbling step away from him.

"I am taking you home tonight, Mattie. One way or the other."

"You…you can't mean that."

He took a step toward her as she took a step back. The back of her calf bumped into the dresser, causing the bottles on it to rattle, but thankfully everything stayed upright. At least, she hoped so, since she didn't want to take her eyes off of Lenny long enough to check.

His mouth curved into a frown, and his eyes were hard and sharp. "Make things easy, Mattie, come home. Because the hard way will hurt, but I'll do it. Better for you to have died, a victim of senseless violence in the corrupted big city, than to live like this. Can't you see? I'm trying to save your soul, Mattie."

The terrible thing was, she knew he believed what he was saying. For him, there was no worse sin than disobeying him. Than not being the perfect, pure wife that he dragged to church every Sunday to show off, like the gaudy wedding ring on his finger. At the end of the day, she was worth more to him as a symbol than a person.

Her hands reached back to feel the edge of the dresser as her gaze flicked to the locked door behind Lenny's shoulder. Even if she could get past him, she'd never get it open in time. None of the House knew what was going on. The sound dampening spells were too good to allow anyone passing by to hear the conversation and come to her rescue. But what had Daniel said? If there was true terror or pain, the wards would alert the Lady. All she had to do was scream and the cavalry would come charging in, because if she had anything in abundance right now, it was fear.

All she had to do was scream and Daniel would come running. Even with their fight, she knew he'd be right there if she needed him. That thought was comforting.

And infuriating.

Because it would mean he'd been right. She couldn't protect herself. It meant that she needed a big, strong man to look after her. To make her problems go away.

The scream died in her throat. She had promised the Lady that Lenny posed no danger to the House. That was still true. He wasn't a threat to the House, only to her. She would make sure it stayed that way.

With every ounce of self-control, she forced her shoulders to relax. Her lips pulled up in a what she hoped was a convincing smile. "Take me home, Lenny."

He narrowed his eyes at her, trying to sniff out if this was a trick.

"You were right—I've been bewitched, corrupted by the glamour of this place, but your devotion to me and your concern for my soul has made me see the error of my ways. Please, let's go home and I'll do everything I can to make up for my wicked sins. To make it up to God."

"And to me?"

"Of course! To you as well."

Her fingers trembled, but she raised her left hand

toward his face. Relief softened his features as he stepped close, his head tilting until her hand cradled his cheek. The switchblade was still in his hand, but at least it was now pointed at the ground rather than directly at her soft middle.

"What did I do to deserve a husband like you?" she murmured.

He made a soft sound of agreement as he closed his eyes. "You got lucky."

"Yes, I did," she replied as she brought her knee up as hard as she could into his gentlemen's marbles.

A harsh grunt of pain accompanied the clatter of the knife against the floorboards. He crumbled to the ground a few seconds later, his hands clutching his manhood, his face as red as a boiled crawfish.

His breath came in rasping gasps. "You cocksucking floozie!"

"Why Lenny, that is not the language a Good Christian boy should know."

The hatred rolled off him like fog as he struggled to get his feet under him, his legs shaking and unable to hold his weight. "I will burn this whole booze-soaked building to the ground. Right around the ears of that uppity one-eyed bitch who runs it. But, first, I will strangle the devil out of you, Satan's whore." He'd made it to his knees and looked like he would lunge for her, the knife forgotten in his rage.

"Better Satan's whore——" She grabbed the sherry bottle from the dresser and brought it down as hard as she could on his head.

The bottle broke, showering them both in bits of glass and the last of the sherry. Lenny collapsed to the ground like a scarecrow dropped from his pole. She stood over him, her chest heaving, the broken neck of the bottle still clutched in her hand.

When he didn't move, she nudged his shoulder with the toe of her shoe. Lenny's bulk didn't even twitch, but his chest rose and fell in a slow, steady rhythm. Not dead then. Only out cold. A muted calm came over Mattie as she stepped over him. She needed to tell the Lady what happened. Her brain slid away from what would happen after that, the thoughts of the future turned as slippery as tadpoles.

She turned the doorknob and tugged, but it stayed firmly shut. Lenny had locked it. It took two tries, but she got the door unlocked. It would have been easier if she had put down the broken sherry bottle, but the thought didn't occur to her. When she finally opened the door, she stopped in her tracks.

Standing in the hallway was the Lady in a pale gold sheath dress, her elegant hands crossed over her middle. Behind her left shoulder, Daniel stood as tense and rigid as the stone he resembled when he shifted. There was no expression on his handsome face.

"Lady!" Mattie managed to squeak out. "How long have you been out here?"

The Lady's gaze flicked to Lenny's sprawled form. "Since the moment he entered your room."

"But, how? Why?"

A small smile tugged at the corners of the Lady's red mouth. She swept into the room, taking Mattie by the elbow and gently removing the broken neck of the sherry bottle from her hand. "In good time. First, cherie, are you harmed?"

Mattie should her head. "It's just sherry. Not blood."

251

The Lady steered her to the table, gently depositing her into a chair, and set Mattie's improvised weapon down. "Daniel."

Daniel stepped into the room, keeping his eyes firmly on the Lady, never once looking at Mattie.

"Please take our guest down to the garage. If he looks like he's about to wake up, ensure that doesn't happen, but make sure he stays alive. Do you understand?"

Daniel ground his teeth but nodded.

"Good. Afterwards, please fetch Caron. I believe he's still in the bar and alert Jimmy that I will be in need of a driver."

With a mechanical nod of his head, Daniel gathered Lenny's unconscious body from the floor and threw it over one of his shoulders. Even in her dazed state, Mattie admired the strength it took to lift and haul that much dead weight as if it was a bag of flour. He didn't look back as he closed the door behind him.

"Cherie." The Lady's voice was gentle but insistent.

Turning her head, Mattie found that the Lady had brought a chair next to her and was now holding Mattie's sherry-covered hands. Their reassuring smoothness so different from Lenny's rough grip.

"I know whenever someone enters the House who isn't supposed to. Under normal circumstances, I would never have allowed him to gain access to your room like that, but after our conversation—this was something you needed to handle on your own. But that doesn't mean I was going to leave you defenseless. If things had taken a turn for the worst, Daniel would have broken down that door and intervened on my command."

Warmth suffused through the cold that had enveloped Mattie. She wasn't even a proper member of the House, but the Lady had not only trusted her, she had also looked out for her. Gave her the space to deal with it on her own while still supporting her. Caring for her.

Mattie threw her arms around the Lady's shoulders. "Thank you." The words came out in a breathless whisper.

Strong, thin arms encircled her. The Lady's hands rubbed gentle circles as Mattie took a ragged breath. The enormity of what had just occurred crashed into her. Tears slid down her face as quiet sobs slipped from her. For a long moment, the Lady let her cry. Eventually, she started making soothing sounds, gently prying Mattie from her and rubbing up and down her arms.

"This has all been a terrible shock, but I fear you now have a choice to make, cherie. You need to decide what happens next to your ex-husband."

Unable to help herself, she looked over her shoulder at the scattered glass and drying sherry that was the only evidence left of their fight. Even the switchblade was gone—Daniel must have taken it when he removed Lenny from the room.

"He's never going to let me go, is he?" She turned back to the Lady, searching her face for the answer.

The Lady gave her a small, sad smile. "That is a question only you can answer. Though, it is my experience that men, like Lenny, rarely see others as whole individuals. Just as objects that can either enhance or detract from their own experience of the world."

Mattie thought of the gleam of his switchblade, the ruthless light in his eyes as he told her she was going home one way or the other.

"He's never going to let me go. You're right. To him, I'm property. Something that should be silent and pretty and make him look good at church on Sundays. I could leave." Though the thought made her heart clench and ache, she forced the words out. "Maybe if I head to Texas or New York? So long as I don't do something silly like sending him a letter asking for a divorce, maybe he'll never find me."

The Lady pinched her mouth and gave Mattie a look that said exactly what she thought of that idea.

"He'd still find me. Wouldn't he?"

"Men like that have never had anyone tell them 'No.' So when someone does finally stand up to them, they have no way of coping with it." The Lady's voice was firm but not unkind. "Even if that wasn't the case, you shouldn't have to flee because of his inability to regulate his own emotions. Not if you don't want to."

"I don't want to leave," Mattie admitted in a whisper.

"Then you won't. Do you want me to make the problem go away?"

Mattie understood the question. Understood what was really being asked. Could she make that decision? Make not just the problem of her ex-husband, but the whole ex-husband himself go away?

The thing that swayed her in the end wasn't her concern for her own safety, but the look of disgust on Lenny's face as he'd looked around the room. The way he had talked about the House as a "den of sin." He had to know Tonique & Lace was an illegal speakeasy. And he'd called the Lady such an ugly phrase. He knew who the Lady was and what her business was. That couldn't stand.

"Please, take care of it." Even though she knew it was the right decision, the words seemed to carve her heart out of her chest, leaving her aching and raw.

The Lady lifted a hand and cradled her cheek. "I'll handle everything, cherie. Come on." She pulled Mattie to her feet and wrapped an arm around Mattie's waist.

"Where are we going?" Mattie asked as the Lady steered her out of her room.

"To Jo's room. After the evening you've had, I think it best if you aren't by yourself."

"You think of everything."

"That's my job, cherie."

And Mattie was happy to let her do that job. She didn't want to think about Lenny's limp body hanging over Daniel's shoulder. Or what would happen to him now. Or Daniel's angry, stone-still face. Those were all worries for the light of day.

Chapter Twenty-Four

Daniel

It took everything in Daniel not to strangle the unconscious form of Mattie's ex-husband. Literally every bit of his willpower was needed not to wrap his hands around the ass's thick neck and squeeze until the son of a bitch was no longer breathing. The only thing that held Daniel back was his orders from the Lady. However, she had said nothing about not smashing the man's head into every doorway they went through. The dull watermelon thunk sound it made brought a vicious smile to his face.

As he made his way down to the garage, he replayed the last hour in his mind. The Lady had not bothered to knock but had simply thrown open the door to his room. He'd been working his way steadily through a bottle of bourbon. The pleasant buzz he'd been nursing vanished with one look at her face.

"The wards were activated, and I believe the intruder is in Mattie's room."

The carefully neutral words had driven Daniel to his feet, sending spikes of fear and anger through his veins. The Lady had stopped him with a firm hand to his chest.

"If you go barging in there, you will lose that girl forever, cherie. This is something she needs to do herself, just like she told you."

"He'll rip her apart," he growled.

"Our Mattie is tougher than you give her credit for." The lady's gold eye flashed in the dim lights of his room as she cut off his protest. "However, that doesn't mean we'll allow harm to befall her. Follow me."

They stood outside Mattie's room. Thanks to the wards, they couldn't hear anything going on behind the door. But that didn't keep Daniel's brain from coming up with every terrible scenario that could have been unfolding behind the flimsy bit of wood. Even though he knew the wards would activate if she was in pain or true peril. He had to trust them.

When words had finally broke through, they were not what he'd been expecting.

"You cocksucking floozie!" It was a male voice, high and filled with pain.

Mattie had to be the source of that pain. His bunny with teeth. Only she wasn't his bunny. Not anymore. And that was entirely his own fucking fault. The feral grin dropped from his face.

"I will end you, Satan's whore."

The voice was still full of pain, but there was an anger there that made Daniel clench his hands into fists, his talons itching to extend themselves.

The Lady held her up hand, but he wasn't going to move. He had to trust Mattie. She knew what she was doing. She'd call for help if she needed it.

The silence stretched out longer and longer. Each moment wound the tension building in him a little tighter. She had to be all right. He couldn't imagine a world without her in it, without her sweet curiosity and enormous heart. Even if she was no longer with him.

The door opened and there she stood, eyes wide, hand clutching the broken neck of a wine bottle. His heart ached with relief to see her, then seized back up as he spotted the red liquid splattered down the front of her dress. His gaze went to the sprawled lump on the floorboard, covered in glass. He'd rip Lenny's throat out with his teeth.

Dimly, he had been aware of the Lady checking on Mattie, and Mattie's reassurance that she wasn't hurt. The red splotches were only sherry.

That mollified him somewhat, but it wouldn't save Lenny's soft, internal organs from exiting his body as slowly as possible.

When the Lady gave him his orders, he had to keep his gaze locked on her. If he looked at Mattie, he wouldn't be able to stop himself from crossing the distance and wrapping her in his arms. Checking every inch of her with his own hands. Just to be sure.

Unfortunately, the Lady had specified that this sack of shit had to be kept alive. It was the first order of the Lady's he ached to disobey. But she had given him a home, a family, the first he'd really had since his parents had died. Mimi had done her best to raise him, but it hadn't been the same. He wouldn't jeopardize that, no matter how much he wanted to erase Mattie's ex-husband from existence himself.

If he was honest though, the thing that held him back from bashing the bastard's head into the floor until it resembled corn pudding, wasn't the Lady's order, it was the fact that Mattie might never forgive him if he did.

He could handle it being over between them, but he would do anything to keep her from hating him for all time.

That didn't stop him from swinging Lenny's head into the doorway of the garage. He turned on the overhead lights, bare lightbulbs that lit Mabel in all her black and chrome glory. It was a beautiful machine, especially if you knew about the modifications Jimmy had done under the hood.

Daniel heaved Lenny off his shoulder onto the floor behind Mabel's boot. Bending down, he scrutinized the man's slack face, looking for any flutter of eyelid or twitch of lips that would warrant Daniel slamming his knuckles into the side of his head as hard as possible. Not even the hint of movement. The sides of Daniel's mouth pulled down as he stood up.

A small workbench sat off to the side. He retrieved a length of rope and used it to hog tie Lenny's wrists and ankles as tight as possible. A flicker of satisfaction went through him as the man's fingers turned bluish-purple. It wouldn't do for Lenny to wake up and wander away while Daniel carried out the rest of the Lady's orders.

A vicious smile exposed sharp teeth as Daniel went to find Caron and Jimmy. Knowing the Lady and Caron, he almost felt sorry for what was about to happen to dear old Lenny. Almost.

Chapter Twenty-Five

Lady Lorna

Moonlight filtered between the branches of the Cyprus trees, dappling the dark water. The gentle sound of paddles mixed with the croaks and chirps of frogs and cicadas. It was a beautiful night in the swamp.

The lump in the bottom of her skiff jerked, rocking the boat and sending little ripples off to each side.

"I wouldn't thrash about like that, Mr. Stumps. Not unless you're up for a swim."

Lenny rolled over with a pained groan, cradling his left arm in front of him. "You heinous bitch, what have you done to me?" The end of his arm ended in a bloody bandage.

"Your hand has been removed. I think that would have been quite obvious." She pulled on the oars, enjoying the slight burn in her muscles.

"Where? Where?" Wild eyes darted around. It was just the two of them in flat-bottomed boat.

"Where is your hand? Somewhere safe." The oars dipped into the water, and she pulled hard on the oars. "It's currently marinating in a crab trap. Though, I'm not sure why you are looking for it. It's not as if it can be reattached."

A dull thunk rang out as Lenny's head dropped against the side of the boat.

"Considering how much damage your head has sustained this evening, I rather think you'd like to avoid further trauma."

"You will burn in hell for this, witch." There was so much venom in his words, it was a wonder they didn't burn a hole through the bottom of the boat.

"Tsk. And here I was hoping we could come to a civil agreement over this whole matter." The boat bumped up against a small hillock rising out of the water. "Ah, we're here."

Lenny looked around with narrowed eyes but kept his mouth shut.

With barely a dip or rock, Lorna stood up and stepped off the boat. The waterlogged soil made a wet squish under her sturdy leather boots. Grabbing the flat back of the skiff, she hauled it half onto the small island.

Seeing an opportunity, Lenny launched himself at her with a vicious gleam in his eye. Her mouth twitched in distaste as she batted his hand away as if he were no more a nuisance than a mosquito. The slap rang out in the quiet air, and Lenny tumbled over the side of the boat, landing half in the water, half on the soggy edge.

Lorna heaved a sigh, grabbed the collar of Lenny's coat, and dragged him into the middle of the hillock where he lay sprawled and dripping, cradling the stump of his left hand. From his little moans of pain, he must have banged it against the edge of the skiff. She stood over him with her hands on her hips.

"Obviously, there was little need to caution Caron about taking too much blood if you have enough energy for such stupidity."

"Fucking cunt." The words were hisses of pain.

"Sssuch a lovely sssurprissse. I didn't expect to sssee you this beautiful evening, Lady Lorna."

Lenny's head whipped toward the sound. His eyes stretched wide with horror. "Honey Island swamp monster."

"Her name is Marjorie," Lorna snapped at the cowering man. She turned to where the swamp lapped at the small hillock. "Always a pleasure, cherie," she said, extending a hand to help Marjorie climb out of the water and stand on an increasingly crowded bit of land.

Moss green fur covered Marjorie's human-esque body, damp and clumping from the water. Talons longer than any of Lorna's gargoyles extended from webbed palms. Marjorie's most striking feature though was her alligator snout, pebbled the same green as her fur and filled with rows of knife-sharp teeth. Golden eyes regarded Lorna and the trembling form of Lenny.

"Have you brought me a presssent?" Marjorie's jaws clacked open and shut in a chitter of excitement.

Lenny's face drained of all color as he mouth moved, making a silent plea to Lorna. One eyebrow rose in amusement at the smell of fear that rolled off him like sour perfume. Took him long enough to fully assess the situation. It appeared Lenny had a habit of underestimating women.

"I had hoped we would be able to resolve our disagreement on the way here, but it seems that Mr. Stumps has already made his choice."

"No. No, I haven't," Lenny cried, his voice high and desperate. "If Mattie wants a divorce, we'll get a divorce. I'll even take responsibility. I'll go back to the farm, and she'll never see me ever again. I swear!"

Lorna crouched down next to him, gathering up her

skirts so they didn't drag in the damp grass. "Oh, Mr. Stumps. If I believed you, we'd get back in that boat and I'd send you on your way. Unfortunately, you have proven yourself untrustworthy time and time again. I'm afraid I can't let you slink home to lick your wounds and plot revenge against our sweet Mattie."

The fear fled Lenny's face as it twisted into anger. "Why are you protecting that worthless harlot? She's the one who ran away from her marriage vows. She's the one who deserves to be fed to that god-awful creature. Not me."

"Just as the Oracle foretold," Lorna muttered to herself. Someone was going to end up in the swamp, and Lorna was going to make damn sure it wasn't Mattie. "Our Grace is so very good at what she does, isn't she? Well, I could waste my breath and half the night trying to explain it to you, but since you have no concept of loyalty except as for how it benefits yourself, I won't bother."

Lorna rose and stood on her toes to press a kiss to the underside of Marjorie's pebbled jaw. "Give my love to the little ones. Despite how sour he is, I'm sure they will enjoy the treat."

"You must visssit sssoon. Though, they make an unholy racket every time they sssee you."

Lorna let out a laugh. "They are darlings—even when they squeak. Au bientot, cherie."

After pushing the skiff back into the water, she leapt and landed lightly in the bottom of the boat. A strangled cry caused her to look back over her shoulder.

Heading toward the water, Marjorie had Lenny by one leg. Panic contorted his face as he scrambled to hold on to the wet grass, not only with his good hand

263

but also with the bandaged stump as well. When his leg hit the water, a ragged scream tore from him, rending the night air. Great plumes of water erupted as Lenny continued to thrash until his head finally went under, cutting his cry short. His flailing arm soon followed after him.

The ripples from Marjorie and Lenny's departure lapped against the side of Lorna's boat. She picked up the handles of the oars and settled into her rowing rhythm. Once again, the only sounds were those of paddles cutting through water and the nocturnal song of the swamp's inhabitants.

Chapter Twenty-Six

Mattie

The next morning, Mattie stood outside of the Lady's door. For the past five minutes, she'd been debating on whether to knock. Who knew how late the Lady had been out dealing with Mattie's mess? The last thing she wanted to do was to deprive the Lady of more sleep.

The door opened, startling Mattie into taking a step back. The Lady was dressed in a simple ebony skirt and ivory satin shirt. The skin under her eyes had a bruised look that sent a ripple of guilt sloshing around Mattie's stomach.

"No use lurking in doorways, cherie. Come in."

Mattie followed her through the bedroom and into the office, but instead of sitting behind the desk, the Lady sank down into one of the armchairs around the polished wooden coffee table. With a wave of her hand, she bade Mattie to take the chair opposite. Mattie sank onto the edge of the plush seat, her hands clutched in her lap.

"Um." Mattie cleared her throat and forced the words out. "May I ask how it went?"

A hard smile crossed the Lady's red lips. "You will never have to worry about your ex-husband again."

Relief flooded through Mattie as she slumped back

into her chair. Dimly, a part of her clamored that she should have been horrified or, at the very least, sad about this news. The only regret she could find, though, was for the husband that Lenny could have been, not the one he had been. She may not want to know the specifics, but she wouldn't lie to herself about the end results.

"The question now is, what are you going to do? There are obviously some logistical concerns, but the farm is now yours."

Mattie looked up at her in confusion. After all this, the Lady was going to kick her out? Send her back to the empty farm?

The Lady leaned forward and took her hand as if she could read Mattie's thoughts. "Oh, cherie, I only meant you will have to decide what to do, not that you have to leave. This is your home."

"Thank you, Lady, for everything." She took a deep breath and let it out. "I know I've only brought trouble, but if you would have me, I'd like to join the House."

Squeezing her hand, the Lady gave her a gentle smile. "You don't owe me or the House anything. I'm certainly not going to require you to join the House as payment."

"I know. That's why I want to. You took me in, gave me work, allowed me to be myself, and dealt with a massive problem of mine, all without asking for anything in return. The House is my home, and you all are my family." Mattie put all her conviction in the words, all the years she'd wanted nothing more, all the joy and relief at finally having them.

Without a word, the Lady stood up and crossed to

the bookshelf. She picked up a small wooden box and returned to her chair, taking a moment to rearrange her skirts over her knees. The box was made of dark, polished wood and carved with a fleur-de-lis surrounded by magnolia blossoms. Mattie's breath caught in her chest as the Lady took out a gold ring adored with a red ruby.

"Are you certain, cherie? Is this what you want?"

She wanted to blurt out 'yes,' but didn't. The Lady wasn't idly asking. She wanted a true answer, and she deserved for Mattie to give her one.

After Jo had gotten Mattie cleaned up the night before, Mattie had lain awake in Jo's unfamiliar bed. The crow-girl a comforting warmth pressed to her side. She had thought about all things she'd believed she wanted when she'd packed up her carpetbag and fled from Lenny's farm—fled from Lenny himself. What she found instead was something beyond what she thought possible. A group of people comfortable in their own skins who lived life as they wished. Who loved hard and fiercely protected their own (even when the one they were protecting was too stubborn to ask for help they desperately needed).

She thought about the gold bracelets that had bought her freedom. When Granny Marie had given her the bangles, she'd grumbled, "Family should never make you change to suit their needs. Family should love you as you are." Looking back, Granny Marie had never thought much of Mattie's marriage to Lenny, but at the time, Mattie had believed it was for the best. Or, at least, that's what her parents had stressed. A man who owned his own land. Attended church every Sunday. What more could Mattie have asked for? Well, now she knew. She could ask for a hell of a lot more.

When she'd come to the House, the idea of a ring she couldn't take off had horrified her. It had seemed worse than her wedding band. A shackle that would bind her. But now she understood. The difference between her ex-husband and the Lady was that Mattie knew, with no room for doubt, that if she ever asked to be released, the Lady would make it happen. She'd remove the ring, kiss Mattie's cheek, and wish her all the best. If Mattie ever said the word "stop" the House would listen.

"I'm certain."

"Give me your right hand, Mattie Logan."

Mattie held out her hand, and the Lady took it in her strong fingers.

"Do you pledge yourself to House Verity and the ideals we hold dear?" The Lady's voice was serious and heavy with the weight of ritual. Similar to how she'd sounded when beginning the prophecy with Grace. "To respect others' boundaries and your own? To cherish your body and its desires? To live as fully and joyously as possible?"

"Yes, I do." The side of her mouth quirked up at the wording.

The Lady gave her an answering smile as she slid the ring onto the pointer finger of Mattie's right hand.

"Bienvenue à la Maison de Verity."

Mattie held up her hand, admiring the wink of the ruby. "Does it fit so well because of the magic?"

The Lady let out a laugh. "No, I'm afraid nothing so mundane. I've a knack for guessing ring sizes."

"But how did you know that I would ask to join?"

"Heads of Houses just know. I had it made after

your first Tuesday Night dinner. You are welcome to try to take it off. Everyone does."

Mattie's cheeks heated. Her fingers hovered over the ring. She had thought she was being stealthy, having stacked her hands back in her lap. But there was no admonishment in the Lady's voice, only gentle amusement. She tugged openly on the ring. It stayed firmly on her finger, as if glued there with paste. Oddly enough, she could still turn it side to side around her finger. It was only the motion of removing it that was thwarted.

"There is one other matter I wished to discuss with you, cherie." The smile on her face faded into a serious line. "The final steps I believe you need to take to put your old life behind you."

As the Lady laid out her plan, Mattie couldn't help but be both amazed at the neat efficiency of it and a little horrified at the brutal necessity. Still, she had come too far not to put the final nail in the coffin of her life as Mrs. Mattie Stumps.

Chapter Twenty-Seven

Officer Boudreaux

It wasn't even ten in the morning and already it was hotter than the gates of, well, heck. At least Officer Boudreaux wasn't on foot patrol today, walking the blistering sidewalks of the French Quarter. Still, even with the overhead fan on and the electric fan pointed straight at him, he had sweated a line down the back of both his undershirt, his dress shirt, and his uniform jacket. His prized mustache was as limp and wet as a catfish's whiskers.

Thankfully, crime slowed to a trickle on days that hot. When breaking the law just required too much effort. Better to sit on the porch with a pitcher of iced tea and complain with your neighbors.

The bell over the precinct door gave a sweaty jingle, and Officer Boudreaux snapped upright, stepped away from the electric fan, and quickly buttoned his jacket. With every shiny button in place, he turned toward the front counter.

"Morning, ma'am. How may I assist you this fine day?"

A young woman stood tense and uncertain on the other side of the counter. Her shin-length flowered dress sported a wide white collar. A matching scarf was tied around her head, and a handbag hung in the crook of one of her elbows. She looked familiar, but Officer Boudreaux couldn't place her. Had he seen her around the French Quarter?

"I do hope so, Officer. My name is Mrs. Mattie Stumps and I'm sure you'll think me terribly silly, but I'm awfully worried about my husband." The woman's voice was sweet as plum jelly.

"As an officer of the law, I can assure you that we take all the concerns from such an upstanding woman, such as yourself, very seriously." His chest puffed, straining the buttons of his jacket. He retrieved a clean pad of paper and a pencil. "My name is Officer Boudreaux, Mrs. Stumps. Now, why don't you tell me what has that pretty little head of yours worried?"

"My husband, Lenny Stumps, recently moved to the city. We had the most darling farm up near Baton Rouge, but Lenny insisted that the money he could make in the big city was too good to pass up. Well, being his day off yesterday, Lenny wanted to go fishing—that man loves to fish."

"Understandable, ma'am. We have excellent fishing around these parts. I myself fish for red snapper on my day off."

Mrs. Stumps gave him a smile, but her lower lip trembled. "He went out in the early morning and never returned. It's been two days and I'm just worried sick about him."

A tear slipped from her eye, and the lady retrieved a handkerchief from her handbag to blot it daintily away. Officer Boudreaux noted the white short gloves she was wearing despite the heat. Here was a proper lady. Not many of those around these days, what with the flappers and their short dresses being all the craze.

Simply indecent, if you asked him.

"Mrs. Stumps, there's no reason to fret. He may have gotten lost or taken a little side trip. I'm sure he'll turn up just fine."

Mrs. Stumps clutched her handkerchief and looked around the lobby of the precinct, even though they were the only ones present. Leaning forward, she revealed in a scandalized whisper, "Officer, I fear there was alcohol involved."

Ah. Now, they were getting into the heart of the matter. There were good reasons hooch had been made illegal. Even though he himself kept a small stash of whiskey for his personal use. Still, some men could not be trusted around alcohol. "That does complicate matters. Do you know where your husband intended to go fishing?"

"Near the Honey Island Swamp. An old friend lent him his boat."

A niggle of worry poked the back of Officer Boudreaux's brain. "Can you please describe your husband for me?"

"He's about as tall as you. Sandy colored hair cut short, bleached from working under the sun. I've tried to get him to wear a hat, but he just won't listen. Oh, and he was wearing his wedding ring. He never takes the thing off. It's a big gold one."

The worry blossomed into disappointed certainty as he remembered the flyer that had come with the morning's correspondence. Still, he was an officer of the law and there were procedures to follow. "Is something monogrammed on the top of the ring?"

"Why yes, it has an 'S' monogrammed on it. On account of his family name." The sweet smile slipped from the woman's lips. "Something terrible has happened to my Lenny. Hasn't it?"

His face settled into what he thought of as his Bad News Face. It was serious and authoritative, with a hint of concern so that the subject receiving the face knew that he cared. Secretly, he wished he didn't have to employ that face as often as he did, but this was the big city.

"Ma'am, it is with deepest regret I must inform you that a local fisherman in the Honey Island Swamp found a ring fitting that description."

The light dimmed in Mrs. Stumps eyes. "They didn't just find his ring, did they? My Lenny didn't lose it fishing, did he?"

He thought back to the flyer with its description of the critter-nibbled hand and its gold wedding ring and surpassed a shudder. This delicate lady did not need to know the specifics of her careless husband's demise. "No, ma'am. You are probably right that the devil's juice was a contributing factor of your husband's death."

He liked phrases like "contributing factor." They had the ring of authority to them. What he thought of as Proper Police Terms. He didn't add that her husband had probably gotten liquored up and fell into the bayou. If the yahoo was lucky, he'd have drowned before the gators, snakes, and other swamp critters got to him.

A sob tore itself from Mrs. Stumps as she held the handkerchief to her face, tears streaming down her cheeks. With a visible effort, she pulled herself together, taking a few deep, ragged breaths and dabbing her tear-streaked face.

"My apologizes, Officer. Oh, how I wish we'd

never left the farm."

Officer Boudreaux cleared his throat. Even stalwart officers of the law could still be moved by tragedy. "Nonsense, ma'am. You've been dealt quite the blow. I'm afraid I have some paperwork you'll need to fill out regarding your husband's accident."

"Anything you need. May I ask if my husband's wedding ring will be returned to me?" Her bottom lip trembled again.

"I'll make sure it's returned to you personally." He'd also ensure the ring was properly cleaned beforehand. Those St. Tammany parish coppers weren't always as factitious with evidence as they ought to be.

"You are a saint, officer. I don't know how I can thank you."

"No need, ma'am. Just doing my duty." He straightened his jacket before retrieving the proper forms from under the counter.

The grieving widow straightened her shoulders, steeling herself for the task ahead as she picked up her pen. The thought occurred to him again—now, there was a proper lady.

Chapter Twenty-Eight

Mattie

Stepping into her bedroom, Mattie stripped off the short white gloves and was, once again, caught off guard by the sight of her House ring. Toward the end, before she'd fled to New Orleans, her plain wedding band had been impossibly heavy. As if the weight of it would snap her finger from her hand if she wasn't careful. But for the last five days, she'd kept forgetting that her House ring was even there. Almost as if it wasn't a separate piece of jewelry at all.

The windows were open, letting in sunlight, and she took a moment to watch the ruby wink as she turned her hand. The small smile on her face slipped as she remembered the other ring still nestled in her handbag.

She set the gloves down on the top of her dresser and placed her handbag next to it. Her fingers hesitated on the clasp. An irrational fear gripped her that she would open it and find the ring gone. That everything that had happened in the last week had been a dream.

"Come on, you Ditzy Dora."

The click of the latch seemed to echo around the room. In the depths of her purse, nestled into a plain handkerchief, was the large gold ring engraved with an 'S' exactly where she had put it after tearfully receiving it from Officer Boudreaux. What had been left of Lenny would go straight to the funeral home. Cremation was the best option. She was sure it would raise some eyebrows back in Prairieville, but she wasn't going to shell out the expense of a casket burial for a single hand.

There were still so many things she needed to take care of. She would have to make a trip up to Prairieville soon. There'd have to be a funeral service, and Pastor Michals would extoll the sins of booze while being hungover himself. Once more she'd have to play the part of the tearful, grieving widow. No matter how ill-fitting the role.

And there was still the problem of what to do with the farm. A part of her almost wished that Lenny had had some relative that actually wanted the farm and to work the land. Especially since that someone was not her. Still, there was the continued problem of the lack of gin. Maybe she could offer the farm up to the Lady for use? Maybe not as a still location, but as a stopover for Jimmy to use on his runs.

Worries for another day.

The metal was cool in her fingertips as she held the heavy ring up. Maybe it would be best if she asked Jimmy to drive her out to Honey Island Swamp. She could hurl the ring into the murky waters to lie for all eternity with the rest of him. The thought was tempting.

With a sigh, she opened her unmentionables drawer and pulled out a small wooden box. She tucked the ring in among the three remaining bangles from Granny Marie. Her finger traced one of the thin gold circles. The ring wouldn't do anyone any good at the bottom of the swamp. Maybe she'd never again need what her Granny Marie had called "safety net" jewelry, not with the money she made from Tonique & Lace collecting in her own bank account or the money coming from Lenny's life insurance policy, but still.

She closed the lid softly and set it back among the mix-match of her underthings. Lace and silk tumbled together with cotton underpants so old and worn thin they had to be classified as underpants, not panties.

So many of them reminded her of Daniel. If she was honest, it wasn't just her lace things that reminded her. Nearly everything in the room did. From the bed where they had spent their first night together, to the table where he'd shown her just a glimpse of what her body had been missing.

Things between them had been a tense stalemate ever since he'd removed her unconscious ex-husband from her bedroom floor. While she no longer avoided getting too close when he stood watch at the door of Tonique & Lace, they hadn't spoken about what had happened either. A large part of her ached to reach out to him, to fix the rift that now separated them. But what could she say?

A bright knock came from the bedroom door.

"Coming," Mattie called as she firmly shut the drawer.

Jo stood in her doorway with a small black velvet box and an envelope clutched in her hand. The crow-girl was nearly vibrating with excitement.

"Jo, what's going on?"

"These are for you," Jo said as she shoved the items into Mattie's hands. "I'll be in my room if you need me." Before Mattie could question her further, Jo planted a kiss on Mattie's lips and headed down the hallway.

Mattie watched her for a moment before closing the door and heading to the table. She set the box to the side and flipped over the envelope. The single word written in a neat hand sent her heart racing.

Bunny

Her fingers shook as she removed the folded piece of paper inside, whether because of fear or anticipation, she couldn't have said. It certainly wasn't a long missive, only about half a page of Daniel's precise handwriting.

Mattie,

I want to apologize for not listening to you. For not respecting your wishes in how you wanted to handle your ex-husband. I could say that it is in a Gargoyle's nature to protect those they love, but that would be a poor excuse for my actions. Protecting someone you care about does not mean you can run roughshod over their boundaries and needs. By letting my fear for your safety rule me, I was proclaiming that you couldn't take care of yourself. And that is far from the truth.

The tension between us is also my fault and while I know we can no longer be friends, I wish to earn the right to be called a friend. This is not something I expect to happen overnight. I can only hope you will forgive me enough to let me start to make amends.

If it would make you more comfortable, I'd be happy to skip Tuesday Night dinner this evening. You deserve to be a member of this House and to have that celebrated. I don't want to do anything that would dim that joy. Please let Jo know if that's the case and I'll make myself scarce.

Daniel

P.S. Welcome (officially) to House Verity.

Such a brief note. She read it twice over, each time her eyes caught on the phrase "to protect those they love" as if the words were fly paper. After the third read through, she set the page aside, pulled the black velvet box in front of her, and lifted the lid.

A silver necklace and chain sat on a satin pillow. The pendant was shaped like a fleur-de-lis and set into its middle band was a small ruby, same as the one in her ring. A sob caught in her throat. She checked the time before snatching up the necklace in one hand and the letter in the other.

Entering the hallway, she didn't head for Jo's room, but turned to go down the stairs, her feet flying over the steps. But when she got near the kitchen door and the familiar sounds and smells of Daniel's cooking wafted out, her feet slowed even as her heart sped up.

Peeking around the corner, she watched as Daniel stirred something in the bottom of the large pot. He'd stripped down to his undershirt, a kitchen towel slung over one shoulder. Her eyes traced down his arm as the muscles bunched and tensed.

The stirring stopped. With precise, deliberate movements, he set the large wood spoon onto the rooster spoon rest and turned the flame down under the pot until it was only a flicker.

Without turning around, he braced his arms against the counter and said softly, "Hello, Mattie. Are you going to come in or just lurk in the doorway?"

Mattie stepped into the kitchen, a small guilty smile stretching her lips. "How did you know?"

"I'd know the smell of you anywhere." Daniel turned around and leaned back on the counter, his eyes flicking to her hands. A look of pain flashed across his face, before he hid it behind a half-smile. "You didn't have to come see me yourself. If you didn't want to keep the gift, you could have sent Jo."

She glanced down at the necklace still clutched in her hand. "Oh, no! That's not…." She took a deep breath and tried again. "Can we talk?"

"Of course." After checking the contents of the pot a final time, he sat down at the kitchen table and gestured to the chair across from him.

Her eyes never left his face as she crossed to the table and sat down.

"There were no expectations with the necklace. I meant it as a Welcome gift. Nothing more."

The edges of the pendant bit into the side of her palms as her hand curled around it. "Did you mean what you said in the letter?"

"Every word." Confusion knit his eyebrows together. "What part specifically are you asking about?"

"That you protect those that you love." The words seemed to hover in the warm, humid air of the kitchen.

She held her breath as the confusion cleared from his face and he smiled.

"I meant those particular words more than the rest. Another failing of mine that I didn't tell you before."

"Is…is it all in the past?"

He shook his head ruefully. "No. Feelings like this don't just disappear, but that is my burden to bear. Not yours."

A flicker of hope wrapped itself around her heart and squeezed.

"I need to apologize to you as well." When it looked like he would argue with her, she shook her head, and he sat back with a small nod. "Over the last week, I've realized some important things. Including the fact that I rejected your offer of help for completely the wrong reasons. A part of me knew Lenny was a danger, even if I didn't want to believe I could have married a man like that. More importantly though, I wanted to take care of the problem on my own because I didn't want to be a burden to you or the House."

She paused, but he didn't say anything, just gave a nod of encouragement. After taking a deep breath, she continued, "I was so afraid that if I caused a fuss or endangered the House, even indirectly, I'd be sent away. What use would y'all have for a country girl who offered nothing but trouble?" The smile faltered from her lips.

Hesitantly, Daniel reached a hand out to cover her hand, clenched around the letter, giving her plenty of time to pull back. Instead, she set the crumpled page down and laced her fingers with his. The feeling of his hand in hers was one of sweet relief. Like jumping into a cool pond on a sweltering summer's day.

He squeezed her fingers. "That's not how this House works."

"No, it's not. It was only afterward that I understood how stubborn and stupid I'd been. He would've killed me, given half a chance."

"I wouldn't have let that happen. Neither would the Lady."

"That's part of what I realized. You and the lady let

me face Lenny on my own, exactly as I had asked, but you also made sure that he couldn't do permanent harm. It was only afterwards, when Jo had cleaned the sherry and glass off me, that I realized how close I'd come to losing everything. Worse than that, though, was what my own pride and fear cost me. You."

Daniel inhaled a sharp breath, his eyes intense and bright. "We can't change the past, but we can choose how to move forward. While I can't promise I won't be an overprotective bastard in the future—"

Mattie let out a startled laugh that earned her a grin.

"—I can promise that I will respect your wishes and support you in whatever way you ask me to."

Tears stung Mattie's eyes. "Then it only seems fair that I promise to ask for help when I need it and to not be such a Ditzy Dora about putting myself in dangerous situations. I don't think Francis will forgive me if I waste any more bottles of sherry."

Leaning over, Daniel grabbed the edge of her chair and hauled her around the side of the table. The speed of it forced a squeak out of her. That wonderful cocky smile split his face as he gathered her into his lap. His long fingers took the necklace from her grasp and fastened it around her neck.

Mattie looked down, admiring the way the bottom point of the fleur-de-lis nestled at the swell of her breasts. Gentle fingers took ahold of her chin and forced her to look up.

"I love you, Mattie Logan, in all your stubborn, curious, and beautiful glory."

Giddy joy suffused her, bubbling through her chest like champagne. She kissed him hard, trying to press all the things she was feeling into the way her lips fit against his, the way her tongue delved into his mouth to dance with his own. One arm snaked around her lower back, pressing her more firmly to his chest. His hand tangled with the hair at the back of her head, and she knew he understood.

Feathering kisses along his jaw, she breathed the words back to him. "I love you."

He groaned, and his hand in her hair clenched, sending a pleasant buzz of pain down her scalp. Gently, he pulled her head back so he could look her in the face.

"If I didn't have to finish preparing dinner, I'd bend you over that table and show you all the ways I missed you until the only thing you could do is scream those words over and over."

Desire made her thighs ache as she sneaked a hand between their bodies to cradle the hard length of him straining against his pants. She gave him a firm squeeze.

"Evil bunny," Daniel groaned, leaning forward to nip her bottom lip.

Giving him a grin, she climbed off his lap and moved her chair back around the table where she sat primly down.

"You'll pay for that later, you know that, right?" As he stood, he rearranged his pants into a more comfortable position.

"Ab-so-lute-ly." She grinned and pulled the cutting board closer.

With a shake of his head, he headed back to the stove. For a few minutes, there was only the sound of cutting vegetables and Daniel's bustling around the kitchen, the two of them working in companionable silence.

"Daniel, I have to ask. Does this change anything?"

He looked over from the stove. "What do you mean?"

"Does the House do couples?"

His grin was wide and a little dirty. "The House does whatever it wants."

"Like the Lady and Caron?"

"Exactly. Hell, Leo and Hazel are married." He turned around and added, "I'm not asking you to marry me. I'm not against the notion myself, but it's not something I need. Being your partner is more than enough. I don't want to own you, Mattie. Or shut you away. If you want to play with Jo or anyone else, that's fine by me. All I ask is that we do it together. I want you to be happy."

A warm glow settled in her belly at his words. She loved that he wasn't making her choose. That he wanted her exactly as she was. He held the primary place in her heart, but she wanted those other experiences, and, most importantly, to have those experiences with Daniel. To baise their amis together as the motto went.

"Deal."

They shared a grin as he turned back to the stove, and she went back to cutting the lettuce for the salad.

"I missed this." Daniel's words were soft. "You helping me with Tuesday dinner. I've never wanted anyone in my kitchen before, but when you weren't here, it didn't feel right. It was too empty."

Mattie got up and wrapped her arms around him, pressing her cheek to his back. His left hand came up to cover hers. "Everything was empty without you."

Lifting one of her hands, he pressed her fingertips to his lips. "Then I'll just have to fill you up later."

Chapter Twenty-Nine

Lady Lorna

"The Zinfandel or the Pinot Noir?" Francis asked as he ran his fingertip along the edge of his mustache.

Lady Lorna knew Francis wasn't really asking her opinion. Rather, she found his habit of talking to the racks of liquor and wine bottles endearing. Still couldn't hurt to help the process along. He'd be muttering about the wine selection and fretting over the growing number of holes in the floor-to-ceiling wine rack all night if she let him. Prohibition's end could not come soon enough.

"I passed the kitchen earlier," Lorna said in an offhanded manner. "By sound of things, Daniel and Mattie have made up. By the smell of things, I believe the gumbo is chicken-based this evening."

"Chicken, hm? The Oak Knoll Zinfandel, it is. About time those two finally kissed and made up," he muttered as he pulled three bottles out of the rack.

"Indeed. Might you want to grab one of the Pinot Grigios as well, cherie? Just in case someone wants a white?"

Lorna savored the look of exasperation that passed over Francis's face. She did so enjoy teasing the uptight barkeep, especially when he made it so easy.

"Fine. Even though they'd be wrong," Francis gave

in with a huff before adding a bottle of the white wine to the growing pile in his arms.

Lorna would have offered to take one but knew from experience that the barkeep would only decline. Besides, he'd never once dropped a bottle in all the years that he'd run her establishments, both legal and less than legal.

He gave a half-bow and said, "After you."

Lorna led the way to the door, past crates of bootleg gin and bourbon. The lack of a fresh rum supply was a heavy weight on her mind, but she pushed it away. It was a problem for another night.

Ducking low, she stepped through the low doorway into the area behind the bar. While Francis set the wine bottles on the polished wood surface, Lorna closed the door to the storage room. Clever hidden hinges and no visible hardware meant the door blended into the dark red wallpaper and carved crown molding. Lorna ran a loving hand along the invisible seam.

Beyond the bar, House Verity prepared for Tuesday Night dinner. Jimmy and Leo bickered good-naturedly while rearranging the tables while Hazel and Clementine twirled and shimmied together on the dance floor. As Francis started pulling out wine glasses, Lorna drifted to where her gramophone rested on the edge of the bar. Duke Ellington's piano filled the room.

Reflexively, Lorna placed a hand over her House ring, checking the wards. All was quiet. Some of the tension went out of her shoulders and she allowed herself to enjoy the sights and sounds of her family preparing for their weekly dinner.

"Are you gals going to help us set up or just dance?" Leo called out as he muscled a table into place.

"Babe, once you big, powerful men get done doing the heavy lifting, we'll set the table," Hazel called back over her shoulder. "Until then…" She deftly spun a giggling Clementine into her arms and then back out. Clementine's pink skirt flared to show off shapely legs.

The clink of glass hitting glass made Lorna's eyebrows crease as she glanced over at Francis. The notoriously steady-handed barkeep had his fingers curled tight around the edge of the bar and tension hummed in every line of his body.

The taste of barrel-aged bourbon, the kind meant to be sipped and savored, flooded Lorna's tongue. It had been so long since she'd tasted Francis's desire, she almost didn't recognize it. With slow movements, Lorna turned back to the gramophone and began flipping through a stack of records while watching Francis from the corner of her eye.

His gaze was locked on Hazel and Clementine as they continued moving to the music. Clementine threw her head back and laughed, the sound bright even over the jazz spilling from the gramophone. Flares of smoke and amber licked through Lorna's mouth as Francis watched Hazel's hands skate down Clementine's arms and wrap around her waist. Now that was interesting.

"As much as we love the show, loves, time to work," Jimmy called out as he set the last chair into place.

The two ladies sagged in each other arms.

"Fine! Fine!" Hazel called back. She nodded to the bar. "Why don't you grab the wine and I'll grab the plates?"

Clementine grinned and sauntered over. Francis seemed to give himself a mental shake as he let go of the bar, pulled several more wine glasses from their shelf, and placed them with the others. Leaning across the bar, Clementine reached up and tweaked the end of his waxed mustache.

"You're the bee's knees, Francis." Her voice was still breathless from dancing.

Another wave of bourbon slipped over Lorna's tongue, rich and spicy. The side of his mouth twitched, but he managed to keep a mostly straight face as she grabbed up several glasses and headed to the table. Francis watched Clementine's hips as they swung to the rhythm of the music.

Only then did Francis seem to remember Lorna at the end of the bar. He swallowed hard as understanding and fear flashed over his face. With a rough tug on his bowtie, he cleared his throat and mumbled something about needing more wine. After flinging open the hidden door, he nearly threw himself into the back room.

Poor Francis, Lady Lorna mused as she swapped the records on the gramophone. She wished she could reassure him that there was no need for embarrassment, but she knew broaching the subject would only make him more anxious and upset.

As strands of violins spilled from the gramophone, Lorna stifled a smile. Francis being sweet on someone might only happen once in a blue moon, but this particular crush was going to be especially painful for him since he'd already turned down Clementine's advances once before. Oh well, at least it was never boring in her House.

Chapter Thirty

Daniel

Mimi would have rolled over in her grave if she'd
seen how Daniel rushed the gumbo. It was cooked.
Mostly. Besides, gumbo was always better the next day.
Granted, leftovers were rare for Tuesday night dinners,
but the sentiment still held.

Anticipation seethed under his skin as he portioned
out the soup into serving bowls. Mattie had already
taken the salad and baskets of French bread to the table.
He picked up the two massive serving dishes, the heat
of the gumbo scalding him through the porcelain sides.
But he wasn't about to take the time to make two trips.

The tables were already set up for the meal. After
depositing the gumbo, he dropped into the empty chair
next to Mattie. Joy crinkled the corners of her eyes as
she smiled at him, and the anticipation in his belly
sharpened into a need so desperate it hurt. Shifting to
hide the erection that strained his pants, he forcibly
reminded himself that it was just dinner. He could make
it through one meal, and then he'd whisk Mattie up to
his room. He'd been without the feeling of her hands on
him, his mouth on her soft skin for days now. Another
hour, tops, wouldn't kill him.

At the head of the table, the Lady stood and raised
her glass. She didn't need to say anything. The quiet

power of her rolled around the room and pulled every eye to her. Daniel raised his own glass along with the others.

"Welcome House Verity to another Tuesday evening dinner. Tonight, we not only are celebrating the bonds of family that have brought all of us together. The bonds we strengthen through shared food, shared drink, and shared company. But we are also welcoming the newest member of House Verity into our loving fold. Bienvenue à la Maison, Mattie Logan."

Cheers and whoops rose from the table as the House welcomed its newest member. A thrill of pride ran through Daniel as he yelled his joy. Through it all, Mattie sat with the biggest grin he'd ever seen on her face. On the other side of her, Jo cawed loudly and wrapped her arms around Mattie's shoulders, squeezing with all her might.

When the celebration had died down, the Lady continued, "To feeding our bodies. To feeding our souls. To House Verity. Baise tes amis!"

"Basie tes amis!"

After taking a long sip of his wine, Daniel leaned over and whispered, "Welcome home, bunny." He indulged himself with the tiniest licks along the curve of her ear. The small inhale of breath it earned him nearly shattered his resolve.

"It's good to be home," was her breathless reply.

He rumbled his agreement and forced himself to turn back to the table. Leo was ladling out gumbo into bowls of rice. Daniel picked up Mattie's and held it out.

As the first ladle of sausage and shrimp gumbo hit the bowl, he felt a small hand press itself to his upper thigh. He flicked a look at Mattie, but she was turned away, chatting with Jo, her hand hidden by the edge of the table. There was nothing tentative or hesitant as it smoothed up and over his hard dick.

His careful control snapped.

He plopped the half-full bowl down, earning him quizzical looks from Leo, who still held a full ladle out. Setting his napkin to the side, he stood and stepped behind's Mattie's chair. Heads up and down the table swiveled to look at him, including the curly-haired one in front of him.

"House Verity, forgive me. You'll have to celebrate Mattie's joining up with our motley crew another night." He yanked her chair away from the table. Its occupant let out an adorable squeak. Before she could protest, he swept her up into his arms, relishing the feeling of her pressed to his chest. He nodded his head. "Please enjoy your dinner. I know I'll be enjoying mine."

Appreciative chuckles and a few catcalls followed them as he carried her into the back hallway. It was all he could do not to sprint up the stairs as Mattie clung to him. Once in his room, he closed the door with his foot. His mouth was already on hers when he set her down and pressed her into the wood of the door.

Her mouth opened for him, eager and needy as his own. With a groan, he claimed her with his tongue, his lips, his teeth. Fire built under his skin as her hands roamed over his shoulders and back, quick and desperate like she was checking that he was still there. Still hers.

When she wrapped one leg around his hip, pulling his aching cock against the sweet heat of her, all his careful plans for the evening went out the window. His hands sank into her hair, pulling it back. His breath was ragged on the column of her neck.

"I'm sorry, Mattie. I need this. Say the word and I'll stop, but I promise I'll make it up to you later." His hands were already pushing up the hem of her dress. One hand kneaded the round globe of her ass as his other fumbled with the buttons on his pants.

Her nails dug into the fabric at his shoulders. "What makes you think I don't need this too?" Her voice was breathy and low. It scraped along his nerves like whiskey. "Take it, Daniel. Take me."

His hand tangled into the flimsy lace panties she wore and tore them off her. He'd buy her more. When she wrapped her other leg around his waist and arched against the door, he drove himself into her with one long, hard stroke. The wet heat of her surrounded him, and he fell into her like the only thing that could save his life was to bury himself deeper into her.

With his hands clenched around her perfect ass, he took most of her weight and rocked out of her, before fucking back into her. There was no finesse to his movements, just raw need as he drove into her over and over.

Even lost in his desire, he watched her face to make sure she was still with him. Not once did she try to hide. Not once did that terrible blank mask fall over her features. He reveled in the pleasure suffusing her face, the feeling of her fingernails digging into his shoulders, the clench of her legs around his waist, pulling him into her harder, faster. The pressure built in his balls and lower back, but he fought it off. Her skin radiated heat and her breathing was coming in the little fast gasps that meant she was close to the edge.

"Say it, bunny." The words were raw, barely more than a growl. His lower back was taut enough to snap, but he couldn't fall. Not just yet.

Mattie's eyes were half-closed, lost in the rhythm of their bodies' collision, but she knew what he was asking of her.

"I love you." The words were soft gasps. A gift offered only to him.

She came hard around him, her exquisite mouth letting out a cry as she shuddered and clenched. He wanted to fuck her through it, to ride her orgasm as long as possible, to stretch it to its limits, but his body had other plans. With a growl, he spilled into her, bright pleasure searing through him with every clench of his balls. One arm wrapped around her lower back. His other hand came up to brace against the door.

He pressed his forehead to hers as they caught their breath. The muscles in her legs softened like she wanted to be put down, but he wasn't ready to let her go just yet and kept a tight grip on her, keeping her suspended between himself and the door.

Her hands were gentle as they slipped up his chest and neck, before caressing his cheeks. Those soft hands smoothed all the jagged feelings that had sliced his insides to ribbons over the days they'd been apart. She pulled him close, brushing her lips against his in a kiss that was sweeter than honeysuckle.

"Welcome home," she whispered against his mouth.

His arm tightened, pressing her soft curves against his chest. He felt the truth of her words settle into his bones. He was home.

Chapter Thirty-One

Mattie

Daniel put Mattie down with a reluctance that brought a sweet ache to her chest. His fingertips trailed along her jaw as if to reassure himself that he hadn't hurt her. Instead, she felt like her entire body was glowing, buzzing off making such a powerful, careful man lose control.

His lips pressed kisses to her jaw, the curve of her ear, the slope of her cheek. She leaned back on the door, floating back down to earth with the help of his careful administrations. When his mouth trailed down her neck, the kisses turned sharper, interspersed with the sting of his teeth. Banked heat flared back to life, and she arched, pressing her aching breasts into his chest.

A small moan escaped her as he sank his teeth into her neck, sucking just enough to leave a mark. As if the whole House didn't already know exactly what they were up to. He pulled her further into the room and stepped behind her, his hands working her dress up and over her head.

"Notice anything new?"

It took Mattie's brain a moment to process the question. Another to actually look around the room.

Her heart beat loudly in her ears. "Is that from the

Lady's room?"

"Yes." He undid her brassier and slid the straps down her arms.

The round leather footstool sat in front of Daniel's sofa. Leather straps and chains were already attached to the four legs.

"How did you get it up here? When did you?"

Fingers slid down her hips, over her garter belt, and to the tops of her thighs, and she remembered that he'd already removed her panties. Well, ripped. A little shiver of pleasure went through her at the memory.

"Earlier today, when I asked you to stir the gumbo while I ran a quick errand. This was the errand."

His hands moved up her stomach. One hand cupped her breast while the other one stroked the fleur-de-lis pendant resting on her skin. She arched back, pushing into his hand as he pinched the hard bud of her nipple. With a grin, he spun her around and guided her to the edge of the footstool. His movements were gentle but insistent, allowing her plenty of time to protest, to say 'stop'. Instead, she sat down and laid back against the leather. Her feet, still in her heels, rested on the floor. Maintaining eye contact with Daniel, she slid her feet along the floorboards, opening herself fully for him.

A rumble of approval accompanied his devouring gaze. "What a delicious sight."

He made quick work of his clothes, tossing them to the side, before dropping to his knees between her legs. Rough stubble brushed up the inside of her thigh. There was the clink of metal, but instead of leather slipping around his ankle, he picked up her leg.

Curiosity forced Mattie's head up. "That looks too

large for my ankle."

"Why yes, it is too large for your ankle." He slid the leather under her thigh. "But, for your thigh…"

Her heart sped up in her chest as he slipped the end of the cuff into its buckle and pulled it tight, before securing it. Her head dropped back to the footstool as he fastened the other thigh strap and adjusted the chains until they pulled her legs apart just enough to leave a pleasant burn in her hips.

After shifting until he was next to Mattie's head, Daniel bent down and kissed her thoroughly. Her hand came up to run her fingernails along his jaw. Strong fingers captured her wrist and brought her hand to his mouth. His lips pressed around her new ring. His tongue darted over the metal and into the soft space between her fingers before placing her wrist up by the side of her head and securing the leather cuff.

He paused for another kiss, murmuring against her lips, "I love the sight of you spread open like this. So soft and willing."

"Just for you."

"That is the best part."

He fixed the last cuff into place and stood. From her vantage point, she got a glorious view of Daniel's cock, hard and rigid once more. Her tongue darted out to run along her lower lip.

"See something you like, bunny?" That mischievous glint was back.

"Yes. Yes, please."

Bracing his hands on either side of her waist, he lowered his hips and stopped. Even stretching out her neck, she couldn't quite reach him and let out a mew of protest.

"Use your words."

"Please, let me lick your cock. Let me taste you."

His hips lowered until she was able to run her tongue along his length.

He let out a deep groan. "How can I say no to that perfect mouth?"

She used that mouth to nuzzle the soft skin of his balls, running her tongue between them. Slowly, he lowered himself to his elbows, allowing Mattie to rest her head back on the footstool. She worked her way to the head of his cock, kissing and licking as she went. Using the tip of her tongue, she pulled him into her mouth and sucked hard.

The angle meant she couldn't take more than a few inches of him, but that didn't stop her from making the most out of what she could reach. When his tongue brushed against her pearl, her hips arched up, but was met with resistance from the bands around her thighs. Her frustrated cry was muffled by her full mouth, which earned her a delighted chuckle from Daniel.

Splayed open and held down like this, she could have felt trapped, but the familiar bands didn't constrict her chest. There was no desire to retreat inside of herself.

The thought that kept the panic at bay was that all she had to say was "stop." Really, she probably only had to mumble the word, and he would immediately release her. A part of her wanted to say it, not as a test for Daniel, but because she wanted to luxuriate in the feeling. In the trust that she had for him.

Of course, if she did say it, that would mean he'd stop lapping at her like a satisfied house cat and that wasn't something she wanted to do.

By the time he finally did let her out of the cuffs, it was late into the night. They were both worn out. With his tongue and hands and cock, he'd made her orgasm so many times, she felt as if her soul was floating somewhere near the moon. Or at the very least, nestled among the stars. With infinite care, he rubbed the feeling back into her wrists and thighs before bundling her into bed.

"Love you, bunny. With everything I am."

Her ear was pressed against his chest, turning his statement more into a rumbling feeling than coherent words. A smile curled her lips, and she rallied enough energy to look up at him, her eyes wide and innocent.

"Does that mean you'll go get us some gumbo and a couple of slices of bread before round three?"

The laugh that roared out of him shook the bed and she smiled so hard her cheeks ached. As his chuckles died down, he pulled her tighter against him.

"Anything for you, bunny. Anything."

Epilogue

The Lady Lorna

With all that had been going on in the last few days, the last few weeks if she was honest, Lorna was grateful to retire to her rooms with Caron for a few hours. They were no closer to finding a new gin bootlegger. She'd bartered for a few cases from a House LeBlanc, but they wouldn't last long. Not with the way this town drank.

Caron poured two glasses of whiskey and pulled her onto his lap. His fingers not holding his drink were working their way into the knots at the base of her neck.

The only sounds in the room were the little pleased noises that slipped from her when his fingers found a particularly tight bit of muscles. She knew that soon he would need to head home, to be safely ensconced in his carefully boarded up room before the sun peaked its head over the sleepy New Orleans streets. Even with her special blackout curtains, it wasn't safe for him to stay with her during the day. The risk was just too high. Though some nights she wanted nothing more in the world than for him to fall asleep next to her, she'd never put the burden of that wish onto his shoulders. He'd given up enough already.

A loud banging echoed through the room. Lorna and Caron tensed, their heads whipping in unison to the door. Her hand went to her House ring. It remained cool against her finger. The wards were still active and not indicating any danger, so it couldn't be a threat. At least, not from the person currently smashing their fist into the door.

"Please, Lady! Please, you must open up!"

"Grace," the Lady exclaimed as she scrambled out of Caron's lap and rushed to open the door.

Before she could get the door fully open, Grace pushed her way into the room. Her normally neat dark hair was a wild snarl around her head. She was only wearing a thin robe and nightdress. Her feet were bare and nearly black with dirt.

"Did you come all the way here dressed like this?" Lorna asked, reaching out to gently grip her tattoo-covered arms. "Cherie, what's wrong?"

Grace's wide and pleading eyes locked onto Lorna's. "Please, help me. I've tried and tried and I can't make it happen. I just know it needs to happen. Please!"

The words made Lorna's heart still in her breast. "You need help to deliver a prophecy?"

"Yes! Yes!" Grace's body seemed to melt in relief, but her hands remained clamped around Lorna's. "I've tried so many times. I can't do it. I used my hands, toys, everything I can think of, but I can't finish. My skin feels like it's crawling with fire ants. Please, help me make this stop."

"Of course, cherie." Lorna's gaze flicked to Caron, who had joined them and now slipped a protective arm around Grace's shoulders. "We'll help you. Do you have any sense of where the prophecy is located?"

Grace shook her head, her mouth pulling down

wretchedly. "No. It's rare for me to have prophecy force themselves on me like this and never with this urgency. I thought I could handle it myself—use the mirrors in my bedroom—and then tell you what I saw afterwards, but this time is different."

"Shhh," Caron said, steering her back to the couch. "Let's sit down and we'll see what that beautiful skin of yours has to tell us." He looked back to where Lorna followed them, his eyebrows quirked in a question.

Pressing her mouth into a line, Lorna nodded. The poor thing looked about ready to collapse. They couldn't make her stand. No, they'd just have to deal with where the prophecy was located when they came time.

After tenderly removing her robe and nightdress, Caron set the trembling Grace down on the edge of the couch. He sat beside her, and Lorna lifted the skirt of her dress as she knelt in front of Grace's parted knees. There was a self-consciousness about the tattoo artist, a lost feeling, that Lorna had never seen before. It broke her heart. With almost painful gratitude, Grace held out her palms to Lorna.

Forcing an encouraging smile to her lips, Lorna placed her palms against the Oracle's. The two women took a deep breath in and out together. The edges of Grace's breath were frayed and ragged, but in sync.

"Oracle, House Verity requests your help. Will you exchange a little death for the answer to our query?"

"Yes, the Oracle accepts." The relief in Grace's voice was plain. She finished the rest of the ritual in a rush. "What is your question? What do you wish to learn?"

Lorna paused. Normally, she had a question

prepared and ready to ask. After some thought, she went with, *What does the Oracle need to tell us?* She held the question on her tongue, in her mind, and near her heart. Instead of her normal press of hands to let the Oracle know the question was set, she curled her fingers around the edges of Grace's palms and gave them an encouraging squeeze. When Grace squeezed back, Lorna nodded to Caron.

Caron snaked a hand to the dark curls between Grace's legs. Despite Grace's desperation, his hand moved slowly in soft circles. Lorna didn't let go of Grace's hands, which clung to her own as Lorna took a deep breath, drawing the air over her tongue.

At first, there was nothing. No desire laced the air. The knot of concern that had settled into Lorna's belly since Grace had first banged on the door tightened further. She pulled another lungful of air across her tongue.

Burnt sugar.

Lorna swallowed her sigh of relief. The next breath had hints of cinnamon and clove. Grace's shoulders relaxed away from her ears, her legs spread just a little wider. Under Caron's skilled hand, Grace was soon panting, the heat and desire radiating off her, coating Lorna's tongue like caramel.

Finally, the Oracle said in a voice sharp with need, "Left thigh. Left thigh."

"Front or back, cherie?"

"Um…fr…front."

That meant they wouldn't have to shift her. There was always a danger of losing the flow and needing to start over if that happened, which was why they usually performed this ritual standing. Lorna gave Grace's hands another squeeze and moved them out of the way so there was an unobstructed view of where a black and white crown graced Grace's thigh. The feeling of foreboding tightened in Lorna's gut even as Grace's body tensed. Strangled and muted, Grace cried out, a sound so different from her usual abandon.

The tattoos on her thigh moved.

A drop of rain fell upon the crown. Then another. Soon it was pouring so fast it was represented by streaks of dark lines. The lines shifted, coming in sideways like rain that shepherded hurricanes. Soon you could see nothing of the crown through the dark slashes of ink. The tattoo stilled, and the crown was visible once more, only now, it was battered and dented.

Lorna blinked, and the crown was whole again. The tattoos were merely ink adorned skin. The Oracle was once again just a young woman panting in Caron's arms.

Though Lorna's heart beat like a drum in her chest, she forced a smile onto her lips. "Thank you, cherie. You did wonderfully." She leaned forward and pressed a kiss to Grace's mouth, and Grace kissed her back with limp relief.

Lorna stood up and pulled the Oracle to her feet, aiming her toward the bathroom door. "Why don't you get cleaned up? Draw yourself a bath and use the lavender oil from Clementine. Either way, you are staying here tonight."

"Thank you, Lady." Bone deep wariness clouded her words now that she had delivered the message. The door closed behind her with a soft click.

Caron stood and rubbed his hands down Lorna's crossed arms. "I couldn't see the prophecy clearly.

What did it say?"

Heaving a sigh, she laid her head on Caron's shoulder, taking comfort in the solid warmth of him.

"A storm is coming for House Verity."

"We've weathered storms before, love," Caron murmured into her hair.

She gave him a nod, but her apprehension only grew. As if what was coming was like nothing they'd seen before.

But just like for a real hurricane, she would batten down the hatches and board up the windows. The Oracle had delivered her warning and House Verity would be ready.

A word about the author…

Victoria is a Southern transplant, living in the Pacific Northwest. When she's not pining for the sun, she enjoys nerdy pastimes with her husband and writing romances full of found families and monsters. Victoria's Website: https://www.victoriaweyland.com/